A DEATH
at
Seascape
HOUSE

A DEATH
at
Seascape
HOUSE

EMMA JAMESON

bookouture

Published by Bookouture in 2021

An imprint of Storyfire Ltd.
Carmelite House
50 Victoria Embankment
London EC4Y 0DZ

www.bookouture.com

ISBN: 978-1-80019-400-7
eBook ISBN: 978-1-80019-399-4

To Barbara Franklin and Melissa Myers, two real-life librarians who are always up for a mystery.

CHAPTER ONE

"Do You Ever Think About Cam Tremayne?"

"You've been stood up," said the bartender, sliding over a second pint.

Jem Jago forced a smile. Bad enough that she felt like a fool. Did she look like one, too?

"What makes you say that?" She drummed her fingers against the mahogany countertop.

"I read auras. Yours is tragic." The bartender, a tall black woman somewhere between thirty-five and forty, gazed seriously at Jem for a moment, then broke into a grin. "Okay, not really. But every time the door opens, your head comes up. You're always checking your phone. And you stretched out that first pint to last nearly an hour."

"You got me. Top marks." Jem took a sip of her second ale, a local brew called Double Drowned. She'd already decided to drink this one quickly, call it an afternoon, and head back to Tregarthen's Hotel. There was a vintage book in her suitcase, a scholarly debunking of Cornish wrecker mythology, that she wanted to get back to. When people let you down, there were always books.

"Sorry. That came off as a bit rude, didn't it?" the bartender said. "Only I'm working on something called cold reading, and I couldn't resist trying it on you. Ever heard of it?"

Apparently, conversation came standard with the two-for-one deal. Jem bit back her annoyance. She wasn't in London anymore, where people were more likely to assume that a silent person desired solitude. Moreover, she and the bartender were currently the only two women in the pub.

It was past six o'clock on a Friday night and the Kernow Arms, a quayside pub in Hugh Town on St. Mary's, largest of the Isles of Scilly, belonged mainly to local men. Fishermen in their woolen caps, waders, and braces, were seated galley-style at a long table, eating burgers and chips. A couple of pensioners were perched on stools at the other end of the bar, watching an arcane satellite game—whomever vs. whomever, beamed in from wherever. Among the booths, a few surfer types were draped languidly, playing surf videos for one another and critiquing the wipeouts. If the bartender wanted a chat, small wonder she'd picked Jem.

"I've heard of cold readings," Jem said, deciding to smile and make an effort. "Fortune tellers at fetes do it. They size you up at a glance and make guesses based on what they see. Makes it seem like they have a sixth sense. Are you planning a second career as a psychic?"

"Something like that." Pulling a dishrag from her apron, the bartender went to work on a long stretch of countertop. It already looked spotless, but she seemed like the type who preferred to keep busy.

"My cousin's trying to make a go of it on St. Morwenna," she said. "He bought a bed and breakfast, but business hasn't taken off like he hoped. So he thought we could do a psychic consultancy on weekends. Not fleecing people. For entertainment purposes, as they say."

"No judgment. People love a tarot card reading or an astrological profile," Jem said. "There used to be a lady on St. Martin's who did that. She also sold bits of shell art. *And* put out jams and jellies in the front garden, in an honesty box, for the emmets to purchase. Everyone in the Scillies runs two or three angles simultaneously to pay the bills. It's the price of living in paradise."

"Emmet?" The bartender wagged a finger at Jem. "I figured you for one. But you're an islander, eh?"

"Ex-islander. Recovering Londoner. Jemima Jago. Call me Jem," she said, putting out a hand.

The other woman gave it a firm, friendly shake. Two of her fingernails, the thumb and first finger, were long and pointed. The other three were short and squared off, like Jem's.

"Pleased to make your acquaintance, darling." The bartender put on a posh accent. "My name is—"

"Micki," Jem cut across her with a grin. She took another sip from her pint, enjoying the other woman's startled look.

"How'd you know?"

"Oh, well, I know all sorts of things," Jem said as if peering into a crystal ball. "Let's see. You've tended bar for a long time, but you're new to this pub. You've worked here… what? Ten days? Call it ten days," she said, watching Micki's eyes widen at the specificity. "You were born in the West Country, but not in the Scillies. You came here to escape something. Oh." She took another sip of ale. "*And* you play guitar in your spare time."

Micki raised her eyebrows. "Now that's a cold read. How'd you do it?"

"I tend to notice little details," Jem said. "Especially when I'm letting my eyes roam. Trying to escape my thoughts."

"You were stood up, weren't you? He's a fool."

"She's an old friend. Well. Not a friend, clearly," Jem said, letting her frustration seep into her voice. "Somebody I used to know."

"A fool," Micki repeated firmly. It was the sort of womanly solidarity Jem had missed for a long time. Not just since moving to Penzance. Even in London she'd been a bit isolated, a bit insulated from deep connections. It was nothing against her new colleagues at the Courtney Library, where the atmosphere was of scholarship and shared purpose. But none of that was quite the same as a loyal mate who'd declare a complete stranger a fool, just because that stranger let you down.

"Back to the cold reading. How did you know I'm called Micki?" She indicated her nameplate-free apron. "And the bit about ten days was spot on. How'd you guess?"

Jem pointed at the calendar pinned to the wall. Someone had penciled names on the squares. Through June 15th, it was all ZAK and BENJY. From June 16th, which was ten days previous, the name MICKI appeared in rotation with ZAK and BENJY.

"That's how. Ten days at work. And Micki with an i is the only female name."

Looking over her shoulder, Micki squinted at the calendar, which was pinned near the swinging kitchen door. "I can't make out a word of that from here."

Jem shrugged. As a teen, she'd had extra keen vision. Over the years, the sharpness had dulled, particularly up close. Jem could still read distant signs better than most, but up close, she often resorted to readers, despite the fact she'd only just turned thirty-three.

"Since I'm a wizard behind the bar, I'm not surprised you guessed this isn't my first pub gig," Micki said, still dissecting the various bullseyes in Jem's cold reading. As if to prove her point, she interrupted the conversation briefly to pull a fresh pint for one customer, made change for another, and directed a third to the Star Castle Hotel, all without missing a beat. She had the smooth assurance of someone whose job is second nature.

Returning to Jem's end of the bar, Micki continued, "How could you tell I didn't grow up in the Scillies?"

"Because I did. I'm not just a recovering Londoner. I was born in Penzance," Jem said. "But when I was six, I came to the Isles of Scilly to live with my grandmother on St. Morwenna. I was there until I was fourteen. Islanders talk with a slightly different cadence. Unhurried. But as far as you coming to St. Mary's to escape something—every cold reading needs a bit of drama. Shot in the dark on my part."

"You weren't wrong. It's two and a half hours to the mainland. Five-hour round trip," Micki said. "I'd never put up with it if I had a partner or kiddies across the water. *Don't* look sympathetic," she added. "I'm a Latham, which means I'm never alone in the world. Lathams are all over Cornwall. Like fungus." She grinned.

"The Scillies are a world apart. Do you like it so far?"

"I quite fancy the climate," Micki said. "And it's lovely not to be at my old dad's beck and call, or always being asked to babysit on a moment's notice. When you're everyone's favorite single auntie, your time isn't your own. Somebody's always in desperate need. But for a place with so many men," she added in a lower voice, nodding toward the fishermen and surfers, "there are no men, if you know what I mean. Haven't had a proper date since I moved in."

With a jangle of bells, the pub's door opened. Jem sat up straighter on her barstool, looking around hopefully. But it was just another fisherman, ruddy-cheeked and big-bellied, with a sad basset hound face. His mates hailed him, demanding to know why he'd washed up so late. He went round the table, shaking hands and swapping good-natured insults.

"Has it changed much, since you lived here?" Micki asked.

"It's like stepping back in time."

Jem didn't mean it as a compliment. The opportunity to work for the Royal Institute of Cornwall and the Courtney Library had lured her back. Returning had been a difficult decision, as it threatened to unbury the past, but when push came to shove, Jem couldn't resist an offer to do the sort of work she'd long dreamed about: authenticating and preserving Cornish history for future generations.

Some might have found her views on history oddly inconsistent. Writ large, she viewed history as a treasure, not merely for knowledge or nostalgia, but to foresee the future. But on the personal level, history was a quagmire. Her life only worked if it went relentlessly in one direction: forward.

Micki said, "All right, now spill. How the hell did you know I played guitar?"

"Your fingernails," Jem said. "They're much longer on the right than the left. Especially your thumb and first finger. My ex played guitar, so I tend to notice these things."

Micki regarded her telltale fingernails and laughed. She had one of those laughs that was funny in itself, and therefore infectious— a soft, deep wheeze in her throat, like a squeaker toy on its last go-round. Jem found herself laughing, too. It felt good to relax. Especially after a tense day that had ended with being stood up—a small but lingering hurt, like a cigarette stubbed out on tender flesh.

"Since I'll never make a cold reader, maybe I'll double up on my guitar playing. Try and turn folk music into a side gig," Micki said. "Emmets love it when you dress like a milkmaid and sing about corn dollies and stargazy pie. Speaking of loving it…" She leaned toward Jem confidentially. "The surfers in the back find you intriguing, m'dear. I reckon any one of them would buy your next drink, and probably the drink after that, should you glance their way."

"Not a sniff of it," Jem said breezily. That sounded better than saying flat out that she wasn't interested. Not today.

"Suit yourself. By the way, if you're peckish, the dinners here aren't bad. Tonight's special is sea bass." Glancing toward the kitchen door to make sure no one from the back of the house was listening in, Micki added, "Under no circumstances should you order it. I know fish that's gone off when I smell it. But everything else on the menu is acceptable. Dare I say it—very acceptable."

As Jem studied the menu, she realized how hungry she was. Breakfast had been a coffee from Costa. Lunch, a plain bagel and an old packet of almonds, which represented the last of the food in her Penzance flat. By the time she finished deciding which books she absolutely had to pack, it was time to take a taxi to the harbor, where the *Scillonian III* was due to set off at half two.

Because traveling aboard the big white steamship was luxurious enough, Jem had economized on board by limiting herself to a cup of tea. She loved her career as a Special Collections Librarian, but it would never make her rich.

Penny wise and pound foolish, she thought. Her job didn't officially start until Monday, but a request from an old friend had enticed her into changing her travel plans and arriving late Friday, rather than on Saturday. That left her personally on the hook for food and lodgings until Monday, when she could begin, within reason, charging to her expense account.

Jem was in an odd position, because the old friend and the job were, to some extent, the same. From age seven until age fourteen, Pauley Gwyn and Jem had been inseparable—swimming, sunbathing, exploring, and attending all the same classes at St. Mary's School. All that had changed one summer night, and they hadn't spoken in almost twenty years. But Pauley was also the Gwyn family heir. Her home on St. Morwenna, Lyonesse House, was the oldest dwelling in the Isles of Scilly. When Pauley contacted the RIC about donating her three-hundred-and-fifty-year-old library, an undifferentiated mass of books, papers, maps, and Gwyn family ephemera, the institute's leadership had been over the moon. The collection even included an exceedingly rare find—what appeared to be a lost poem by none other than Oscar Wilde. Their search for a librarian with the training, knowledge, and desire to undertake such a project—not to mention a willingness to live on St. Morwenna for up to a month—had led them to Jem.

Not long after Jem accepted the job, Pauley had rung her out of the blue, suggesting they meet up in Hugh Town to break the ice.

The conversation had been brief. Awkward. In a word, *cringe*—there was twenty years' worth of ice, after all. Jem suspected she was mostly to blame. Everything she said had come out in a weird little voice, like she was beaming in from Andromeda. Pauley, by contrast, had gone full manic pixie. Clearly, they'd both been overcompensating in their own way—Jem by talking like a paper doll, and Pauley by chattering like a cartoon character. But in the end, they'd gotten through the conversation, and Jem had agreed to come a day early.

When Pauley suggested they meet up in Hugh Town rather than St. Morwenna, Jem hadn't been suspicious. St. Morwenna had about two hundred residents, half of those second-homers. So unless things had radically changed, gossip traveled along the island grapevine quicker than megabits along fiber-optic cable. The number one topic among islanders was, naturally, other islanders. If Jem and Pauley wanted a private, no pressure meeting without eavesdroppers, interlopers, and real-time social media commentary, they needed to meet somewhere besides St. Morwenna.

I left myself wide open for this, Jem thought. *I should've asked to meet in Penzance, on my own turf. I just never thought she'd stoop so low. If Pauley wanted to make me squirm, she could've told me off over the phone. Or rung my boss at the RIC and said the donation was canceled unless they sent somebody else.*

Sighing, Jem pulled out her mobile, compulsively rereading Pauley's text from the previous day, the cheery exclamation point at the end especially rankling. *Looking forward to seeing you!*

But apparently not, since she wasn't here. She wasn't answering calls or texts. Even the landline at Lyonesse House rolled over to voicemail.

I suppose something might have happened…

But no. Jem rejected that the moment it crossed her mind. The Isles of Scilly were quiet and peaceful.

Maybe she changed her mind about clearing the air. Maybe she can't face me. Probably because she can't forgive me.

Dwelling on that notion made Jem's stomach drop, so she shifted her thoughts to something she was fiercely protective of: her career.

If she thinks I'll slink away with my tail between my legs, she's got another think coming.

I'll still turn up at Lyonesse House tomorrow at ten a.m., ready to work. If she can't stand the sight of me, she can lurk in the residential wing. And she'll have only herself to blame for making the process as unpleasant as humanly possible.

It occurred to Jem that Pauley's endgame might be to draw her into some sort of emotional confrontation. Was that the idea, to get Jem to leave a nasty voicemail, or arrive at Lyonesse House spoiling for a fight? If she behaved in a manner that reflected poorly on the RIC or the Courtney Library, she'd lose more than the Gwyn family collection assignment. The world of Special Collections Librarians was small, and reputation was important. As far as Jem knew, none of her superiors were aware of the years she'd spent on St. Morwenna, or the black cloud under which she'd left.

I can't blow this opportunity. I refuse to, Jem thought, turning her mobile upside down on the bar top. She wouldn't keep looking, and deliberately inflaming her emotions. Whatever the game was, she simply wouldn't play.

Micki drifted back into Jem's orbit. "What about it? You still look hungry."

"Veering toward hangry," Jem agreed. "Put me down for fish and chips with mushy peas."

"Lovely! And look, a booth in the back's opening up. I'll have it cleared in a jiff," Micki said.

Sliding off the barstool, Jem stretched her neck and shoulders. She felt overdressed in her professional attire—skirt, blouse, jacket, and a deceptively named pair of kitten heels that qualified as instruments of torture. Starting tomorrow, and for however long the job kept her in the Isles of Scilly, she'd wear nothing but island togs: T-shirts, linen trousers, and breezy cotton sundresses. Simple pieces requiring nothing but to be handwashed and pegged up to dry.

One of the surfers ambled to the exit, nodding at Jem as he went. His surrendered booth was in decent shape, with only a few empty glasses and crumpled napkins left behind. Jem was about to clear it herself—Micki had been waylaid by another patron—when her mobile buzzed. She turned it over. The lock screen preview read PAULEY GWYN.

She let out her breath, grinning in relief. An explanation. Thank God. She thumbed open the message. It read: *Do you ever think about Cam Tremayne?*

Jem let out her breath in a rush. Staring at the words, she read them again. Then again. The meaning was plain. Inescapable. She felt like a paper airplane. Not the proper sort kids have fun with, but a blank page, folded halfway, then crushed in one sudden move. The kind that takes flight only once—straight into the bin.

"Are you okay?" It was Micki, back at her elbow with a bus pan balanced on her hip. "You look like you've seen a ghost. Or you're about to turn somebody into one."

"No, I… I got a weird message. A text meant for someone else," Jem mumbled. For years, she'd been careful never to discuss Cam Tremayne. To shift focus from whatever tale her face was telling, Jem said, "Don't worry about the table, I can clear it." She held out her hands for the bus pan and bar rag. "Take care of that bloke standing by the taps."

Micki obeyed, looking pleasantly surprised. Apparently no customer had offered to help her in a very long time. Still numb from the shock of the text, Jem cleared the booth, wiped it down, and took a seat, telling herself sternly to think about something else.

But it was like repeating the words, "Don't imagine an elephant." The more you say it, the more you see a trunk and tusks.

Her mobile buzzed again. Warily, Jem turned it over. It wasn't another text. Pauley was ringing her.

Her line was set to roll to voicemail on the sixth ring. Jem stared at the phone, counting vibrations. Just before it buzzed for the sixth time, she snatched up the phone and said calmly, "Jemima Jago."

"Jem! Thank goodness. That text—it wasn't from me. Someone picked up my mobile." Pauley had gone manic pixie again. She also sounded out of breath, as if she'd been running.

"I've ordered dinner. It just arrived," Jem lied, again in the manufactured tones of the Robot Queen of Andromeda. "Let's discuss things tomorrow, after I arrive at Lyonesse House, shall we?"

Pauley made an odd little noise. It took Jem's brain a moment to decode it after so many years. It was the sound Pauley emitted just before calling you on your bullshit.

"I know you're upset, Jem, and I don't blame you. But I'm in the middle of a disaster. I'm at St. Mary's Hospital. I'll probably be there all night. And I just found out some of my books were stolen. Including *the* book. *A Child's Garden of Verses.* With the Wilde poem."

Jem's stomach dropped. "Who would do that?"

Pauley's voice dropped to a whisper. "Mrs. Reddy would. I'm almost certain she took them. And if she did, there's only one reason."

"To spite me," Jem said.

CHAPTER TWO

Ancient History

By the time Micki returned from the kitchen bearing her plate of fish and chips, Jem no longer had much appetite. The Kernow Arms really heaped on the food. It was twice as much as she'd expected.

"You sure you're all right?" Micki asked, setting the food in front of her. "Bad phone call?"

It was on the tip of Jem's tongue to say it was just a wrong number and she'd feel better as soon as she tucked in. Then her gaze met Micki's and she realized, in the same way she'd belatedly decoded the sound Pauley made when calling her on her bullshit, that Micki was really asking. It wasn't a polite query. She wanted to hear the answer.

"I don't know what to think. Or feel. First I'm gutted. Then I'm suspicious. Then I'm concerned. And then I'm mad as hell." As Micki's eyes widened, Jem added, "I don't suppose you're due for a supper break? I'll go splitsies with you on the food and buy you a drink to wash it down with, if you're willing to listen."

Micki looked pleased to be asked. She headed back to the kitchen, brought out one of the Kernow Arms' other employees to man the bar, peeled off her apron, and sat down across from Jem in her booth.

"Don't worry about the drink," she said, placing a fizzy soda on the table. "Employees get free soft drinks. Besides, I never touch a drop on the job. Tequila makes my clothes come off, as they say. Now spill."

"Okay. So. I told you I used to live on St. Morwenna," Jem began, indicating the malt vinegar cruet to see if Micki found it as essential to good fish and chips as she did. When the other woman nodded, Jem shook it over the food, continuing, "My best friend on the island was a girl named Pauley Gwyn. They lived at the oldest house in the Isles of Scilly, Lyonesse House—"

"I've seen it," Micki broke in. "While I was visiting my cousin, Clarence—the one with the B&B. When he mentioned how old it was, I expected something poncy, like Prideaux Place. But Lyonesse looks every minute of its age. Like the Old Post Office in Tintagel, with those wavy-gravy roof tiles."

"Exactly." Jem popped a fry in her mouth. It was perfect, and she was relieved to find her appetite had returned. "The main part of the house could probably be classified as Grade I Listed. The residential wing is from the seventies, and when we were growing up we thought it was ghastly. But the large wing is pure magic. When you step into it, you're transported back to the days of pirates and wooden sailing ships. It has a library that dates from the eighteenth century. That's why I came back. I'm a Special Collections Librarian."

"Is that a fun job?" Micki asked, sounding a bit skeptical.

"It's the best job," Jem said, pausing only for a bite of fish. "I always liked to read, especially on rainy days when I couldn't get outside. But the library at Lyonesse made me think, for the first time, maybe I'll be a librarian someday. As a kid, I was in the Hugh Town Library every week, but it was pretty typical—utilitarian metal shelves, ugly, super-Scotchgarded carpets, and green paint on the walls.

"In the library at Lyonesse House, the wallpaper is that French turquoise color you never see anymore. The pattern is hand-drawn with gilt accents. The shelves go right up to the ceiling. They're made from elder wood, and they don't match—different Gwyns added them when the books started piling up on the floor. Even the rugs feel different when you walk on them. Like they're steeped in secrets."

Micki let out that amusing, wheezy laugh. "I thought you'd been away a long time?"

"I have. But it made an impression on me." Jem decided not to add that she still dreamed about the library sometimes. It was the only dream of St. Morwenna that she still welcomed, all these years later. "Besides, when they offered me the job, they emailed photos. It's amazing how many details I'd forgotten. There's over three hundred years of history squirreled away in there. Scrolls. Books with latching covers. Old leather sea chests containing God knows what."

"Then I stand corrected. It's a crazy-fun job. But will Pauley still donate the collection to the institute if you unearth something valuable?"

"I think so," Jem said. "From my point of view, by curating the collection and getting it into the Courtney Library's archives, I'll be making a huge contribution to British history. There will be scholarly papers to write, talks to give, maybe even a book. To be read by up to two hundred *very* interested researchers," she added with a grin. "From Pauley's point of view, it's a heap of stuff too potentially important to chuck out, and too troublesome to maintain. Old books and papers don't do well, long-term, in a subtropical climate. There's only one item that was pre-identified as potentially valuable apart from just to historians."

"Hey. Don't go back to your fish. Tell me!"

"Sorry. It's just… it's still kind of a niche thing. The collection might include a previously undiscovered Oscar Wilde poem," Jem said after a sip of ale. "Pauley's mum found it written on the back flyleaf of a first edition of *A Child's Garden of Verses*. A William Blake first edition in good shape is already worth a bit at auction. If the poem, 'Isola'—which seems to be about Wilde's dead sister—is authenticated, the book will be worth thousands." Even as she said it, Jem couldn't suppress a sigh.

"This all sounds wonderful. So I don't get it. Why are you all woe-is-me?"

"The book has been stolen. By someone who has hated me for a long time. And wanted to ruin this for me, apparently."

"What? You're telling me you have a nemesis?" Micki gave another wheezy laugh. "Please. You with your demure heels and your hair up in a chignon and that buff-color nail polish? You in the Witness Protection Scheme or something?"

"I turned over a new leaf. But I was a bit of a wild child, back in the day."

"No kidding? Well, me too. I used to run away from home," Micki offered. "Not because I was mistreated. There were just too many Lathams, and never any privacy. The constables in our neighborhood were always scooping me up and bringing me back. They called me the Wanderer."

"They called me Stargazer," Jem said. "I was always outdoors. Slept in the back garden sometimes, or camped all night on the beach. Knew all the constellations by sight. I just needed a distraction from—well, everything. When Kenneth, my dad, dumped me on St. Morwenna, I was so confused and miserable. The only thing that took my mind off it was to lie on my back and watch the stars. I used to pretend if I wished upon the right one, things would miraculously get better."

"I used to wish aliens would swoop down and whisk me away to another planet," Micki said. "Why did your dad dump you?"

"My mum fell ill with ovarian cancer. She died when I was six. Afterward, Kenneth had a sort of breakdown."

"You mean a clinical breakdown? As in, sectioned?"

Jem shook her head. "Nothing like that. More of a resign-from-your-job, send-away-your-only-child, get-a-twenty-year-old-supermarket-assistant-up-the-duff-and-move-in-with-her sort of breakdown."

"Bastard! Really, a twenty-year-old? Up the duff?"

"With twins," Jem said. "So Kenneth decided I should stay with his mum, Sue Jago, until he got his new life sorted."

"And that took—how long? Five or six years?"

"Eight," Jem said. "To be honest, I don't think he ever would've had me back, except Gran had a heart attack and died. Went to bed one night and never woke up."

Sue died to escape you, Mrs. Reddy's voice said in her mind. She'd made that accusation years ago on St. Morwenna's Quay, in front of dozens of people, as fourteen-year-old Jem climbed into a water taxi bound for the mainland. Over the years, Jem had become adept at turning down the volume on Mrs. Reddy's outlandish accusations, but she'd never succeeded in shutting them out entirely. Would proximity make them louder again?

"Parents." Micki's sigh was somewhere between fondness and exasperation. "Mine split up when I was still in nappies. Mum had two more blokes before I was sixteen. They weren't terrible. Wouldn't work, for the most part, and wouldn't tidy up after themselves, but I wouldn't call them terrible.

"Still," she continued after a pause to polish off the last of her dinner, "I used to sneak off to see my old dad and beg him to come back home. I had this idea of what a household should be—a neat little nuclear family, like on telly. All the boyfriends and cousins and whatnot trooping in and out like a train station seemed wrong to me. But as I look back, I think it was all for the best. Taught me how to get along with all sorts. And to not take TV bullshit too much to heart. Especially when it comes to romance."

"Very wise. So as far as you're concerned, there are no men in the Scillies? Despite"—Jem glanced around at the pub's otherwise entirely male clientele—"all the men?"

"It's not that I'm choosy. Well. Not terribly choosy. I'm just in a bit of a drought. Not looking to get married or make babies. That's not me," Micki added firmly. Pointing at Jem's ringless left hand, she asked, "What about you?"

"Divorced."

"Oh. Sorry to hear that, love," Micki said.

"I'm fine." Jem smiled to prove she meant it. "My London friends—and by friends, I mean acquaintances, colleagues, and so forth—all assumed I was gutted because Dean and I were so close. The fact is, he was my only real friend. We met at uni and just clicked. I'd got out of the habit of… well, letting people in. But I made an exception for him. So we started dating, and became joined at the hip. Married right out of uni."

"But…?"

"But it was a flatmate kind of marriage. Still BFFs. Loved to binge-watch the same shows on telly, plan mini-breaks, try new restaurants. We had absolutely identical tastes. Right down to—"

"Right down to the fellows you fancied, am I right?" Micki cut in.

"Well spotted. It wasn't Dean's fault he didn't come out sooner. His family is so repressed. Almost Victorian. He knew they'd never accept him as gay, so he tried to be not-gay. It took him a long time to face the truth. Once he told me the truth, he was terribly relieved."

"But what about you?"

"I was even more relieved," Jem admitted. "But that's not something you can go around telling your colleagues, is it? 'No worries, it was a sexless marriage. Euthanization was the only humane option.' So they assumed I was gutted and I, well, let them. Otherwise, they would have been offering to arrange blind dates, or recommending dating apps, when all I wanted was time to…"

"To what?" Micki asked.

"I don't know. Focus on my career for a while," Jem said. "I mean, how Dean got into his predicament is obvious. *I'm* the question mark. Why did I say yes when he proposed? Why did I stay in a flatmate marriage for years? When he came out to me, it was the least shocking news I ever heard. Now if he'd dumped me for another woman, or done a legger with our joint finances, or any breach of trust, really, I would've been gobsmacked. That was the thing about Dean. Five minutes after I met him, I knew he'd never hurt me."

Micki allowed the statement to stand for a moment. Then she said, "That's as good an answer as any. To why you said yes, I mean. Especially if there was someone before him who did harm you."

"There was," Jem murmured, again surprising herself with the readiness of the revelation. Instantly she saw Rhys Tremayne's face, as he'd been twenty years ago: sixteen, square-jawed and handsome, with blond-highlighted hair and dark blue eyes. She saw his brother's face, too. They'd resembled one another, but Cam had been two years younger, the lines of his face less defined, his eyes brown instead of blue. When she imagined Cam, he always looked sad. Sad, and accusing.

Micki was still waiting patiently for Jem to finish her sentence. Automatically, Jem's forefinger crept up to trace the small, deep scar above her left eyebrow. She daubed concealer over it each morning, but it still stood out like a warning in Braille, inscribed on her face so it could never be forgotten.

"I suppose I said yes to Dean because he was the polar opposite of… someone else," Jem said.

Micki seemed to consider that. Then, after a brief silence, she said, "Sounds as if you've contemplated the whole thing a bit more than you realized."

"I knew what I didn't want," she said at last. "Sometimes, first love leaves a scar."

"No argument there." Micki glanced over her shoulder at the man who'd taken over her bartending duties. "I can get away with a few more minutes. So. Let's get back to your nemesis, the antiquarian book thief. Is your friend Pauley doing anything about it? Ringing the police, for a start?"

"Not yet. She's dealing with a lot," Jem said, relating the essence of her conversation with Pauley. "She said she only realized the book had gone missing a little while ago. St. Morwenna didn't take kindly to the news Pauley was donating the library. They seemed to think it was community property—even though they'd never lifted a finger to help her organize or preserve it."

"Shocker," Micki said.

"Anyway, there was a teen called Kenzie who saw Mrs. Reddy hovering nearby before it went missing. Pauley didn't know what to do—it's hard to accuse anyone, much less Mrs. Reddy, without proof. Then she had a message from St. Mary's Hospital. Her mum's in the hospice unit. The nurses called to say she's taken a turn, and Pauley needs to stay with her, just in case."

Micki made a face. "That stinks. Doesn't she have someone who can help her? Make the police report for her, or at least go confront the person who nicked the book?"

"To be honest," Jem said, finishing her ale, "I've half a mind to do it. Not call the Isles of Scilly Police Department—the chief's an arse, and if he's still running the show, he'll probably try to turn it around so Pauley is the guilty party. No point bringing in the police unless there's proof. But I could go to St. Morwenna. Knock on a certain someone's door and see how she likes dealing with me when I'm all grown up."

"Oooh, wish I could be there. What's the nemesis' name? My cousin Clar likes everyone on St. Morwenna except this one right old cow called Reddy. She roars around the island on a golf cart, spying on everyone."

"That's her! Edith Reddy. *Mrs.* Reddy, to be exact. She's very keen that the proprieties be observed at all times. What did Clarence do to incur her wrath?"

"Left his clothes on the line a bit longer than she thought necessary."

"Sounds about right. Mrs. Reddy made life miserable for kids all around the Scillies," Jem said. "Only a few of us actually lived on St. Morwenna—St. Mary's was more popular with families, because of the school—but Scillonians are island-hoppers, and Mrs. Reddy was the secret police. When she wasn't actually watching and listening, her snouts were gathering intelligence to report back to her."

"And you really think she hated you personally enough to steal that book, just to spite you?"

It's possible that plenty of people still hate me, Jem thought, remembering the text. *I don't care. I committed to this job and I'll see it through. Then I can walk away from St. Morwenna on my terms and never look back.*

"Yep. Anyway. Thanks for listening to ancient history," Jem said, gathering her things and readying to leave.

"Thanks for inviting me to eat." Micki glanced over her shoulder at the relief bartender, who caught her eye and pointed at his wristwatch. "So do you mean it? You're really off to confront the old witch?"

"If I can find a water taxi, yes."

"Then unlock your mobile and I'll put in my number. I'm dying to hear what happens next."

Marveling at Micki's deft offer of friendship, Jem did so. Maybe her return to the Isles of Scilly wouldn't be all work and old grudges. Her post-London, post-divorce life could certainly do with some new friends.

The bell over the pub's front door jangled. Glancing over, Jem saw a newcomer who filled the door frame so completely, he seemed to wear it. Then he squeezed through, popping into Kernow Arms to reveal himself as even taller and wider than Jem had first assumed. Perhaps six foot six, he was pale and blue-eyed, with a faint blond halo around his otherwise bald head. On his lumpy face, his jowls slid into his chin, and his chin melted into his neck. His patchy beard and overbroad grin made him seem simultaneously affable and disreputable.

"Bart the Ferryman," the relief bartender called.

"Bart the Ferryman," a surfer echoed. His mates joined in, making the name into a chant.

Bart glanced around almost furtively, as if he hadn't expected to be recognized. He was dressed like a boatman, in hip waders and braces. On top of his shirt was the kind of reflective yellow vest worn by builders and police officers.

"Bart! Where's that tenner you owe me, then?" a man called from the other side of the pub.

Casting off his furtive look, Bart put on a friendly grin. "Soon, mate. Soon!"

Bart's eyes roved around the room. When his gaze fell on Micki, he loped over, turning sideways to keep from colliding with the tables in his path. "All right, Micki, my love. It's been a terrible day. Hardly any emmets on the ferry. I don't suppose you'd pour a broken man one on the house?"

"I can do better than that. How about a paying customer?" Micki asked, indicating Jem.

CHAPTER THREE

In the Presence of the Dead

It wasn't a long walk from the Kernow Arms to Hugh Town's Old Quay, and Bart the Ferryman kept up a running commentary all the way. Jem was in no mood for chit-chat—now that she'd decided to confront Mrs. Reddy, she wanted to work herself up for the process, to imagine every possible outcome and how she could triumph over whatever the old bat threw at her. Fortunately, Bart's running commentary required no input from his listeners.

Bart strove to present himself as a sort of Renaissance man: gentleman, scholar, and romantic wanderer.

"Instinct brought me to the islands three months ago," he said, escorting Jem along the stone jetty. The orange sun was halfway below the horizon, and Bart's shadow stretched behind him, melting into shadows and then chasing him again.

"I was done with Devon. Done," he added emphatically, as if Jem had asked. "The problem I have, and some say it's a blessing but I say it's a curse, is that I'm an honest man. My word is my bond. The *villains* in charge of Brixham Harbor have never met an honest man. They're all tricksy legal types. Refused to accept a handshake deal. With them it's all paperwork and non-refundable deposits and signing your life away…"

Between two sleek yachts, Jem glimpsed a converted fishing boat. It was in such pitiful shape, cosmetically speaking, that it looked little better than a recent salvage, up from the depths. Its blue-gray hull was patched with a square of bright red corrugated steel, probably cut from a shipping container. It looked like an open wound.

"Thar she blows!" Bart called proudly, pointing. "I call her *Merry Maid.* I've been all over the world, but I'll always be Cornish at heart."

Jem hadn't lost her critical eye for watercraft. *Merry Maid* had been nominally renovated for passengers. Its trawling apparatus was gone, along with the station for cleaning fish. Crude wooden benches were bolted along the gunwale, creating space to seat about twenty people. That was the only amenity she could see. No wonder Bart had appended "the Ferryman" to his name—without it, people might see the *Merry Maid* and never guess its purpose.

A man leaning against a lamppost, head down as he scrolled on his mobile, glanced up at them and called, "Bart! You're a hard man to reach."

"What?" Bart patted at his Day-Glo jacket, coming up with a smartphone. "No unanswered calls, mate."

The man, who Jem couldn't help noticing was better-looking than average, with dark hair and a neatly sculpted, pointed beard, scowled. He called out a number from memory, suggesting he'd tried it many times.

"Oh!" Bart patted himself down again. From the vest's inner pocket, he came out with two cheap, anonymous black flip phones. "Burners," as the crime dramas called them. He opened one, checked, re-pocketed it, opened the second, and said, "Ah! Ringer's muted. Sorry, mate. I give out different numbers sometimes. It's, ah, a marketing tactic. A/B testing."

The man looked skeptical, but didn't argue. "There doesn't seem to be a lot of water taxis doing inter-island runs tonight. Are you free? Or…" He shifted his gaze to Jem, trailing off.

"Hmm?" Bart turned to look down at Jem from his great height. "I don't know, the little woman and I were just about to embark on a romantic sunset cruise, but—"

"I'm a paying fare. Bound for St. Morwenna," Jem cut in. She glared at the bearded man for daring to suggest that in addition to being seen with Bart the Ferryman, she might actually be *with* him.

"I knew it," the man announced, as if accurately interpreting her tone. "I'm new to the Isles of Scilly. I want to make the circuit. Ramble about and get a feel for the place. Perhaps you could advise me where to start?" He shook out his visitor's map, placing it across his knees, where Jem could see the cartoonish, not-to-scale image of Scilly's five largest islands.

"He can drop us at St. Morwenna, then when you're done, take you on to Bryher," Jem said. "By the time he comes back round to St. Morwenna, I'll be ready to go and you'll have made the circuit, as long as you don't spend more than, say, fifteen minutes per island."

"Fifteen minutes?" the man asked.

"More than enough at this time of night. This is a Dark Sky Reserve," Jem said, then glanced at Bart. "Isn't it?"

"If not, it might as well be," he said, heaving massive shoulders. "Once the sun sets, it's nothing out there but the moon and stars. Blacker than black. Where're you from?" he asked the man.

"Exeter."

"All right, Exeter. I was about to call it a night, it being a long and profitable day," Bart told him, eyes flicking toward Jem as if to ask for her complicity in the lie, "but out of the goodness of my heart, I'll give you a ride. Still, I must charge you an extra tenner on top of the usual circuit fare, though, for the darkness and the added bother."

"Five," the man said, in the flat voice of someone accustomed to being obeyed.

Bart groaned. "I've already taken one charity case," he said, indicating Jem. "Just when I was settled in the pub with a pint in my future…"

"Except you couldn't pay for it," Jem said helpfully. "So the charity goes both ways."

Looking slightly betrayed, Bart turned back to the bearded man. "All right. Usual circuit price, plus five."

"Usual circuit price, final," the man said, tucking his mobile into his jacket, which was hot-rod red. So were the earpieces of his specs. The color choice intrigued her. He was at least forty, with silver at his temples and a fleck or two in his neat beard, but there was a vitality in his bearing.

Live wire, she thought. A first impression based not on fact, but on instinct.

Jem was first up *Merry Maid's* metal gangplank, with the bearded man coming up behind, and Bart's heavy tread following. Jem sat on the starboard bench, which was none-too-firmly attached; when she sat down, the whole thing shuddered. Chuckling, the bearded man took the port bench.

"I'm Hack, by the way." He flashed a grin at Jem.

She nodded, then shifted her gaze to the water. Her brain kept trying to resume running Mrs. Reddy worst-case scenarios.

But that's bollocks. I'm a grown-up now. She's an old lady. The sort of nonsense that worked when I was fourteen won't fly anymore. I'll get the book back, and that will be that.

Her fellow passenger, Hack, had said something. Shaken out of her musings, Jem looked across the boat. He was taking advantage of the wide-open space by lounging, legs stretched out on the bench. Were those cowboy boots? Who came to the Isles of Scilly in a hot-rod red windcheater and black cowboy boots?

"And you are?" he repeated.

"Miles away." She turned back to the water. From inside *Merry Maid's* wheelhouse, Bart said over the boat's PA system, "Secure all valuables. Hands and feet inside the ride. Off we go to serene

St. Morwenna, home of the Tremayne Lighthouse and everyone's favorite Scilly tradition, the Ice Cream Hut."

"Sounds amazing," Hack said sardonically. "I take it you're a native? Didn't have to consult a map to figure that Bart ought to take us to St. Morwenna first."

"I lived on St. Morwenna as a child," she said. "I'm back to do a job for the Royal Institute of Cornwall."

"Is it a sunset-on-a-Friday sort of job?" Hack asked. "Or does serene St. Morwenna have a nightlife?"

Jem shrugged. "There's a pub that's open late. I suppose there might be a few shops that stay open till nine o'clock. Otherwise, it's all rocks, sand, and stars."

"You don't give up much under interrogation, do you?" Hack sounded pleased. "I've asked you two direct questions and you've sloughed them off like rainwater."

"Do I owe you answers?"

"No. But I'd still like to know what you're thinking about. Your face just now looked a bit…"

"What?"

"Fierce." He flashed the grin again. "Are you storming off St. Mary's, or storming onto St. Morwenna?"

"I'm a librarian. I'm going to confront someone over a misappropriated book."

Hack burst out laughing. "No, really."

"Really."

"Remind me never to let one fall overdue."

They spent the rest of the short jaunt in comfortable silence, watching St. Mary's recede and St. Morwenna rise out of the darkening sea. It was exactly as Jem remembered: craggy and crenellated, like an island created with natural battlements. The beaches facing *Merry Maid*'s approach were of stony shingle, dotted with bracken and heather, but there were white sand beaches on the northwest side. On St. Morwenna's highest point, the stout white bulk of the lighthouse stood out against the purpling sky.

"When do they turn on the beacon?" Hack asked.

"Never." Jem smiled at his consternation. "Seriously. It's been deactivated forever."

"I could learn a lot about St. Morwenna with you as a guide. Sure you don't want to forego the book errand and check out that pub you mentioned?" Hack put his head to one side, charmingly, like a dog performing a trick that usually works in his favor. "I'm buying."

He's chatting me up, Jem thought, feeling ridiculous for taking so long to realize it. Though her divorce had been final in January, she still wasn't used to thinking of herself as free to respond. It was always nice to realize someone found you attractive. As for Hack—well, he wasn't her type. Not a bit of it. She'd spent twenty years avoiding men who put out his kind of signals.

It was like the Tremayne Lighthouse was staring at her, waiting to see how she would respond. And both Tremayne brothers: the living, and the dead.

"Sorry," she said, smiling gently. "I've been waiting a long time to tell this woman off. I can't wait to look her in the eye and say—" She broke off.

"What?"

"That despite everything she said and did, here I am. She's beneath my notice."

Hack bit his lower lip, eyes dancing.

"I know. I know it's ridiculous to come back after twenty years, knock on somebody's door, and shout, 'You're beneath my notice,'" Jem said. "But I'll do it. And I'll enjoy it."

"Wish I could tag along," Hack said, but in a pleasant tone to tell her there were no hard feelings.

"Just ahead, Porth St. Morwenna," Bart bellowed over the PA, giving the island's little quay a title it never had, nor aspired to.

"As there are no berths, I'll approach the sea stairs and allow you to alight via the portside gunwale. Please make no attempt to disembark until I arrive to render assistance."

Merry Maid chugged toward the sea wall, which was lit only by a few dim, shielded light posts. The boat seemed on a collision course, then righted itself rather suddenly as something deep in the vessel's innards let out a groan.

"Sorry. Coming around again at a better angle," Bart said over the PA.

"As skippers go, do you think Bart is… qualified?" Hack asked Jem.

"I wouldn't bet on it."

"I suppose if he strands me, I can ring the IoS PD for help."

"I wouldn't bet on them, either. If you find yourself in difficulty, ring the coastguard," Jem said. "But with any luck, I'll see you back here in a couple of hours—book in hand."

*

Jem was glad of the twilight, which blunted the visceral impact of returning to St. Morwenna after so long. It was almost dreamlike to step onto the old, cobbled jetty as the light faded, with the familiar shops of the Square, St. Morwenna's marketplace, rendered mostly in shadow. Ahead was the Ice Cream Hut, its crown of fairy lights proclaiming it was still open for business, but behind the service counter, the hut's metal shutters were pulled down.

Another relief. Jem wasn't looking forward to reconnecting with many people on St. Morwenna, and apart from the demon of the pantheon—Mrs. Reddy—the islander she least wanted to see was Bettie Quick, owner of the Ice Cream Hut. Once upon a time, Bettie had been a fixture in Jem's life, since she and Jem's gran had been very close friends. But Mrs. Reddy had put an end to that, and Gran had died before the rift could be healed. As far as Jem was concerned, Bettie's betrayal of Gran had contributed to her sudden death. But, of course, that could never be proved.

Following Quay Road through the Square, Jem walked as fast as her uncomfortable kitten heels allowed, determined to blaze through the little cluster of shops and cottages without giving anyone the chance to recognize her. The text—*Do you ever think about Cam Tremayne?*—was probably a fair barometer of how she was remembered on St. Morwenna. She couldn't let anyone engage her, bog her down. She had to save all her firepower, all her confrontational energy, for the woman who'd caused it all.

The Square was tiny by most standards. Once Jem had passed the Duke's Head Inn, the brightest spot on St. Morwenna after dark, Quay Road flattened into the cross-island pedestrian lane called the Byway. After the first bend, trees clustered in close and the profound darkness of St. Morwenna swallowed her up. After two decades, she had forgotten just how lost you could feel on a murky, silent stretch of the Byway. As a teen, it had given her a pleasant thrill, making her feel daring and up for anything. Now it gave rise to a stab of uncertainty.

No one asked me to confront Mrs. Reddy about the missing book. If I handle this wrong, I could make a fool of myself. I could get myself sacked.

Pauley had made it clear that while she believed Mrs. Reddy nicked the book, she had no proof. Her eyewitness of the event, someone named Kenzie, had seen Mrs. Reddy hovering near the precious first edition of *A Child's Garden of Verses,* a red tote bag at hand. Like most of the community, Mrs. Reddy had stopped by Lyonesse House to bid the library goodbye. Its loss had become an unexpectedly tender subject, as many in the community thought Pauley had no right to dispense with the Gwyn family collection, even to a historical society. According to Kenzie, after Mrs. Reddy was glimpsed near the book, it was discovered to be missing.

Jem tried to tell herself that this all depended on the testimony of someone she'd never met, and it certainly wasn't worth enraging her boss, Mr. Atherton. Much less getting sacked over. But the moment she began to make such arguments, her heart sped up—not with fear, but with rebellion. Mrs. Reddy might have ruled the roost in the Isles of Scilly since time out of mind, but it was high time someone held her accountable. Jem had already poured out her heart—by her normally tight-lipped standards, at least—to Micki and then impulsively hopped on the *Merry Maid* to St. Morwenna. So what if Mrs. Reddy didn't actually have the book? It wasn't really about that. It was about facing down an old fear.

Besides, I'm already on Mrs. Reddy's land. Too late to back out now, Jem thought.

Along this stretch of the Byway, palm trees predominated, shading the path. Pulling out her mobile, Jem flicked on the torch app and trained the beam ahead of her.

There it is. She picked out the shape of Seascape House. The house had been built in the place of an original four-room stone cottage typical of island homes. Mrs. Reddy's first act upon arriving on St. Morwenna, husband and daughter in tow, had been to buy a home in need of renovation and knock it down without a second thought. That event, which had occurred long before Jem, aged six, arrived on the island, perfectly encapsulated Mrs. Reddy's relationship with her new community. What she wanted, she purchased. What she found lacking, she destroyed.

With the moon and stars blotted out by tree canopies and only her mobile's torch to light the way, Jem couldn't tell if Seascape House had been improved over the intervening years. But judging from the greenery encroaching on her path, it seemed that Mrs. Reddy's front garden had been abandoned to go wild ages ago. King Protea flowers, six to eight feet tall, rippled in the slight breeze; the once-neat stone path leading from the Byway to the porch was thick with creepers. Only one area looked exactly as Jem remembered it. The sacred space dedicated to Mrs. Reddy's mechanical soulmate, Big Orange.

The golf cart sat on a concrete rectangle measuring roughly eight feet by twelve feet, looking as self-satisfied and quietly menacing as a fat ginger tabby. Its bonnet and awning flashed metallic orange as Jem's torchlight slid over it. A second air horn had been installed on the dash. Maybe Mrs. Reddy needed twice the weaponry to bully today's kids. Jem hoped so. She liked the idea of contemporary teens giving the old woman a jaundiced stare, popping in earbuds, and calmly scrolling on their phones until she spontaneously combusted.

The nape of Jem's neck prickled suddenly. Was someone watching her?

She looked at the house. In the islands, people tended to eat late. Most of Seascape House was lit up, golden light spilling out of the front room's bay windows, though gauzy curtains shielded the living space from view. With Big Orange parked and all the lights on, Mrs. Reddy was probably cooking supper, or perhaps settling down to eat. It was the perfect time to knock on the door and demand a word.

That feeling of not being alone, of being watched, intensified. All around her, the overgrown garden seemed to hold its breath, the insects and tiny night sounds going silent. From nearby Scorch Cove came the sound of the breakers crashing. It was so gentle, it might have been pure imagination.

Marching up the steps, Jem rapped smartly on the door. She expected the familiar call—"It's open!"—or perhaps a bit of Mrs. Reddy's signature abruptness, such as "Who's there?" or even, "Piss off!" Instead, she could only hear shuffling from the other side of the door.

She waited. Another deep breath. There was no peephole on the door, and the gauzy curtains in the bay window didn't twitch.

She rapped again, louder this time, hard enough to make her knuckles smart. From inside, something fell with a crash.

BANG.

For a crazy second, Jem thought she'd heard a gun go off. But no, she'd felt the impact of something heavy striking the floor with sufficient force to make the dwelling shiver.

"Mrs. Reddy!" Jem called, surging through the unlocked door. Only when she was inside did it cross her mind that something sinister might be afoot. In London, you kept your eyes open for your neighbors, but your own safety came first. Better to hang back and ring 999 than to blunder into a mugging or drug deal gone bad, and end up getting robbed or knifed.

Sod that, Jem thought. She'd once stopped a youth from snatching her bag by sprinting after him, snatching it back, and kicking him in the shins for good measure. Of course, he'd been a featherweight, strung out on God knew what, but Jem hadn't noticed those details until after she'd taken her bag back.

"Mrs. Reddy!"

Small wonder the old woman kept the curtains drawn. The front room was wildly cluttered. In the opposite space, probably meant to be the dining room, there was nothing much except the source of that shattering bang. A curio cabinet lay on its side, glass-paned door cracked, interior glass shelves smashed to pieces.

Jem didn't have time to focus on the fallen cabinet. Deeper inside the house, something else gave way with a loud crack. Jem didn't know what it was. The scrabbling, rattling sounds seemed to issue from inside one of the bedrooms. Was there a scuffle going on? An intruder, perhaps, struggling with Mrs. Reddy?

Jem surged into the house's dimly lit central passage. In front of an open door—*bedroom,* she thought, taking in a flash of its contents—one of her kitten heels hit a wet patch. Before Jem knew it, she was arse over teakettle, hitting the cold marble tiles with a thud.

The scuffling sounds in the room died away. Jem thought she heard something else now, farther away, like branches snapping. The fall hadn't injured her—she'd landed on the part of her anatomy best equipped for a hard jolt—but it had shaken her out of her single-minded pursuit. What was going on? And what on earth had she slipped on?

Her mobile, which had slipped from her grasp as she tumbled, had fallen in the stuff. When she automatically retrieved the phone, it smeared, red and sticky, across the palm of her hand. And though there wasn't a lot of it, Jem recognized the blood at once. It stood out, garish against Mrs. Reddy's white travertine marble floors, like mountains on the moon.

Up came the hackles on her neck and forearms. "Mrs. Reddy?" she called, rising slowly. She'd lost a shoe, and the remainder of the blood—probably just a few big drops, as opposed to a puddle—had become a long smear with a pointed end. A shaky red arrow, pointing into what Jem now saw was the master bedroom.

Kicking off her remaining shoe, Jem stepped into the room, mindful for other little blood spatters. Even before she laid eyes on the bed, which was half concealed by the bend of the wall, her heart thudded crazily. She was in the presence of the dead. It was the skin-crawling sensation of being close to a corpse—of inhaling air that had once passed through dead lungs—and even while her higher mind denied it, accusing her of jumping to conclusions, her animal instincts knew the truth.

The queen-sized bed stood tall on its platform, massive green headboard reaching halfway to the ceiling. The quilted coverlet, patterned in green leaves and orange bird of paradise flowers, was neatly tucked in. Near the pile of frilled and tasseled throw pillows lay the richest woman on St. Morwenna, the most disliked woman in the Isles of Scilly, and the demon of Jem's personal pantheon. It was Mrs. Edith Reddy, and she was stone dead.

CHAPTER FOUR

Murder by Duct Tape

Mrs. Reddy wasn't lying on the bed, as if to take a nap. Rather, she bisected it, head and torso on the mattress, feet on the floor. It looked like she'd sat on the side of the bed, possibly to remove a shoe, and fallen backward. Something covered her mouth and nose. Silver-gray duct tape.

Somebody made a noise. A strangled intake of breath. For an awful moment, Jem thought the old woman was trying to speak. Unreality washed over her, insisting frantically that this was all a dream, that it couldn't be happening. Then Jem realized the sound of surprise and horror had come from her.

She forced herself to inch closer to Mrs. Reddy's body. The old woman's eyes were half-open, the whites marred by burst blood vessels, the corneas frosted over like a pond in winter. If there were cuts, contusions, or other signs of violence, Jem couldn't see them. There was nothing in the way of a murder weapon except the duct tape covering the old woman's nose and mouth. And that was enough. Whoever had applied it hadn't been content with simply covering Mrs. Reddy's mouth. They'd wound the stuff all the way around her head several times, sticking her hair, still worn in a frizzy white bob after all these years, against her ears.

The cracking noise, Jem saw now, had come from the bedroom window. The blinds hung askew, the curtains had fallen off the rod, and the casement window had been torn off its hinges, breaking the wooden sill in the process. Someone had escaped via that route only moments before. Now a square of blackness peered into the bedroom, like a malevolent island spirit watching over the old woman's corpse.

The killer might still be out there. Behind the house, Jem thought, rushing headlong to the gaping black hole. Her foot trod on something slippery, almost landing her on her arse again. Clutching the bed's quilted footboard, Jem caught her breath, forcing down her rising panic until rationality returned. Then she *saw* the rest of the room, and what had tripped her up. Mrs. Reddy's wardrobe stood wide open. Every stitch of clothing she owned had been swept onto the floor. One of Mrs. Reddy's signature nautical pieces, a boat neck top decorated with red embroidered crabs, was under her foot. A pale pink mark—a bit of blood transfer—stood out beside one of the whimsical crabs, stamped there by Jem's big toe.

Something about that little pink toeprint brought the full horror of Jem's situation home to her. What was she even doing here, inside Seascape House, tracking blood through a crime scene?

Through the open window, Jem heard the soft crash of something pushing through the back garden's overgrown greenery. The sound was soft enough to be a cat or other small creature. Or it might be the killer, doubling back in the direction of the Byway. Was Mrs. Reddy's murder a robbery gone wrong? The act of someone who'd come to the Scillies to party or hide out from mainland authorities, and found themselves desperate for cash? Such a person would have no idea how to escape through the wilds behind Seascape House. Jem knew a narrow path led to a flower farm, and then to a cliff overlooking Crescent Beach, but a stranger might feel hopelessly lost in the dark. If the killer was returning to the Byway, this might be Jem's only chance to get a look.

Picking her way over the piles of clothing, Jem reached the window and stuck her head out. It took a moment for her eyes to adapt to the darkness. Something shook a dwarf palm, shivering its fronds. Squinting, Jem picked out something small circling the dwarf palm's base. It didn't move stealthily, like a cat. Instead, it pushed ahead with its nose to the ground, something long and shaggy lashing behind.

A puppy, she thought, shoulders slumping as she let out her breath. Turning right to be certain the area was clear, she found herself staring into the eyes of a wild-haired man. He was big and broad-shouldered, with a beard as thick as a rhododendron.

Jem screamed, or tried to. What came out was a high, thin sound, strangled by pure shock. She pulled her head into the bedroom and backpedaled, turning her ankle in the process. Then she was falling again, this time onto a soft pile of nautical-themed sets of matching shirts and capris. If she'd been an old-school cartoon character, the classic twittering birds circling her head would've been replaced with blue whales, red crabs, and silver dolphins.

Outside the window, the wild-haired man was—laughing? Not cackling maniacally, but definitely laughing.

"Buck! Come on." He whistled, presumably at the puppy, who issued a good-natured bark. "Let's go, Buck."

Jem tried to process the voice. Was it familiar? Maybe, but she couldn't reconcile it with the startling wild man who'd emerged from the blackness. Heart thudding against her ribs, she had to reassure herself that she wasn't dreaming, that this chain of mad events was actually happening. She'd dropped her mobile again. It had fallen nearby, the smear of crimson on its screen rebuking her. On her right forefinger, a matching band of crimson stood out. Jem stared at it with rising horror. She was dreaming. If Mrs. Reddy's blood was on her hands, she *must* be dreaming.

Heavy steps fell upon the porch. Seascape House's door opened. As Jem scrabbled to her feet, shocked back to rationality, the wild man shouted, "Buck! Sit. No." Another whistle. "No. I mean it. Out. Out, buddy. No... no... come on, now."

As Jem listened, the heavy footfalls thumped out of the house. Whoever the man was, he apparently wasn't coming to murder her until he'd brought his dog to heel. And it sounded as if the dog had ignored his master's commands, forcing the wild man to retrace his steps and escort the canine out.

I got this, Jem told herself, even as her heart kept up its double-time beat. *He's no desperado. He's pleading with his dog, for heaven's sake.*

The man was returning. Jem retrieved her mobile, picked up her wayward shoe—the other one was apparently still in the passageway near the blood smear—and smoothed down her skirt. She'd faced down a handbag snatcher. If this hairy creep made one false move, she'd throw her shoe at his head, then escape through the broken window. Even after almost twenty years, her feet would instinctively find the path to Crescent Beach. It had been *their* beach, after all—the special refuge for her, Pauley, Cam, and Rhys, once upon a time.

Footfalls sounded down the passageway. Something skittered across the marble tiles, and the man swore.

"Lose a shoe, Jemmie?" he asked, entering the bedroom.

The casual use of her name startled her. This man was tall, perhaps six foot four, and looked even wilder in a well-lighted room. He wore swim trunks and a sleeveless white cotton vest, the kind Americans call a "wife beater." His feet were bare, and none too clean. Neither was the wife beater; it was smeared all over with black, gray, and red. He was so intent on her, he actually appeared unaware of the body on the bed.

Jem stared at the man, trying to separate the planes of his face from that wild beard and mane of ragged hair. It was like staring at an autostereogram—one of those "magic" pictures that morphs into a 3D image once the viewer relaxes enough to perceive it. For a frozen moment, she had no idea who she was looking at, or why he'd called her Jemmie. But the moment she gave up—the moment she decided he was no one to her, that it was mistaken identity—she relaxed. Instantly, the constellations rotated in the heavens, the earth shifted beneath her feet, and Jem knew him. The first boy she'd ever kissed. The first boy she'd ever loved.

"Rhys."

She didn't decide to go to him. Jem's body made that decision, completely independent of her higher faculties. Making her way through the piles of fallen clothing, Jem made it within arm's length of him before her brain finally intervened to stop her. He was taller than she remembered, and broader in the shoulder, his stained vest straining across the center of his chest. Teenage Rhys had been a lithe surfer with a pretty face. This man was… she didn't know what he was. He looked like the sort of unfortunate that sometimes slept rough around Penzance Harbor.

As if uncomfortable with her proximity, Rhys's gaze flicked away from Jem. When it crossed the bed, he recoiled with a gasp.

"Christ Almighty," he said, his gaze shifting away from Mrs. Reddy's pale, motionless body as he locked eyes with her again. "Jem. What have you done?"

CHAPTER FIVE

A Jump-Scare from Poundland Chewbacca

"What have I done?" she repeated stupidly.

"To Mrs. Reddy. You've killed her!"

A pulse of sheer anger overcame Jem and she slapped him. The shock of impact shot through up her arm, but she registered the jolt without truly feeling it. All she could feel was the anvil Rhys had dropped on her chest when he accused her.

If the crack of her palm against his bearded cheek hurt, Rhys didn't show it. Neither did he look all that surprised. Apparently finding her standing over a corpse was just what he expected from Jem Jago.

"I came here to ask Mrs. Reddy about a missing book," Jem said. Her voice trembled slightly, but she was absolutely determined not to lose control. She'd see Rhys Tremayne in hell before she gave him the satisfaction of seeing her weep, or watching a single tear roll down her face.

"Pauley's at St. Mary's Hospital with her mum. We spoke on the phone. Apparently, folks weren't best pleased to hear that Pauley was donating the library, despite never lifting a finger to help her with it," Jem said with more bitterness toward St. Morwenna than Pauley herself had expressed. "So last week, she threw a party with open access to the Lyonesse library—"

"I know that. I live here," Rhys cut across her.

As if he hadn't spoken, Jem continued, "The book in question—a first edition of *A Child's Garden of Verses,* the one with an undiscovered Wilde poem written inside—was on display. Someone nicked it. Probably Mrs. Reddy. Pauley said someone named Kenzie saw Mrs. Reddy touching everything, with a red canvas tote bag over her shoulder."

Rhys groaned. "Kenzie? Kenzie sees a lot of things. She's thirteen years old, if Pauley forgot to mention it." He ran his hands through his shoulder-length hair, but the smoothing effect lasted only as long as direct pressure was applied. The moment it stopped, the mane sprang up again, wild as ever. "So what are you saying? You came here to confront her, and things got out of hand?"

Jem let her breath out all at once. Damn him for seeing her that way. The way Mrs. Reddy had taught him, and all of St. Morwenna, to see her—as a killer.

"No," she said, speaking with a cold precision that sounded like someone else. She spit out each word like a clockwork mechanism emitting brass tokens: all gears grinding, no warmth. "I knocked on the door. All the lights were on, and Big Orange was parked outside, so when Mrs. Reddy didn't answer, I tried again. I could hear something going on inside. And then the curio cabinet fell over with a bang.

"I burst in, because any decent person would at that point," she added, voice expressionless even as she glared daggers into his dark blue eyes. "Then I heard the casement window break. I knew there was someone in here. Before I reached the bedroom, I stepped in a bit of blood and fell. That's how I lost a shoe and got blood on my fingers. I got up, found Mrs. Reddy, and heard something outside. I stuck my head out the window to see what it was. I saw the dog. Then I glanced the other way and saw you."

Rhys appeared to take this in, although his expression remained somewhere between skepticism and faint disgust.

He's judging me, Jem thought. Young Jem had thrown punches, kicked shins, and disrespected every adult that tried to give her a kind word. Time and gentleness had taught her a better way, but the look on Rhys's face brought her early belligerence back in a rush.

"If you're just an innocent bystander, why haven't you rung 999?" He said it as if he'd put his finger on her story's fatal flaw.

"Because I just had a jump-scare from Poundland Chewbacca!" To prove her willingness to involve the authorities, Jem stabbed 999 into her mobile. It rang twice, and then a flat female voice announced herself as representing Exeter police dispatch.

"I need to report a death," Jem said, turning her back on Rhys so she wouldn't have to stare at his stained vest, filthy bare feet, or rhododendron beard. "A murder."

*

Jem had actually never called the police before in her life. When she discovered Gran dead in her bed all those years ago, she'd run out of the cottage and into the closest neighbor's yard, desperate for someone to come back with her and rouse Gran from what seemed like an impenetrable slumber. After tussling with the handbag snatcher, she'd gone straight to the nearest pub for a large one. Calling the authorities was something she'd witnessed in a thousand television dramas and read about in countless books, but the actual experience proved slower and far more frustrating than she'd imagined.

Because the Isles of Scilly were lightly populated and mostly peaceful, the little police station on St. Mary's wasn't manned 24/7. Ordinarily, they had their own dispatcher to perform a mini-intake before routing the caller to a constable, but on this particular Friday, the station had shut down at four o'clock. The Exeter dispatcher didn't offer an apology or explanation, but she had endless questions for Jem. They spent at least five full minutes establishing that Mrs. Reddy was absolutely, without a doubt, no-take-backsies dead, which obliged Jem to get up close and personal with the old woman's corpse in various unappealing ways. Even in death, Mrs. Reddy was getting back a little of her own.

The moment Jem became committed to the Exeter dispatcher's interrogation, Rhys wandered out of the bedroom, as if he'd suddenly remembered he had something better to do. At first, Jem was relieved not to have to see his face, or indeed any part of him, as she paced the room answering questions. But after her third recitation of the story's constituent parts—she was Jem Jago, no, she didn't live on St. Morwenna, yes, the circumstances of her coming across the dead woman were strange, no, she hadn't seen the perpetrator—she decided to make certain Rhys got his share of forensic attention.

"There's a bloke here with me," she said loudly, hoping Rhys hadn't already slipped out, reunited with his puppy, and buggered off home to Tremayne Lighthouse, which was situated on the island's northwest side. "I didn't catch his name. He looks like a rough sleeper. I saw him crashing around the bushes behind the house…"

Rapid footsteps sounded in the passage. Rhys had clearly been within earshot, probably in the front room, because he hurried back into Mrs. Reddy's clothes-strewn bedroom with a face like thunder.

"Don't—" he began.

"For all I know, *he's* your man," Jem added recklessly, staring directly into Rhys's eyes as she poured poison into the dispatcher's ear. "He frightened me to death at the window, then burst into the house. He's six feet away from me right now. Make that five."

"Are you safe?" the dispatcher asked, still in that flat tone, as if potentially imminent assault was no more interesting than whether Jago was spelled J-A-Y-G-O or J-A-G-O.

Placing the mobile on the bed well away from Mrs. Reddy's body, Jem thumbed the speakerphone button. "Say again?"

"Are you safe, ma'am?" the dispatcher repeated. The question rang out between Jem and Rhys.

Jem mouthed, "Am I?"

"She's safe," Rhys told the dispatcher. "I'm here as a concerned citizen. I was passing Mrs. Reddy's house with my dog when I saw this woman inside. She didn't like being questioned. I'd pick up her phone to tell you more, but I can see blood on it. There's blood on her hand, too."

"What about that great red splotch on your vest?" Jem burst out, reverting all the way back to her heedless, angry former self.

"She's referring to a bit of polyurethane paint. I do bodywork on dinged-up boats, ma'am," Rhys told the dispatcher, suddenly sounding not only like a concerned citizen, but a model one. "I might add, it's *obviously* paint. No one could mistake it for blood. This woman appears quite unhinged. Which I think you can perhaps hear in her voice."

As Rhys gave the dispatcher his personal info, Jem warned herself to take a breath. The room didn't seem to have enough oxygen. Heading back to the open window for a double lungful of fresh air, she stopped herself at the last possible moment from putting her hands on the broken sill. That was all she needed—to seed this room with more of her DNA, fingerprints, and even toeprints. She'd watched enough true crime and mystery programs to know the scene could be spoiled by careless handling before the forensics team arrived.

With the facts fully established, the Exeter dispatcher put them on hold. During that time, Rhys appeared to absorb himself in the wordless study of Mrs. Reddy's body. Because Jem childishly refused to even look at the same thing he was looking at, she focused on the bedroom instead.

What she was seeing wasn't signs of a struggle, she decided. Either Mrs. Reddy had surprised an intruder in the act, or once she was dead, the murderer had tossed the room. The wardrobe wasn't the only thing that had been dumped. The bedside table's modest contents had been tipped out, too. To Jem, none of it looked worth stealing—puzzle magazines, flowery stationery, arthritis ointment, a bottle of pain reliever. The same thing had happened to the lowboy—the clothes flung out, the drawers yanked free. Whoever had searched the bedroom was either in a rage, or looking for something specific. Something they thought might be tucked inside a piece of furniture, in the narrow space between frame and drawers.

"Thank you for waiting," the Exeter dispatcher said, cutting through the soft canned music. "Hold for Chief Anderson, Isles of Scilly Police."

"This is Anderson," a man said. At the same moment, a burst of violent music came through. At first, Jem thought the dispatcher had somehow patched through the policeman and canned music at the same time. Then she realized Anderson was shouting to be heard over the din of a pub or nightclub.

"Sorry to bother you, Chief. We're in Seascape House. Mrs. Reddy is dead," Rhys said, infuriating Jem by taking control of the conversation.

"Tremayne?" Anderson sounded aggrieved. "This is my retirement party. Couldn't you keep the plug in the jug for three more days?"

"I'm not drunk," Rhys protested.

Jem, seized by another wave of childish defiance, snatched up her phone and disabled the speakerphone. Holding the mobile close to her face, she said, "This is Jem Jago. I discovered Mrs. Reddy. I can assure you, this isn't a prank. I think she's been murdered."

For what seemed like a long time, Jem only heard distant vocalizing, chatter, and the thump of that driving beat. Then the noise lessened considerably, as if the policeman had stepped outside to finish the call.

"I heard something about you coming back," Anderson said after a moment. "I'll round up my constables, get the RIB, and be over to St. Morwenna with all speed. Thirty minutes at the most. Tell Rhys he's not to set foot off the premises. In fact, I urge both you and Rhys to wait outside the house. That will protect the scene from any, er... accidental soiling." Anderson cleared his throat. "Is that understood? Make Rhys say he'll obey my instructions."

Jem started to relay the message, but there was no need. In the room's chilly stillness, the words traveled only a little more softly than they would have on speakerphone.

"I'll be here," Rhys called. The chief's attitude seemed to have infuriated him; his shoulders were tensed, his hands balled at his side. When Jem's eyes fell upon those fists, Rhys unclenched them with what looked like effort.

"Ms. Jago," Anderson said in his signature tone of weariness, the one he'd used with her many times during her teen years. "I must caution you not to leave the scene as well. While you await our arrival, I suggest you sit quietly and think about your future. If you're responsible for Mrs. Reddy's death, it's best you make a clean breast of it right away. Trying to deny the truth will only harm your defense. These days, the forensic lab can establish guilt in a matter of days. Or hours. But not every death is ruled a murder, and cooperation counts for a great deal. Consider that."

Jem stared at her iPhone in disbelief after Anderson rang off. When she finally lifted her eyes to Rhys, he was smiling.

"What a snake," she muttered. It took everything she had not to chuck her mobile at that big, white grin.

CHAPTER SIX

Rigor Mortis and Randy Andy

"Right. Well. We have our orders," Rhys said. Pushing Jem to the brink seemed to have restored his good humor. He sounded almost friendly, in a diabolical sort of way. "Outside, to await the authorities."

Jem watched him troop out of the bedroom. She'd been so overwhelmed by the circumstances—Mrs. Reddy's corpse, a sudden face outside the window, and all of Rhys's overgrown hair, as if he'd spent the last few years manacled to a dungeon wall—she'd done nothing for the last half-hour but react. Time to stem the adrenaline rush and start thinking rationally. And for that she needed as much information as she could gather before Chief Anderson and his constables arrived.

The first order of business was Mrs. Reddy. Jem looked the old woman over again, from her wrinkled throat above the buttoned navy boat neck tee, to her bent legs in their white capris with little whale appliqués sewn on the pockets. Apart from the duct tape over her nose and mouth, encircling her head multiple times like the rings of Saturn, she had no visible injuries. No livid marks on her throat. No wounds or foreign bodies, like a knife sticking out from between the ribs. And because the Exeter police dispatcher had insisted Jem go through various procedures to verify that Mrs. Reddy was categorically deceased, Jem knew her neck wasn't broken. But the corpse seemed to be stiffing rapidly, which probably meant she'd been dead for several hours already.

Maybe longer than I've been on St. Morwenna. But do I have that right? Jem wondered.

One of the best things about being a librarian was constantly drinking in knowledge, like a blue whale straining the ocean for krill. And as with the whale, a great deal of what she took in was completely random. Small snippets and factoids were always rising out of her subconscious, bobbing on the surface of her mind and giving her tremendous firepower during quiz nights at her local. But she often couldn't remember where she'd picked up the information, or if it was true.

Take rigor mortis. She might be remembering part of a scholarly article, or she might be remembering a line of dialogue from *Luther.* If it were the former, the question was, had the article been up to date, or from the Cornish archives, where it might have been published anytime in the last four hundred years? If it was from *Luther,* or another bit of cracking telly, there was no reason to assume the writer's first objective was unimpeachable scientific accuracy.

A noise from the bedroom doorway cut through Jem's thoughts. Rhys was back. Judging by his expression, he was none too pleased with her for failing to follow him outside Seascape House like a good little girl.

"Why," he asked with exaggerated patience, "are you poking Mrs. Reddy's leg when the chief told us both to keep the scene unspoiled?"

It was on the tip of Jem's tongue to say, "Because Randy Andy's not the boss of me, and neither are you." But that was ridiculously childish. She had to stop falling back into old ways of reacting to Rhys.

Before *it* happened—the accident, and all the trouble that followed—Jem and Rhys had spent the summer in each other's arms. He'd been her first boyfriend; she'd been his first girlfriend, if you discounted all the mild flirtations that came before. And as 'tweens, they'd been part of the Fab Four, as Mrs. Gwyn had called them, along with Pauley and Rhys's younger brother, Cam. And before *that,* when Jem and Pauley were still playing with stuffed teddy bears and Barbies, Rhys and Cam had been their sworn enemies. Rhys in particular had been Jem's nemesis for most of Year Three at St. Mary's School.

"Randy Andy," he muttered. "I'd forgotten that. He's being forced out of his job, you know. Finally made a grab for a subordinate who wasn't afraid to speak up."

Jem wasn't sure if Rhys had mentioned this morsel of IoS PD gossip as a peace offering, or if he was just indulging in a bit of character assassination as vengeance because Chief Anderson had accused him of inebriation. Her instinct was to poke her finger in that wound. To demand to know exactly what he'd done while intoxicated that was so heinous that Randy Andy had heard his voice and immediately assumed he was talking to a drunk. But deliberately riling up the islanders wouldn't sit well with her boss at the RIC, should it get back to him. With an effort, she changed the subject.

"Does the house feel really cold to you?"

"No. I don't know. Maybe." He gestured impatiently toward the window. "There's a gaping hole where the glass is meant to be."

"Pretty sure that's making this room warmer. Didn't Mrs. Reddy have central air conditioning installed, way back when?"

Rhys nodded.

"There should be a thermostat nearby. In the passage, maybe. Check it. I have a feeling the temp setting has been cranked down to arctic. Feels like an American hotel lobby in here."

"What," Rhys said, with even more exaggerated patience, "does the temperature have to do with anything?"

"Rigor mortis." Jem tugged on the leg of Mrs. Reddy's white capris, trying and failing to flex the knee. She'd already been forced to touch the body several times; the soon-to-arrive SOCO team could handle a little more. "If Seascape House's ambient temperature has been cold enough, I think it might have influenced how quickly her body stiffened up."

"I don't know how to tell you this, but there are people paid to evaluate these things. Specialists. Scientists." Rhys folded his arms across his chest. "What are you? A librarian?"

She ignored that. "That's an awful lot of duct tape wrapped around Mrs. Reddy's mouth."

"Don't tell me you've forgotten the way she ran her mouth."

Jem hadn't forgotten. The Mrs. Reddy of her childhood could scarcely be made to stop talking, even when other people screamed in her face, or turned their backs and walked away.

"My point is, Mrs. Reddy wouldn't have stood still for it. Think she could have been unconscious?"

Rhys made a noncommittal sound. "She looks unhurt. Besides being dead, I mean."

In the mystery novels Jem devoured as regularly as she read every other form of fiction, there were endless ways to render a victim unconscious. Toxic vapors piped into a closed room; a tablet dissolved in a teacup; even a merciless gloved hand simply pinching the nostrils of a sleeper closed. That last one, from P. D. James, epitomized the sort of ruthless calculation killers in novels tended to employ. But in the news accounts Jem subjected herself to—only when she had some compelling reason to do so—real-life murderers were anything but elegant. They tended to erupt spontaneously, commit their crime with whatever was near to hand, and draw a blank when it came to hiding a corpse.

On a hunch, Jem pushed up Mrs. Reddy's buttoned navy boat neck tee. Beneath it was a plain white bra, the buttressed and bulletproof sort many older ladies seem to prefer. Beneath its thick elastic band, her torso's pale flesh was decorated with three round pink depressions. The top mark sank deeply into the flesh. The second mark was half as deep, the third only a shallow mark.

"What on earth are you doing?" Rhys asked at her elbow. "Hey! Don't!"

Mobile raised, Jem snapped a picture of the pink depressions, ignoring his protests.

Rhys seized her arm. "You are the most reckless, arrogant person I ever met," he said, fingers digging into her bicep and making her gasp.

"Don't touch me!"

It took all her strength to wrestle away from him. The iPhone clattered to the floor again as Jem, propelled backward, collided with a torchiere lamp. It struck the wall, shade cracking open as its bulb exploded.

A bark rang out, startling Jem. Rhys whirled on his puppy, a mottled brown, white, and black creature.

"Buck." Rhys sighed. He sounded relieved to be interrupted, but assumed a stern face. "I said wait outside. Outside!" He pointed helpfully toward the door.

Buck was far more interested in Jem. He wandered toward her, head down, tail lashing. He seemed uncertain if she was a threat, or a misunderstood ally in need of support.

"Good boy," Jem said warily, easing toward her fallen mobile. Buck allowed her to retrieve it without growling or putting his ears back. He seemed like a baseline friendly dog, perhaps six months old, his liquid-brown eyes immediately disarming.

The iPhone was undamaged. It had even snapped a pic of Mrs. Reddy's feet as it fell. Relieved, Jem tucked the mobile back into her jacket's inner pocket. Her arm throbbed where Rhys's vise-like grip had fastened upon it. She wanted to rub the spot, but she wouldn't give him the satisfaction of seeing he'd harmed her. Instead, she edged over to Mrs. Reddy, gave Buck another soft "That's a good fellow," and pulled the old woman's nautical tee back in place.

"Look. I didn't mean to…" Rhys let the sentence tail off. "Point is, if you're innocent—if you just came to ask about the book and found her this way—you have nothing to worry about. The police will collect samples and dust for fingerprints and tell the chief who to arrest. In the meantime, he told us to wait outside. Why can't you just do as you're told?"

Buck was now wagging his tail at her. He'd rendered his verdict—ally—and Jem felt a surge of affection for the little mutt.

"Lead your master out to the porch, will you?" she asked him. "If Randy Andy has the raw nerve to tell me I'm his number one suspect, I'm not leaving this place without a look-see. Maybe the person who did this left a calling card." Giving Buck a gentle pat on the head, she added, "I hope for your sake that big ugly git you run with isn't the real killer."

That was over the top, but Jem couldn't bruise Rhys's body the way he'd bruised hers, so an insult would have to do. Judging by the thunderhead on his brow, her offhand slur had hit home.

"You really haven't changed. Except I reckon you're worse. Little Miss London, back to lord it over the rustic islanders. Do you ever even *think* about Cam?"

Jem gave Buck another pat. Mechanically, she smoothed her skirt, at the same time trying to smooth her face. Was that the question everyone on St. Morwenna was asking themselves, now that she'd had the gall to return?

"Buck!" Hearing genuine anger in Rhys's tone made the puppy's head come up. He trotted briskly back to his master's side.

"Forget I asked about Cam," Rhys told Jem. "Do what you want. You will, anyway. Consequences be damned."

CHAPTER SEVEN

Cereals of the Adult Bowels Variety

Rhys's exit was a relief. Having examined as much as she could in Mrs. Reddy's bedroom without touching anything else, Jem moved to the passageway. Her dropped shoe and a thin pink smear was all that remained of the blood. To help prevent a careless officer from treading in what little remained for forensic analysis, Jem blocked the area by leaving her other shoe in a conspicuous spot. Barefoot, she proceeded toward the living area of Seascape House.

The air conditioning's thermostat was in the house's central passage. As she'd surmised, the temperature was turned all the way down to eighteen degrees Celsius, which appeared to be as low as it would go. The unit was rumbling as it fought to compensate for the master bedroom's open window, butchering BTUs in the process.

Jem couldn't believe a woman in her seventies would ever choose to keep her home so cold. But if the intruder had set the thermostat so low, then to what purpose?

Maybe the killer thought the longer Mrs. Reddy's death went unnoticed, the better shot they'd have at getting off scot-free.

That made sense. In June in the Isles of Scilly, the warm weather would quickly nudge any corpse over the line into stinking decomposition.

Beyond the master bedroom, three doors opened off the passageway. The bathroom looked untouched. From a pop-up box of tissues, Jem gathered a handful, then eased the medicine cabinet open.

There were prescription drugs on every shelf, including a couple of moderately strong painkillers. So much for drug seeking as a motive.

The other two rooms, guest bedrooms, contained little except for beds and bits of unfussy furniture. There were no rugs on the floor and no decorations on the wall, although Jem could see the empty hooks and dust outlines where pictures and knick-knacks had once been displayed. The spartan look of each room didn't square with Jem's memories of Mrs. Reddy, who'd lived well and made sure all her neighbors knew it.

As a girl, Jem had never been invited inside Seascape House. Not even during her unsuccessful attempt to become friends with Mrs. Reddy's only child, Dahlia.

Mrs. Reddy had not been on board. House-proud in the extreme, she'd refused to allow Dahlia to bring other children into their home, or even play in the Reddy garden. She'd made no secret of her distrust for them, saying they'd only trample her prize flowers or track sand through the house.

Moreover, Dahlia wasn't much fun. She'd been afraid of everything under the sun, probably because she lived in terror of her mum's acid tongue. One day they'd quarreled over a tea party, which Jem had wanted to transform from the Queen's Birthday into a pirate's grog ration. In the end, Dahlia had packed up her miniature tea things and gone home for good.

Jem headed for the back of the house, where the laundry room, breakfast nook, and kitchen awaited. As older kids, she and Dahlia had more or less hated each other, but Jem couldn't remember any concrete reasons why. Now she felt a ripple of automatic sympathy for anyone losing their mum. They'd surely see one another in the coming days. Perhaps Dahlia had changed as much in the intervening years as Jem had.

The laundry room proved mostly spotless, but the kitchen was in complete disarray. Every cupboard stood open, their contents swept onto the counters. Every drawer had been pulled free and tipped out. The result was cutlery, tinned goods, dry ready meals, and crockery flung about as if by a tornado. Not even the cereal boxes were safe. Four of them, apparently new, had been broken open and emptied on the breakfast table, inside the porcelain sink, and directly onto the white travertine floor. Muesli, oat hoops, and unappetizing clumps of toasted bran had been dumped indiscriminately, as if someone had been fishing for prizes. But these cereals were of the Adult Bowels variety, so none of those boxes would've contained a prize, except possibly lower cholesterol.

Desperation, Jem thought. *But does that indicate a thwarted thief? Or is this pure rage? And did it happen after Mrs. Reddy's murder, or before? Am I looking at the row that came before things turned deadly?*

When she returned to the front of the house, she was dismayed to find Rhys back inside. Having apparently left Buck outside, Rhys had draped his long, muscular frame in Mrs. Reddy's leather recliner, the kind with an extendable footrest. The bottom of his feet looked as if he'd strolled through a tar pit.

"Don't believe in shoes?" she asked, not because she cared, but because she refused to slink silently into the front room. That might imply she was cowed after his parting shot about Cam, and Jem would be damned if she gave him that satisfaction.

"Don't believe in shoes, she asked him, whilst traipsing about barefoot herself," Rhys retorted in a sing-song tone. Either the chilly air conditioning had cooled him down, or he was manufacturing his own frost.

"I told you. I accidentally trod in blood. Which probably belongs to the killer," Jem added, not for Rhys's benefit, but thinking aloud. "I don't think Mrs. Reddy had some hidden wound. She was wearing white. If she'd been bleeding, it would've stained her somewhere. You should see the kitchen. I can't tell if Mrs. Reddy threw a fit, or if the killer had a meltdown after she was dead."

Rhys declined to answer.

Jem bit back a sigh. It was on her tongue to inquire if he'd perhaps joined some cult that required him to go about unwashed and unkempt. But no. One remark was a powerplay. Repeated attempts to engage him, even with insults, might give him the impression she actually cared.

She refocused her attention on the room around him. When she'd rushed into Seascape House, all she'd cared about was the fallen curio cabinet and the *crack* as the bedroom's windowsill snapped. Now she could see Mrs. Reddy's leisure command center, as it were, in its full glory. There was a lot of orange. Not the Day-Glo of Big Orange, which demanded supplicants cower before its gauche grandeur. Rather, the natural oranges found in the tropics: mango and sherbet and apricot and grenadine. There was loads of silver duct tape, too. It appeared to be Mrs. Reddy's go-to item, used for sealing torn cushions, affixing small rugs in place, mending a lampshade, and so on. After a couple of minutes to take it all in, Jem still didn't know what she was looking at.

Was the duct tape over her mouth a matter of convenience? The killer saw a roll and made use of it? Or was it a statement? Jem wondered. *Perhaps someone who knew Mrs. Reddy—knew her well—saying, if you love the stuff so much, try and breathe through it, why don't you?*

Jem could feel Rhys watching her. She hoped if she blushed under his gaze, the summer tan she'd developed since relocating to Penzance would conceal it. But it was no good letting her thoughts slide to the move from London to Penzance, and how if she'd stuck with her old job, she might be currently enjoying a perfectly normal evening in her comfy Putney flat. Nothing could've induced her to miss her chance to catalog the Gwyn family collection. Not even if she'd peered into a crystal ball and glimpsed Mrs. Reddy's corpse—or Rhys Tremayne's nasty feet.

Turning her back on him, she studied the rest of the front room. The TV remote, which had been wrapped with duct tape to compensate for a missing battery compartment lid, was broken open. The batteries lay beside it on a mango-colored pouf. Jem was reminded of the bedroom, where drawers had been yanked all the way out of the dresser frame. Again she wondered, was this the work of an opportunist? Someone trying to make the most of a robbery turned murder, searching even the most unlikely hiding places? Or was it the work of someone on a mission? In pursuit of a specific item, one small enough to be concealed in the battery compartment of a TV remote?

She shifted her gaze to the walls, which were almost bare. A pair of framed prints, an orange hibiscus flower and a bird of paradise plant, had been removed from their hooks and left propped against the wall. The coffee table had been swept clean, its contents strewn on the floor. Jem noted a couple of tabloids, a teacup, and empty packets of pig snacks called OINK ME LAD, a brand she'd never heard of. There was also a scattered handful of wrapped hard candies, Blu-ray discs, and a library book.

The Blu-rays revealed Mrs. Reddy had a fondness for Christmas movies featuring Dolly Parton. The library book was called *How to Use a Personal Computer*. Unable to resist, Jem used a tissue-swathed hand to open the book and view the card in the back. St. Mary's Library still used the old-fashioned date stamp method to indicate when the book had been loaned out and when it was due back. Apparently, Mrs. Reddy had found *How to Use a Personal Computer* useful, because it was six months overdue.

Beneath the coffee table, a white cord with a square transformer ran to the electric point. Although plugged into nothing, it struck Jem as the sort of power cord used for laptops. Phone or headphone charging cords didn't require an integrated transformer to generate sufficient energy. Yet she hadn't seen a computer in any of the rooms.

Jem drifted over to the fallen curio cabinet. This large space was surely intended as a dining room, but appeared to have been cleared out. Mrs. Reddy had definitely either been downsizing or clearing out Seascape House for redecorating.

Apart from the upended curio cabinet, the dining room's only remaining remnant was an antique sideboard. As with the kitchen, its cupboards were open, its drawers pulled out. The burgundy velvet interiors, meant to nestle fine flatware, were empty. Had the intruder made off with the silver—every ruddy piece of it? Even the dessert spoons, the ice tongs, and the olive picks?

"I'm receiving quite an education, watching you breathe on everything. Not to mention poke at the crime scene with a Kleenex wrapped around your paw," Rhys said.

Jem smiled. He'd been that way as a boy, too. No matter how cold and disaffected he behaved, if she mirrored his silence, he always broke first.

"I remember Mrs. Reddy as quite house-proud," Jem said, deciding to give him another chance to be helpful. "So why is this place in such a state?"

Rhys made a contemptuous noise. "As if that mad old bat ever tells me her plans. We haven't spoken—hadn't spoken in years."

Jem noted the quick change from present to past tense. Innocent people, she'd read, routinely spoke of the newly dead in the present tense. They were still coping with full acceptance, and the process took time. Not so with killers, who sometimes revealed themselves by transitioning instantly into phrases like "she was" and "she used to be." After all, the killer knew better than anyone that the victim belonged in the land of eternal past tense.

She was surprised by how relieved she felt. Despite her complicated feelings toward Rhys, she didn't want him to be the one who'd killed Mrs. Reddy. Nothing in the boy she'd known and loved had telegraphed any tendency toward violence, much less murder. Yet Rhys had clearly matured into a very different person. He looked dangerous, if she were being honest. And that spiteful remark she'd tossed off to the Exeter police dispatcher—that Rhys could've killed Mrs. Reddy, escaped through the bedroom window, then doubled back and pretended to have discovered Jem inside Seascape House—wasn't particularly far-fetched.

Jem leaned down to re-examine the fallen curio cabinet. One of those look-at-my-stuff shrines, filled with interior bulbs to spotlight the kitsch. Yet when the intruder pushed it over, it had been practically empty. No Kate and Wills commemorative plates, porcelain shepherdesses, or framed family portraits. The only thing that had fallen out of it, apart from broken glass and wires, was a handful of unframed photos.

If Rhys hadn't been watching her, Jem might have used her tissue-swathed fingers to review the stack. Now she contented herself by squatting next to the fallen pictures for a better look.

Two had fallen where she could study them easily. The first was an 8 x 10 portrait of Mr. and Mrs. Reddy on their wedding day.

Jem had never known Mr. Reddy. In his wedding portrait, he was smiling broadly, as if he'd never been happier. Mrs. Reddy, swathed in white and clutching a bouquet of marigolds, stared past the photographer impassively. She looked impossibly young and sad. It was strange to look on the picture and perceive her in a new way—as a human being—when one look at her stiffening remains made it clear that everything that made her human had fled.

The other picture was a 4 x 6 snap. Mrs. Reddy standing in front of the water at what might be St. Mary's Quay, or might be another modest port like Mousehole or St. Ives. She wore her cat-got-the-cream grin, the one she most often used in photos, like she was queen of the world. Square black shades hid her eyes. They were the sort of oversized, medical-grade black sunglasses favored by eye surgery patients. Her matching capri set featured orange starfish.

Beside her stood someone familiar: a very tall, rather fat man with pale skin and a scant halo of blond fuzz. He wore rubberized waders held up by thick braces and a smarmy expression that made Mrs. Reddy's I-own-you smile look sincere by comparison.

Bart the Ferryman knew Mrs. Reddy? Well enough to pose for a picture with her?

The other question seemed just as relevant—why were the pictures unframed, and who had done it? It seemed unlikely to think an intruder who'd just committed murder, possibly on the spur of the moment, would take the time to painstakingly remove each Reddy family photo before stealing the frames. He or she would've filched first and flung later.

Plus he would've been hauling a sack fit for Santa Claus, if he nicked all the things Seascape House is clearly missing, Jem thought.

In the front garden, Buck started barking. Not an alarm, watchdog sort of bark, but a friendly sound.

"Buck, be good," Rhys called. Pulling the recliner's handle so the footrest folded in on itself, he stood up and stretched. To Jem, he said, "Isn't it time you left off snooping?"

Buck barked again, rapid-fire like a canine machine gun, as Jem sprang up and "accidentally" gave the pile of pictures a kick. She wanted to see if Bart the Ferryman turned up in more snaps. A lover's quarrel could certainly inspire a mass un-framing of photographs. Or a sell-off of items that sparked unhappy memories. Or a murder, when you came right down to it.

"That was careless of you, Jemima. Excuse me… Ms. Jago," a man said just as Jem's big toe scattered the pictures.

It was a hodgepodge of faces and places. Over and over she saw Dahlia Reddy at various ages—in her school kit, wearing her Sunday frock, at the Christmas lunch table with a paper crown on her head. Bart the Ferryman's big blond bulk wasn't in any of them.

"Ms. Jago?"

Taking a deep breath, Jem turned to see Chief Anderson and a pair of uniformed constables on Seascape House's porch. Rhys, who'd opened the door for them, accorded her a serene smile that was somehow more infuriating than a grin. Clearly, he'd known they were on the cusp of arrival from Buck's first bark.

"Hello, Chief."

Twenty years had changed Chief Anderson, and not for the better. The roguish "Randy Andy" was gone, replaced by a pinch-faced bureaucrat. His hair was paler and thinner, and his jowls had taken an express train toward his expanding waistline. But he looked at Jem the same way he'd looked at her when he discovered her, Pauley, Rhys and Cam perched on the roof of the Duke's Head Inn, with no excuse except curiosity. Or the way he'd looked when ordering her to surrender the powerboat she'd "borrowed" from a drunken emmet. Or the way he'd looked at her after… after *it* happened. When Jem was already persona non grata all over the Scillies, but he simply couldn't resist saying, "I told you so," if only with his eyes.

"I thought I told you both to exit my crime scene and stay outside."

Jem said nothing.

"I did," Rhys said. "But she was still inside, snooping about, so I came back inside to keep an eye on her," he added virtuously.

Anderson closed the distance between himself and Rhys. He said nothing, only gave a long, lingering sniff.

Rhys glared at him.

"Well. At least malt liquor isn't wafting out of your pores, this time," Anderson said. "But look at the state of you. Worse than I've ever seen you, if you want the truth."

"He doesn't, sir," one of the constables, a dark-haired woman, piped up. "But I've seen him worse. Many times."

"I stand corrected. All right. Mel," Anderson addressed the woman, "go and find the deceased. You're on interior scene duty until Devon

& Cornwall's team arrives. Newt." He turned to address the other constable, a young man with large ears and big, brown bunny eyes. "Tape off the exterior and stand watch. We're rustic folk out here in the Isles of Scilly. Our role is simply to mind the baby until our gracious overlords, the off-islanders, arrive to show us what's what."

He sounded genuinely bitter. Perhaps a superior from the world of top brass had cast aspersions on the ability of IoS PD to handle a murder. Jem wasn't surprised; the Scillies were famously safe and peaceful. Not being a well-oiled murder investigating machine was something the IoS PD could be proud of, in her opinion.

"Mel," Jem said, using the female constable's given name despite the fact she didn't think they'd ever met.

The policewoman turned, eyebrow lifted. Something in the way her eyes flicked over Jem suggested that she'd formed an opinion. Or been told in advance what to think about Jem Jago.

"You'll find my shoes in the passageway. There was some blood on the floor. I slipped in it," Jem said. "So I left my shoes to mark the place, in case it can be salvaged by the forensics team."

Anderson made a contemptuous noise. "Still bleating out of turn, just like when you were a little delinquent. What did you grow up to be, *Ms.* Jago? Human rights activist? Counsel for the defense?"

The sneering tone in his voice set her teeth on edge. "Librarian."

He laughed. "Let me guess. You're the one loaning sex manuals and bomb-making cookbooks to the kiddies? Creating a whole new generation of menaces to society?"

"Listen, Chief." Rhys sounded as if the comments about his sobriety and appearance had stung him. "I know your retirement is signed and sealed. But remember, I can and will lodge a complaint about abusive behavior. An inquiry might hold up your pension. If you mean to have one final rampage, think again."

"Shut it. For all I know, you did this," Anderson said. "Or she did, and you're helping to cover it up. The moment I heard that

Jago girl was coming back, my antennae went up. When it comes to her, I would've thought you'd learned your lesson," he added, glaring at Rhys. "But some men never wise up."

"Here's the shoes," Mel the constable said, holding out Jem's kitten heels in her blue-gloved hands.

"I'll take those," Anderson said, stepping in front of Jem. "Mel, please take Ms. Jago into custody. Secure the handcuffs and I'll read her the caution."

Jem gaped at him. "Are you mad? For what crime?"

"Suspicion of murder."

CHAPTER EIGHT

"Once You Go Bart..."

"Jem. You look like death," Micki said, sliding into Jem's booth. She was positioned by a window overlooking the quay, her silver suitcase parked beside her. The Kernow Arms wasn't open yet—it was nine o'clock in the morning—so Micki had agreed to meet Jem at a Hugh Town restaurant called Piper's Hole. They served hot coffee, unfussy breakfasts, and were inexpensive. Anything was preferable to the inside of a cell.

"Seriously. What happened?" Micki asked.

"Rough night. Rough morning. Rough everything," Jem said, curling her hands around her coffee mug.

"You have dark circles under your eyes. And your shirt's on backward," Micki said, tweaking the exposed tag under Jem's chin.

"Oh, for the love of Pete." Jem pulled her arms inside the T-shirt, doing a quick turnaround while no one but Micki was looking.

"You didn't do anything mental, did you?" Micki continued. "Meet some bloke and do the walk of shame to this grease bucket?"

The waitress sailed up. "Right," she told Micki. "If you're not ordering from this grease bucket, you'll have to clear off."

"Tetchy." Micki beamed her brightest smile at the waitress, who didn't look much fresher than Jem. "I cast no aspersions. Work over at the Kernow Arms myself. What do you recommend?"

"Sausages. Swimming in grease," the waitress said flatly.

"I don't suppose you could do a frittata?"

"Aye."

"One of those, then. With mushrooms, if you can. And more coffee. Cheers, love."

Thawing slightly, the waitress headed for the kitchen. When she was out of earshot, Jem whispered, "Last night, I was arrested."

"No!" Micki cried, full volume. Glancing around at the mostly empty tables, she said in a softer voice, "Did it happen on St. Morwenna? I saw something on telly about a suspicious death. The reporter even said it might be murder, but this is the Scillies," she scoffed. "There's no way—" She broke off, eyes widening. "No. *No.*"

"Not quite," Jem said, holding up a hand. "I found the body. I went over to Mrs. Reddy's place to see about the missing book, remember? Once I found it, I had to ring 999 and wait for the officers to arrive. Chief Anderson had to know I didn't do it, but there's no love lost between us, so he arrested me on a suspicion of murder charge. Growing up, he didn't care for me, or my friends. Seems like absence hasn't made the heart grow fonder." She choked back another mouthful of her coffee, which had gone cold. "Hope the server brings a fresh carafe. That was two clichés. If I don't get some more caffeine on board, I'll be talking in nothing but."

"So you've been up all night?"

"Yeah. I was taken in around midnight, I think. Rode in one of those rigid inflatable boats to St. Mary's to be processed at the station," Jem said softly. A family with small children had just entered Piper's Hole, and despite a wealth of choices, settled at a table nearby, forcing her to keep her voice low.

"I was so angry, I couldn't see straight. I used to live for boating, once upon a time. Last night I barely even noticed being on the water, except for wanting to grab the chief and throw him overboard," she said. "Once we got to the station, he put me through the whole ordeal of processing—mugshot, fingerprints, cheek swab. Then PC Newt, the young constable—"

"Looks like a bunny rabbit?" Micki interrupted.

"That's him. He hopped over with big, scared eyes and said the chief was charging me with Section 89(2) of the Police Act, 1996."

"Which is?"

"Obstructing a police officer."

"But what does that mean?"

"Whatever our authoritarian overlords want it to mean, apparently. Told you he hated me," Jem said sourly. "By the time PC Newt was sent to tell me I was no longer being held on suspicion of murder, and therefore free to go, it was almost three o'clock in the morning. All I could do was slink back to Tregarthen's Hotel. Took forever for the night manager to let me in. I took a shower and changed, but I couldn't get to sleep. I was too furious."

"Fresh coffee," the waitress announced, placing a plastic carafe on the table between Jem and Micki. "Are you ladies tourists or residents?" There was a new vitality about her, as if her morning had suddenly taken a turn for the better.

"I live here," Micki said.

"St. Morwenna. Eight years," Jem said, leaving out her long absence.

"In that case…" The waitress leaned in and whispered triumphantly, "It's official. The murder victim is Edith Reddy."

Micki gaped at Jem. "Lady Doom Buggy!"

The waitress's face brightened. "Brill. She finally stepped over the line, I reckon. Astonished it took this long."

"So you don't think it might have been a stranger?" Jem asked. Even after a miserable night, her intellect was still humming, searching for more puzzle pieces to engross and distract. "A robbery gone wrong?"

The waitress goggled at her. "Didn't you say you live on St. Morwenna? Pull the other one." Glancing behind her at the newcomer family, which had the bright and shiny air of tourists at the beginning of their holiday, she added in a lower voice, "You'd think when a woman was past seventy, she'd start to worry about the hereafter. Stay in her own patch, at least. But ever since Mrs. Reddy adopted that young constable, she's been to Hugh Town once a week. And—"

"Which constable?" Jem cut in. "Mel Robbins or Newt McDowell?"

"The giddy goat. PC Newt, as he calls himself," the waitress replied. Apparently a bit of gossip had loosened her up. She looked miles happier and more energetic than when she'd first dragged herself to Jem's table.

"Mrs. Reddy believes in divide and conquer. She's been feuding with the chief for years. So when he hired that idiot lad, she moved in, plying him with gifts and assignments. If there's one sincere mourner for her in the Isles of Scilly, it's probably him." She glanced again at the tourist family. "Let me serve these emmets and I'll be back directly."

As the waitress moved away, Jem refilled her mug. "I didn't notice PC Newt looking especially broken up over Mrs. Reddy's death. And I was around him for hours."

"He's a numpty," Micki said, dismissing him with a wave of her hand. "But are you telling me you literally didn't sleep a wink?"

Jem nodded. "I mean, Randy Andy—that's what we kids used to call the chief, because he always had a bit of stuff on the side—*did* offer to let me kip inside one of his cells. You should've seen his face when he floated the idea. So bloody smug, I would've died before doing it. I stormed out. I kept reliving that moment until it was time for breakfast."

"Why didn't you call me?" Micki cried, back to her upper register. "You needed to talk through it."

"I didn't want to presume," Jem said. "Besides, I did call you for breakfast."

Micki stared at her. Then she said, "Jem. If you ever get yourself into a situation like that again, call me, no matter the time of day or night. I mean it."

"I will," Jem said, and smiled at Micki. For the first time in hours, she saw her situation as more intriguing than infuriating.

"The cheek of that man, arresting you," Micki continued. "I mean, was there any reason? A bit of blood on you? Anything?"

"A smear on my finger and the bottom of my shoe," Jem said. "My boss, Mr. Atherton, provided counsel. I had to rouse him out of a sound sleep, so I don't think I'm his favorite person at the moment. But I doubt I'll be prosecuted. I mean… unless the chief finds himself completely stymied, and decides to fit me up for a big career finish."

Jem tried to follow this statement, meant as a joke, with a laugh, but it sounded like a distinct possibility when she said it aloud. Micki's sober reception didn't help.

"You hear about these things," she murmured.

"Yeah. Section 364.1—that's True Crime in the Dewey Decimal system—is packed with stories of people who've been unjustly accused or convicted. Usually because they fit a profile, or turned up in the wrong place at the wrong time."

"The emmets are listening," Micki whispered.

Jem cut her eyes to the table. The four tourists, including the wide-eyed children, seemed riveted by their conversation. It probably didn't matter that she'd been too tired to maintain a discreet undertone. Even if Randy Andy resisted the temptation to spread news of her arrest around—unlikely—his constables and support staff might spill the beans. In a sleepy community where gossip was king, a morsel like "that Jago girl" returning after twenty years and promptly getting banged up for murder would be too good not to share.

"It doesn't matter. There's no keeping a lid on something like this." Jem pinched the bridge of her nose. "I just need to pull myself together, find a water taxi, and get to St. Morwenna. Then I'm going to sleep seven hours or know the reason why not. Phone be damned," she added grimly. "I had to silence it because of all the notifications. My boss wants a word—not Monday, but today. Pauley's mum made it through the night, but she's as knackered as I am, so embarking on our big library adventure is postponed until tomorrow. And the lodgings the RCI booked for me—a place on St. Morwenna called *Gwin & Gweli*—has been leaving voicemails. Somehow the proprietor heard I was arrested and seems keen to hear the complete story."

Micki's eyes had grown round at the words *Gwin & Gweli,* which translated into Wine & Bed in the old Cornish. "Of course he has! That's my cousin Clarence's place. You'd better believe he has his ear to the ground. Nothing escapes him." Digging in her bag, she came up with her mobile. "I'm calling you a water taxi. Then I'll personally walk you down to the drink and—"

"Is that Bart?" Jem asked, her gaze attracted to the window as a tall, broad shape ambled past the Piper's Hole.

"Who else?"

"Think he'd take me? I know it's probably close to his usual time for ferrying full boatloads, but I'd like to ask him a thing or two," Jem said, recalling that unframed portrait of Bart the Ferryman at Mrs. Reddy's side. They'd both been beaming like they'd formed a business partnership—or the other sort of partnership, bizarre as it might seem.

"Give me a sec." Extricating herself from the booth, Micki dashed out of Piper's Hole and jogged down the street to catch up with Bart. Soon, she'd got him turned around and ducking his head to enter the restaurant. He looked a bit too eager for her liking, grinning the moment they made eye contact. Jem hoped Micki hadn't promised him a heftier fare. If so, the last of her pocket money would be gone and she'd be living on thin air until her per diems kicked in.

"Can you believe it? Terrible news. Just shocking. I'll never get over it," he said by way of greeting. "Crikey, that's a lot of food you've left on your plate. Mind if I snag that sausage?"

"Go ahead," Jem said.

"There's no free coffee here," the waitress said sternly, arriving back at the booth to place Micki's frittata in front of her.

"Nancy." Bart sounded hurt. "I'm conducting business."

"And I'll buy him a cup. No, don't try to shoehorn yourself in next to me," Micki said, glaring. "Pull up a chair."

Bart did as he was bid, accepted a clean mug from Nancy, filled it from Jem's carafe, and at her nod, started working his way through the remains of her breakfast without need of cutlery. "Cold but delicious. Delicious!" he called to the waitress, who turned her back.

"I hear you need another ride. So soon, eh?" Bart said to Jem around a mouthful of toast. "It's only to be expected. Once you go Bart, you never go back."

"How you make it from day to day without getting your teeth put down the back of your throat, I'll never know," Micki said, less with malice than astonishment. "I suppose you're big enough to take all comers."

Bart sniggered. "Never threw a punch in my life. Never had to. Size and charm have their advantages. Besides, I'm a lover, not a fighter."

"Speaking of that… did you know I'm the one who found Mrs. Reddy's body?" Jem asked.

He managed to grunt while drinking his coffee. When he put down the mug, he said, "I heard Weirdy Beardy from the lighthouse found her. And the killer was taken in. A woman who used to—" He broke off, goggling at her. "You?"

"Released and cleared of the murder charge," Jem said. That was what she planned on telling everyone, whether Chief Anderson still considered her a prime suspect or not. It was interesting how Bart the Ferryman showed no emotion but delight, as if he'd stumbled onto the best gossip in the islands.

"While I was in Seascape House, I noticed something," Jem continued. "A photograph of you and Mrs. Reddy."

"Hmh? Oh. That." He sat up straighter. "Her, er, daughter came for a visit, Easter last. I ferried them to Penzance and back. Dahlia snapped it, I think." He chuckled. "Poor thing, keeping a picture like that at her house."

"Were you close?"

"Of course. The old girl practically lived for me. She'd have had no life at all if not for me and *Merry Maid,*" Bart said, digging into his food again. "Another satisfied and loyal customer."

Jem and Micki swapped glances. Most people, Jem thought, would commiserate with Jem over the shock of discovering a dead person. They'd also express curiosity over the sort of inside info that the press, as of necessity, always left out. How did the house seem? What was the apparent cause of death? Or did Rhys—whom she'd absolutely be calling "Weirdy Beardy" the next time she saw him—seem responsible? But Bart seemed curious only about one thing: the time of departure.

"How soon can we leave?" he asked, using the heel of his cold toast to mop up what remained of Jem's eggs. "I don't mind squeezing in an extra trip. Not when Micki's promised me a Guinness followed by a whisky chaser at the pub tonight, *gratis,*" he added, causing Jem to shoot her friend a look of thanks. "But time and tide wait for no man. And once word gets about that St. Morwenna is now the murder capital of the Scillies, well—I expect to do a lot of business."

CHAPTER NINE

Snooping

"Careful! Elephant in the pottery studio, aren't you?" Bart cried as Jem sat down too quickly on one of *Merry Maid*'s retrofitted passenger benches, causing the whole benighted structure to shake.

"Pay me no mind, it's my fault," he amended himself, as if suddenly remembering he was in the customer service trade. Leaning down to inspect the bolt, he finger-tightened it, muttering, "If a certain someone was here, she'd tell me to stick it fast with duct tape."

"You mean Mrs. Reddy," Jem said, wedging her suitcase into a corner so it wouldn't roll around once they got underway.

Rising, he looked down at her from his great height, all chins and shrewd blue eyes. "It occurs to me I never asked—how did you come to discover her body, if she was found dead in her house?"

Finally, Jem thought. She wasn't sure if she liked Bart for the killer—that was what the mystery novel detectives called it, "liking" a suspect, meaning presuming their guilt most plausible—but no one with half a brain could discount him. The photo posed with the old woman was odd. The fact it had been unframed—that could go either way, since Mrs. Reddy had also unframed portraits of herself and her family. Having his own boat gave him premium mobility in the islands, unlike most of St. Morwenna's natives, who would be obliged to pay for a water taxi and risk having their movements remembered, perhaps even recorded.

"You ever know Mrs. Reddy to be light-fingered?" Jem asked.

"A question with a question. Well played," Bart said. "Care to accompany me into the wheelhouse? We can talk while I get us underway." She must've looked dubious, because he held up his hands, adding, "Perfect gentleman. I swear on all that's holy. Bring me a prayer book and I'll kiss the ruddy thing."

"You should've stopped on 'gentleman,'" Jem said. But she followed Bart into the *Merry Maid*'s cramped wheelhouse nonetheless. If the situation grew dangerous, she'd jump overboard and swim to safety.

If I can still do it, she thought. *It's been a hell of a long time. Do people forget? Does the water let you forget?*

Bart did his best to make starting the *Merry Maid*'s ancient engine and sputtering into the channel look complicated and mysterious. Jem, charmed by the sensation of nearly skippering a vessel again after so long, felt herself beaming out at the sea's light choppiness and the dreamy blue sky.

Do you ever even think about Cam? Rhys's voice demanded in her head. She swallowed the smile.

"Don't frown that way. What are you? Seasick?" Bart asked.

"A bit," Jem lied. "So about Mrs. Reddy. Was she ever one to steal?"

"Oh, we're all thieves at heart, aren't we?" Bart said easily, as if tackling a trick question was something he'd learned as a little child. "I'd never throw stones or grass on another living soul. But, yes, now you mention it, she had a habit of taking what she thought was hers. Or picking up little *objets,* now and again, to settle a score. If she considered herself badly treated, she might help herself to your soap dish, or whatnot, next time she used your loo."

"Right. Well. It appears she took something from my friend Pauley Gwyn. A book," Jem said, remembering what she'd told Hack, Mr. Hot Rod Red, aboard the *Merry Maid* less than twenty-four hours ago. "I'm a librarian. You nick a valuable book, you'll answer to me."

"You don't say." Bart looked slightly alarmed. "Power of the state's getting out of hand, if you ask me. Sending out ninja librarians to repossess books. The bailiffs are bad enough." He studied Jem so thoroughly, she felt X-rayed. "Are you having me on? I'm just interested." It seemed that in his world, identities were slippery things, liable to twist and shift like the colors of a kaleidoscope when you least expected it.

"All true," she assured him. Pretending to study her fingernails, Jem added in a neutral tone, "Seascape House looked like she'd been flogging everything she owned on eBay."

"Selling it in person, she was," Bart said, keeping his hand on the helm and occasionally checking gauges in an important manner. Jem knew the *Merry Maid* was in the designated lane between St. Mary's and St. Morwenna, and there was nothing for him to do between now and dropping her off, apart from watching the scenery. But Bart was fully committed to pretending his navigatory skills were being taxed to the limit.

"The old bird was mad for selling off bits and bobs," he went on amiably. "I took her to Penzance twice a week or more. She always left St. Morwenna with a red tote bag bursting and came back with it fully deflated. Richer for the trip, I would think."

"Pawning things?" Jem considered it. "When I was growing up on St. Morwenna, she liked to brag about how she could buy and sell every last one of us."

"Oh, Edie still did that," Bart agreed. "But between you and me and *Merry Maid,* I think she was just putting up a brave face. Bringing suit against all and sundry in the Scillies was an expensive business."

"Edie? She let you call her that?"

"Of course. Edie and I were great friends. The relationship started out rocky. She, er, heard something irregular about my ferry business and decided to hold it over my head. Said she'd like to be my silent partner."

"What?"

"Oh, yes. Edie played hardball, surely you knew that if you ever knew her," Bart said. "She told me if I didn't give her free ferry rides whenever she liked, she'd complain about my business to Chief Anderson. Or the Dorrien-Smiths, if you can believe it. Even in the Isles of Scilly, it's a 'papers, please' mentality. If you haven't bought all the correct permits and whatsits, you'll be up on charges."

"She blackmailed you?"

"Not at all. She extorted me," Bart said matter-of-factly. "The terms are like libel and slander. Similar, but not the same. Often confused. Any road, I made the best of it, like I always do. You saw the picture. Once you go Bart…"

"Yes, you already said. So… were you two together? As a couple?"

Bart looked at her sidelong. "Why do you want to know?"

Jem found herself unable to think of any persuasive answer. She couldn't very well hit him with statistics—that when a woman died suddenly by violence, her male partner was always the first person the police looked at. Or that, despite Bart's protestations of being a lover and not a fighter, it was clear that if his temper was roused, those long arms and powerful hands could easily end a smaller, frailer person's existence.

"I'm… I'm sorry," she muttered. Time to change tack. "I do have a bad tummy. Is there a toilet below?"

"Ordinarily I'd say no. But for you… why not," Bart said generously. "In the center of the passenger area, you'll see the caution tape. The stairs into the hold are just beyond. Be careful. My insurance isn't paid up. Anyone who takes a dive on the way to the loo and tries to sue is in for a disappointment. Can't get blood from a stone."

Rather than waste time taking offense, Jem let that pass, exiting the wheelhouse and following the stairs into *Merry Maid*'s hold. For the most part it was empty, but there were brackets on the walls with tough plastic straps. Jem thought they could be used to tightly belt in place almost any kind of cargo, whether boxed, crated, or bagged.

As Jem expected, the skipper's cabin was small enough to be claustrophobic by most standards. Most she'd seen were, however, cunningly designed, with areas that performed double duty. The built-in chest of drawers was also a writing desk; with the flip of a panel, the bunk became a dining table. Of course, to take advantage of these innovations, everything had to be in its place—shipshape and Bristol fashion. Bart's cabin was an open landfill.

Dirty clothes. Empty crisp packets. Plastic drinks bottles with an inch of leftover brown liquid. A few unsavory magazines and old newspapers. Even the floor was covered in crumbs, old spills, and dropped advertising inserts. An empty OINK ME LAD packet, featuring a cartoon rapper-pig giving the consumer a double thumbs up, caught her eye. She'd spied the same empty packets in Seascape House.

Does he like that brand, too? Or is it proof Mrs. Reddy shared the cabin sometimes?

The thought of Bart's pigsty cabin as a love nest was revolting. True, Jem had hated Mrs. Reddy for decades. But she'd always assumed the old woman had *standards*.

She couldn't climb back on deck without flushing the toilet; sounds carried clearly on boats. Therefore, even though the prospect of Bart's lavatory hygiene was terrifying—Jem opened the door and edged inside.

It was wretched.

Breathing through her mouth, Jem flushed the toilet, promising herself copious squirts of hand sanitizer the moment it became available. In the course of not looking in the bowl, she focused on the shaving mirror over the sink. It was cracked. To keep the fragments together, someone had firmed up the frame with silver duct tape.

Jem gaped at it, foul surroundings forgotten. Then she whipped out her iPhone and snapped a picture. After doing the same for the discarded pig snacks packet, she retraced her steps to the stairs.

The hold looked just as empty on her second trip, but because she came from the opposite direction, something small in one corner stood out. Jem, mobile at the ready, moved in for a closer look.

Was it sand? More like a bit of spilled powder. Too fine to be beach sand, and more tan than pearlescent white.

Could it be cocaine?

The notion leapt to mind because in the cinema, scenes with drug smugglers always involved shipping bricks of cocaine. Perhaps she was being silly. But it wasn't as if coke had disappeared along with shoulder pads after the Thatcher era. A recent survey of the Thames water quality had turned up plenty of cocaine, revealing that a large number of Brits had effectively failed a drugs test.

"Snooping!"

Jem almost jumped out of her skin. Bart's disembodied head was stuck through the deck opening into the hold, allowing him to watch her progress. Getting down on his knees to do so clearly wasn't the easiest task for a man his size. His pink scalp glistened like a tinned ham.

"I charge extra for snooping," he added, tone somewhere between accusing and jolly. She really couldn't tell if she'd affronted him or not. "Don't know what you think you'll find here. All the good stuff was in my cabin. Hope my reading material didn't shock you. It's lonely out at sea."

"Who's steering the boat?" she asked, ascending from the hold into the mid-morning sunshine.

"It's chugging away on autopilot," he said, clambering back to his feet with difficulty. "Land in sight. I'll take back over in a moment and put you off on St. Morwenna as planned. By the way, it's a no."

"What?"

"No, there wasn't any naughty business between me and Edie. I daresay she would've liked it," he added, as if his moral compass would not allow him to discuss the matter without acknowledging his own irresistible sex appeal. "But while age is only a number, I prefer using that line on sweet young things half my age. Not letting stringy old birds use it on me. Speaking of sweet young things…"

Jem's mind went immediately to how she might use her bag as a weapon, but fortunately, Bart finished his sentence in a less offensive, not to mention more interesting, way.

"… If you want to know who I fancy for the murderer, look no further than Kenzie DeYoung. She's St. Morwenna's wild child," Bart said. "Edie hated the girl with a passion. And Kenzie felt the same about her. If anyone on the island would've lost their temper with Edie and struck her down in a fit of passion, my money's on Kenzie."

CHAPTER TEN

Fauxhawk Savior

Not long after Bart leveled his accusation, their arrival on St. Morwenna was at hand. It looked pretty, the shallow turquoise waters giving way to indigo depths. The inner island was deep green and lush, while the irregular perimeter offered a little of everything. There were white sand beaches and patches of shingle. There were cliffs that dropped off into deep, rocky vales. Seagrasses waved, palm trees swayed, and sticker bushes grew in clusters, providing cover for birds and insects. At the island's highest point sat a short white lighthouse, like a chess piece plunked down on a black square. Tremayne Lighthouse, dark for almost a century but still romantic when glimpsed from the sea.

Across the tombolo, currently underwater but semi-visible, lay the rockier, sandier islet called Penlan. Jem had played there as a girl, first with Pauley, then with Rhys and Cam. Their favorite game had been Drowned Lands. They'd pretended Penlan was the lost kingdom of Lyonesse and the rising waters would soon carry them off, all the way down to the bottom of the sea.

Jem caught her breath. There was St. Morwenna, not just a dark shape on the water, but in its full glory. She was home again.

That feeling of rightness, of belonging, vanished the moment Jem set foot on St. Morwenna's Quay. She was grateful she'd opened up her suitcase prior to disembarking and augmented her sundress with a floppy-brimmed hat and big, dark sunglasses. Even so, she'd been a

fool to think it would keep the islanders on the Square from recogniz-
ing her instantly. They'd known she was coming, as Pauley and Rhys
had attested. And after her arrest, she was notorious all over again.

Feeling exposed, Jem threw her shoulders back, stuck her chin
out, and rolled her suitcase up the cobbles of Quay Road like she
owned it.

Channel Mrs. Reddy on Big Orange, she told herself, aware that
a few people with especially good vision had already begun to stare
and point. *Worst comes to worst, I'm still a fast runner.*

Fortunately, it was only a ten-minute walk ahead of her. Built
in the seventeenth century and rebuilt, to some extent, in the early
1950s, the Square's low buildings were placed on the clifftop with a
three-sided view of the water. So if you wanted to reach the Byway,
you had to pass through the Square. There was no "back way" that
didn't involve hiking boots or a helicopter. Last night, it had been
easy, in no small part because the Ice Cream Hut was temporarily
closed. On this fine Saturday in June, it was open for business.
That meant Bettie Quick or her daughter, Saoirse.

Like a guardhouse in a medieval courtyard, the Ice Cream Hut
squatted at the Square's entrance, impossible to miss. It billed
itself as "St. Morwenna's Most Beloved Tradition," and that was
probably true. Jem herself had visited it several times a week as a
girl, whenever she scraped up a few pence. In those days it had
been operated by Bettie, a sly woman who tailored her opinions
to the taste of whichever person currently stood before her. This
flexibility of conviction had made her the perfect toady for Mrs.
Reddy. Whenever Mrs. Reddy took up a new crusade, Bettie was
at her side, cheering her on.

After what happened to Cam, during that purgatorial stretch
when Jem and Gran had still hoped St. Morwenna might eventually
forgive them, Bettie had turned her back on Gran. She'd made it
plain that she despised Jem, too.

As Jem marched on, determined, the woman inside the hut stared back, leaning over the counter for a better look. Sunlight glinted off her specs. That wasn't Bettie. Not unless Bettie had lost five stone and taken to wearing her gray-streaked hair in double braids. It was Bettie's peculiar daughter, Saoirse.

When she was close enough to read all the types of ice cream on offer at the hut, Jem noticed that a professional-looking camera was positioned at Saoirse's right hand, the sort with detachable lenses and a carrying strap. It jogged Jem's memory; Saoirse served in the family business, but preferred her hobby, photography, over all else.

"I thought it was you," Saoirse said. "Jemima."

Years ago, when Jem was still quite new to St. Morwenna and Saoirse, then about twenty-five, had been helping Bettie serve ice cream, Gran had introduced her as "Jemima." Saoirse had never called Jem anything else, despite corrections and pleas. As her mum, Bettie, explained, "In that one's brain, once the groove is made, it can't be unmade. Just live with it. That's how I cope."

"Hello, Saoirse," Jem said, and kept walking.

"Did you do it?" Saoirse called.

Jem bit her lip and kept going. Everyone in St. Morwenna knew that Saoirse came out with odd questions and inappropriate statements. She wasn't stupid, or simple. She was just one of those people who wandered about in a world of her own, crossing over into regular society on her own terms and receiving—at least for her—decidedly mixed results.

On the hut's rear side, papered with old picture menus showing frozen novelties and every conceivable permutation of the whippy flake, the door opened.

"Did you hear? I asked you—did you do it?" Saoirse called a little louder.

Now that Jem was properly within the Square, she had an audience on all sides. In Island Gifts, the clerk peered out the door.

In Hen N' Chicks, a restaurant that had sprung up where the old video arcade used to be, the servers had stopped dead and the bistro patrons were watching with interest. Up the hill at the Duke's Head Inn, a few pensioners Jem vaguely recognized stood clustered under the swinging wooden sign. All the men, including the bearded Duke, clutched a pint and appeared mightily entertained.

Jem turned. As she expected, Saoirse didn't look vicious or even unkind. Simply curious, and a little bewildered. A lot probably happened in Saoirse's world that made no sense. Wide eyes behind round lenses, as well as those childish double braids, turned her middle-aged face into little girl lost.

"Of course I didn't do it," Jem said, gentle in spite of her frustration and mounting fatigue.

"Sorry. Only… you killed…" Saoirse tailed off, shrugging.

Jem fought down another surge of helpless fury. There was no point losing it with Saoirse. That particular groove had been worn into St. Morwenna's collective brain. And at least Saoirse, in her odd way, was forthright enough to ask Jem to her face, instead of nattering about it behind her back.

"That was an accident," Jem said. "It's good to see you, Saoirse. I'll get a whippy flake later. Right now, I just want to settle into my B&B and have a kip."

"Jem," a girl cried. "Jem Jago!"

Turning, Jem saw a girl marching toward her. A skinny young thing with lavender hair sculpted into a fauxhawk, dressed in what appeared to be Army surplus, right down to the combat boots. How many outré teens lived on St. Morwenna? Probably not many.

"Kenzie," she guessed.

The girl seized her arm with a grip like a Terminator robot. "I've been so worried about you! Let's get you to *Gwin & Gweli.*" Under her breath she added, "Go with it," as if they were secret agents.

"Can you believe the great nosy parkers of the world? Staring and gaping with their mouths hanging open?" she all but shouted, glaring around the Square at her fellow islanders.

The hint struck home. At the Co-op, the man in a green apron—Jem thought she might have gone to school with him—ushered his rubbernecking customers back into the shop. Around the bistro tables, the waitstaff resumed scratching at notepads and a murmur of conversation resumed. The bell above Island Gifts' door jangled as the clerk went back inside.

"I'm glad you handled Saoirse with kid gloves," Kenzie added softly. "She doesn't mean any harm."

"I know. How old are you, Kenzie?"

The girl made a little sound of displeasure. "Why do adults think they can just go around interrogating people about their age? How old are *you*?"

"Thirty-three," Jem said.

"Fine. I'm thirteen," Kenzie said.

Still in the girl's iron grip, Jem allowed herself to be propelled up Quay Road, her rolling suitcase bumping along behind her. The pub-going pensioners under the wooden sign *were* familiar, she realized as they drew closer. In fact, that particular trio had been day-drinking at the Duke's Head her entire life. Remarkably, they didn't look much the worse for wear for it—a bit shrunken, perhaps, with a little less hair on their heads and a few additional broken veins across their noses, but otherwise unchanged.

"You give 'em hell, Kenzie," one said.

"Don't need Chief Anderson when we got you, girl," another said.

"Mind, there's a murderer among us," a peevish-sounding drinker added. "I reckon it's that Jago girl. Don't go getting killed, sweetheart."

"Piss off, sweetheart," Kenzie retorted before Jem could say the same. The old men roared.

Once they were on the Byway and around the first bend, putting them out of sight of everyone, Jem finally pulled free. "Thanks for the assist."

"My pleasure," Kenzie said with a thirteen-going-on-thirty air of self-assurance. There was something familiar about her that Jem couldn't quite place. Was it the set of her mouth? The way she held herself?

"Those people are the worst," Kenzie continued. "I've heard stories about you from everyone. Including Pauley Gwyn. You're my hero."

Jem blinked at the girl. "Why?"

"Because you got the hell out of this place. And because of Snoggy Cove."

"What do you know about Snoggy Cove?"

But Kenzie only smiled in a way that suggested she knew all. "Tell Clarence I said hiya. He owns *Gwin & Gweli,* if you didn't know. Must be off." She spun on her heel as if to end the conversation by sprinting off like a hare, just as Jem had once been prone to do.

"Wait!" Jem cried before the girl could take off. "You told Pauley that you thought Mrs. Reddy stole the book, is that right?"

Kenzie nodded, looking suddenly wary.

"Do you really think she did it? Or did you just dislike her? Want to make a bit of trouble for her?"

"What do you mean?" Kenzie's light expression had shut down like the retracting doors of a cuckoo clock.

"Look, if you know about me, you know they used to call me a bit wild, too," Jem said. "Mrs. Reddy was always watching me and my friends, grassing on us, exaggerating whatever we were up to. She made us sound like hardcore criminals. Unless she's grown a whole new personality in the last twenty years, I imagine she's done the same to you."

"I didn't lie on her, if that's what you mean," Kenzie said. "You've got a funny way of saying thank you."

"I'm not accusing you," Jem said. "I'm just trying to work out what's happening here. Somebody told me she was known for nicking things, as a way of hurting people who'd upset her."

"True." Kenzie's arms remained tightly folded across her flat chest.

"Do you know of anyone who might have retaliated by killing her?"

The girl's eyes narrowed. She seemed to be putting together possibilities with amazing rapidity. Either she'd guessed that someone—in this case, Bart—had floated her as a person with an ax to grind against Mrs. Reddy, or suffered from a guilty conscience. Either way, she made up her mind how to reply in a flash.

"I don't have to answer you. I know my rights," she snapped, and ran past Jem, down the Byway into St. Morwenna's deep green heart.

CHAPTER ELEVEN

"The Sea Always Wins"

When Jem finally opened her eyes, she thought it was morning. It felt possible. There had been so many dreams, vivid but tangled. She'd dreamed of Gran, lighting up a fag and muttering something about docs not knowing everything. Of Bettie Quick at the Ice Cream Hut, counting out change. Of Bart the Ferryman taking a casketed Mrs. Reddy to Penzance for reasons that only made sense in the dream. And of Kenzie finding the cache, which still contained the lockbox and Cam's rope ladder, and climbing down to their secret beach. "Their" meaning Jem's, and Pauley's, and Rhys's, and Cam's, of course, and the beach: Snoggy Cove.

Rubbing her eyes, Jem found her mobile on the bedside table and checked the time. 5:30 p.m. She hadn't even missed dinner, or sunset. Time to finally deal with the messages on her phone.

Most were from Pauley. Jem listened to them in reverse order, newest first, hoping to hear that Mrs. Reddy's killer had confessed or been arrested. No such luck.

Pauley's most recent message was an invitation to dinner at Lyonesse House. The one before that said she was home again. The one before that said her mum was doing better and back to status quo. Per the oncologist, Mrs. Gwyn might live another month. Or she might go into distress and slip away that very night. There were simply no guarantees. But all in all, the hospice team thought it was safe for Pauley to go home for the night, rather than sleep on a cot in her mum's room.

There was another message from Mr. Atherton at the Courtney Library, clearly not happy to leave all discussion until Monday.

"I now understand there's a history in St. Morwenna involving you," he said, in a pinched tone he'd never used with her before. "I should have liked to have been made aware before you accepted the assignment. Please understand, should the situation generate too much negative attention for the RIC, your participation in this assignment will be re-evaluated."

Translation: I'll be sacked, Jem thought.

"Moreover, there's the matter of Mr. Reed," Mr. Atherton went on. He meant Jem's lawyer, the one who'd spoken to Chief Anderson and got the charges reduced to obstructing a police officer. "We provide representation in the event of damage to a donor's home, or some sort of unhappy accident whilst working in the field. I'm sure you must understand that if you're accused of crimes, as it were," he coughed, as though saying the sentence aloud had touched off an allergic reaction, "you must retain your own private counsel to facilitate your, ah, navigation of such treacherous waters."

This is how people talk when they spend all their time reading antiquarian books, Jem thought sourly. She was glad Atherton had left so detailed a message. It spared her the necessity of ringing him back. Of course, she'd still have to put in a call on Monday. Perhaps Chief Anderson would have a real suspect by then.

He can't fit me up for a crime I didn't commit, Jem told herself, rising from the bed, a creaky antique with a white-spindled head-board, and slipping a dressing gown over her shortie pjs. *He can't go about accusing me publicly, either.*

She made her way down the hall to the bathroom, which was free, of course, since she was *Gwin & Gweli*'s only guest. The shower was much like the one in Gran's house. The water came out weakly, didn't get terribly hot, and carried a familiar scent Jem associated with the islands. Still, it felt wonderful to wash her dark hair, which fell to the middle of her back when she released it from its bun.

It was a pleasure, scrubbing off the previous night's shocks and indignities, but Jem found she couldn't focus properly. Perhaps she'd read too much crime fiction, or watched too many detective programs, but the longer she thought about it, the more her earlier conclusion about Chief Anderson seemed impossibly naïve.

Of course he could fit her up for the crime, if he had a mind to. For starters, he'd never liked her or been inclined to give her the benefit of the doubt. For another, he was loyal to his community, among which Jem would not be counted. No matter how often he'd clashed with Mrs. Reddy, who'd ridden roughshod over him just like everyone else, her life had been his to protect. Jem was an off-islander, no more to him than an emmet.

All he has to do is find a witness who'll say they saw Mrs. Reddy answer the door for me, Jem thought. *There are always desperate types, sleeping on the beach and panhandling for their next pint who will swear to anything, if there's a bit of money in it.*

There was also the matter of access to the crime scene. Jem had managed a cursory look around. She'd even snapped a pic of the curious marks on Mrs. Reddy's torso. But after the chief had her arrested, he would've had untold hours in charge of Seascape House and its surroundings before the forensics team turned up. Anything he found that she didn't know about—anything that fit the profile of, say, a male intruder—could've been done away with to make Jem's guilt seem clearer. Anyone who'd spent time in section 364.1 knew that sometimes when an officer of the law felt certain they'd identified the correct suspect, they planted or subtracted evidence so as to leave no doubt. In some cases, they didn't even think what they were doing was wrong. They thought of it as simplifying matters so lawyers, juries, and judges couldn't muck about with the "right" result.

By the time Jem climbed out of the shower, her heart was pounding like she'd run a half-marathon. The scenarios were dire. Even if she eliminated active malice on Chief Anderson's part—if she imagined him shambling around in his usual manner, then dumping his job in a newcomer's lap and letting the real killer off in the process—that didn't mean she'd be exonerated. If Mrs. Reddy's death became an unsolved murder, the cloud might hang over Jem's head indefinitely.

I already live in a world where Saoirse could ask me in front of the Square if I'd killed Mrs. Reddy. No one laughed. No one told her she was being ridiculous.

And while it was true that Saoirse was peculiar on her best day, if her question got back to the likes of Mr. Atherton, he wouldn't view it as a ludicrous question from a local oddball. He'd see it as a successful small business owner questioning the propriety—the human decency—of someone representing *him*.

"Oh, shit," Jem muttered.

*

After ringing Pauley to say she'd be over by seven o'clock, Jem chose something simple to wear. The pencil skirt, blouse, and jacket wouldn't be making another appearance during her time in the Isles of Scilly. *Not unless I have to wear it to my arraignment,* she thought with grim good humor. But until and unless her situation turned so dire, she never wanted to wear the wretched ensemble again. She'd found a corpse in it, met *Planet of the Apes* Rhys in it, been arrested in it, booked, fingerprinted and cheek-swabbed in it. The bloody thing was spent.

Besides, one of the joys of island living was practical togs. Despite the fact she was going to Lyonesse House for dinner, Jem decided the inner layer of her outfit would be a swimsuit. St. Morwenna had four white sand beaches. It wasn't impossible that after dinner, Jem and Pauley would end up walking along one. They might even swim, if Jem could get past her complicated feelings on the matter and just do it.

After the accident and all that followed, fourteen-year-old Jem had vowed never to swim or set foot in a boat again. Time had demolished the latter oath: during their Scottish honeymoon, Jem and Dean had done a boat tour of the Orkney Islands. And only yesterday, she'd traveled to the islands aboard the *Scillonian III*. In both cases, her conscience hadn't troubled her; a professional had been handling the boat, and she'd merely been a passenger. But swimming was different.

Floating is the first thing a human ever does. Life itself comes from the sea, and while people are no longer suited to dwell there, in some essential corner of our psyche, we've never forgotten. When Jem came to St. Morwenna as an angry, confused little girl, deposited with a thud on Sue Jago's metaphorical doorstep, she hadn't known how to swim. Sue—Gran—had taught her by taking her into the milky turquoise cove on Porthennis Beach and showing her how to float on her back.

"The water will hold you up," Gran had said over and over. She hadn't wanted this duty her only son, Kenneth, had dropped at her feet, but she'd borne up to it with grit, something Jem had only appreciated in hindsight. "Trust the water. It will always hold you up."

It was true, but when it came to the sea, there were many truths. "The water you sail on is the very water that will swallow you," a fisherman mending lobster pots had once told Jem. She'd been playing at the quayside in her lonely, pre-Pauley days, and he'd taken it upon himself to lecture her, in the rusted-out, breathy tones of one who should've been long retired.

"The water is my living," he'd said. "It's my daily bread. My home when I berth at sea. But I never forget it will kill me if I mistake it for a friend. Do not tempt the sea, for the sea always wins."

At the time, she believed she'd taken his words to heart. Certainly she remembered them, even today, with a ringing clarity, like the sound of a fork striking a crystal glass. But she'd heard the fisherman's warning as one that applied to other people, not to her. And she never once thought of it while swimming, or wading, or diving to look at shipwrecks, or exploring the granite rocks and reefs around St. Morwenna. Swimming had come so naturally to Jem, it seemed impossible that Gran or anyone else had ever needed to teach her. Then the accident had happened, and she'd given it up. A joy voluntarily surrendered as a sort of penance.

Nevertheless, a part of Jem seemed to be signaling that maybe, just maybe, she could put her toe in the water again. That it wouldn't be so bad to backslide a little, now that she was back in the islands again. So before leaving Penzance, she'd gone to a surf shop and purchased her first swimsuit in almost two decades. Now it awaited her on the bed, tags newly clipped: a modest navy one-piece, no frills, no JUICY written across the backside in sequins, just a bit of spandex suitable for diving and laps. Did she have nerve enough to try it on?

She shimmied into the suit, then stepped back to inspect herself in her room's cheval mirror. Hers was naturally a swimmer's build: wide through the shoulders and narrow in the hips, with strong arms and long legs. The suit was high-necked, so her small breasts almost disappeared, but it showed her legs off to full advantage.

With that barrier broken, she layered on a long blue cotton sundress. Shoes were a no-brainer—in the islands, sandals were de rigueur. But what about her hair? Should she wear it up, or down? Most of her nervousness about seeing Pauley face to face again had faded—she had better things to fret about, after all. But she still wanted to look nice. She might bump into Rhys.

Why do I keep coming back to Rhys?

The thought was irritating. To chase it out of her head, Jem amused herself by striking a couple of poses, complete with haute couture scowl. Were Dean present, he would've whistled and tossed out racy comments. That was the paradox of the closeted gay husband; he might not want to sleep with you, but he was the best cheerleader a woman evaluating her looks in a full-length mirror would ever need.

Note to self: call and commiserate with Dean.

Smiling, Jem twisted her hair into a bun. Because it was all one length, her hair did buns, chignons, and ponytails with ease. Jem occasionally flirted with the idea of layers, or bangs, or even chopping it all off and bleaching whatever was left. But the simple truth was, her long hair was too much a part of her identity; she couldn't say goodbye to it now.

In her late teens, she'd combed it forward, using it as a shield to hide behind. In her early twenties, she'd rolled it into waves, or put it up in pigtails, or worn it in a French twist, depending on whom she wanted to be that day. Nowadays there was something gratifyingly simple about going from work updo to evening tresses just by pulling out a couple of combs.

For makeup, she applied some carmine lipstick. She had a good face, all told. High cheekbones, rather deep-set brown eyes, a firm brow and a generous mouth. Over her left eyebrow, the white scar stood out. Before work each morning, she covered it with concealer. But was it really all that noticeable? Maybe not. She decided to skip the concealer for a while and see.

Evaluating the scar on her face prompted her to take a peek at its counterpart, located on her right ankle. Her sundress's flowing hem covered some, but not all, of it. Unlike the scar above her eyebrow, this was a true disfigurement: raised, ugly, more pink than white. She didn't remember exactly when it had happened. Nor did she recall the pain she'd surely felt when ragged granite bit into her flesh. At St. Mary's Hospital, she'd received first aid on the day of the rescue, but missed most of the follow-up appointments. In the wake of two funerals, fussing over minor injuries would have felt obscene.

By the time she settled into Penzance with Kenneth, Wendy, and the twins, Jem's wound had worsened. It throbbed angrily, oozing pus and scabbing over, only to break open again. Despite the pain, Jem had kept shtum. To keep it hidden, she'd bathed in secrecy, dressing in woolly socks and trousers. Eventually, her youthful immune system won out, and the wound quieted down on its own.

The first time she'd examined the resultant scar in bright daylight, its ugliness had given her a perverse sense of satisfaction. At the time, she'd felt strongly that there had to be punishment. And for punishment to mean anything, it had to be forever. The scar served as a constant reminder.

Fastening the strap of her sandals, she was ready. What's more, she was hungry. Refusing to acknowledge so much as a shiver of nervousness, Jem set off for Lyonesse House.

CHAPTER TWELVE

From Misfit Waterfowl to Sophisticated Swan

Instead of taking the Byway, Jem cut across the flower fields of Hobson's Farm. It had been her after-school habit for years—home for a snack and to check in with Gran, then a zigzag across the farm, which grew bulbs for mainland wholesalers and cut flowers for a select few shops and hospitality services. Beyond the hedgerows, wind-sown wildflowers grew. Mostly, Jem came across pink carnations, hearty little sun lovers soaking up what remained of the long summer afternoon. She picked a handful for Pauley's table, as they used to do as girls. Neither had really been one for tea parties with dolls and teddy bears, but they'd often played Mab the Faerie Queen—in which case, the flowers were necessary in the brewing of potions, to bind mortals to their will.

Behind Lyonesse House a stone table and chairs were laid ready for dinner. A white tablecloth fluttered in the breeze, held down by a big glass pitcher. As Jem approached, she saw there were three people present. Slowing, she squinted at the table. Pauley hadn't said anything about other guests.

"Jem!"

Pauley stood up and waved. "Move your arse! I've been worried sick about you."

Jem approached, a little shy. Pauley hadn't been changed by the years so much as she'd grown into her habits and quirks, the way a young lioness grows into her paws. Large and pale-skinned, her hair was such a deep red, it could be called magenta. Her bright red lipstick was boldly applied, and her sunglasses had that vintage cat's-eye shape, rhinestones accentuating each upturned point. Her black dress, tight at the waist with three-quarter sleeves, suited her curves perfectly.

"You look like vintage Hollywood," Jem said.

Laughing, Pauley went in for the hug. It was an embrace that rattled Jem to her back teeth, emotionally as well as physically. Eyes stinging and throat going tight, Jem willed herself to be calm. She didn't even know who the other two people at the table were, except they were both women. She hated breaking down in front of other people. She'd be boiled if she let it happen in front of someone who might have been in the Square when Saoirse asked her if she was a murderer, quietly enjoying the scene without speaking up in Jem's defense.

Pauley whipped off her rhinestone-studded sunnies. Holding Jem out at arm's length, she inspected her, grinning all the while. "You look exactly the same! Except taller. *Prettier.* With legs that go all the way up, damn you."

"But no baps," Jem said lightly, smiling down at Pauley, who'd never grown beyond five foot four and possessed the same magnificent cleavage she'd had at fourteen. "You're gorgeous."

"Hah! Now. Turn around," Pauley said, nudging Jem in the correct direction, "and say hello to two ladies you might remember. Lissa DeYoung, and Dahlia Reddy."

Jem caught her breath at the second name. Looking from woman to woman, she said, "Oh. Hello."

Lissa DeYoung looked nothing like her daughter Kenzie, apart from her fine bone structure and narrow shoulders. She was a year or two older than Jem and Pauley, chronologically speaking. Yet her eyes had the look of one who'd been in the wars, and bore all the scars inside. Her short blonde hair was shaved over one ear, in a sort of punk affectation, and she had multiple piercings—little hoops, bone studs, and a lip piercing Jem thought might be called a labret. Her T-shirt, which bore a band logo too faded to be made out, was pulled to one side by the way she sat, right foot tucked under her left thigh. The gap at the shoulder revealed a black bra strap and part of a tattoo—wavy blue lines, Jem noted.

"Hiya, Jemmie. Betcha don't remember me. We never mixed," Lissa said. Her chirpy, birdlike voice sounded like Kenzie's, only higher and younger, somehow. "I want to shake. Just…" She turned her head, and Jem realized she was sitting in that awkward position so she could hold her cigarette downwind. She'd turned her head in pursuit of one long, last drag. Final nicotine hit accomplished, Lissa dropped the dog-end, ground it under her heel, and reached across the table to shake Jem's hand.

"I do remember you. It's good to see you," Jem said. "I've met Kenzie already. I like her very much."

"And here's poor Dahlia," Pauley said, presenting the woman whom Jem had already locked eyes with. "I keep telling her how sorry I am. We both do. I reckoned with my dad gone two years ago and my mum in a hospice now, I was a grief expert. Never have another awkward moment offering condolences again. But then Dahlia turned up, and I just keep stumbling and bumbling."

"Same," Lissa said, fingers fidgeting. She seemed to already regret snuffing her cigarette.

"It's fine," Dahlia said, her voice low. "Mum was… not the sort of person you can believe is really gone. You expect people like her to go on forever. Know what I mean, Jem?"

Jem nodded. Noticing a trace of anger in Dahlia's expression, she'd turned first to Lissa to ease into the conversation. People grieved in different ways, after all—what Jem read as hostility might actually be sadness, or anger at the situation that had stolen her mother's life. But now that Dahlia spoke, the note of accusation rang through, loud and clear.

"I… I'm very sorry for your loss," Jem said, her mouth issuing its default phrase as she stared at Mrs. Reddy's daughter, who'd physically transformed almost beyond recognition.

Dahlia, like Pauley, had always been a plump child, teased relentlessly about her weight. Teasing was universal at St. Mary's School, where the teachers turned a blind eye to bullying and had seemed content to initiate a *Lord of the Flies* scenario every afternoon playtime. Jem had been called flamingo because of her long legs, and Pauley's weight-related travails had been far worse than Dahlia's. But here was Pauley, big and bold, with a light in her eyes and an aura of confident surety that Jem instinctively believed. And here was Dahlia, looking like she'd undergone one of those surgical quick fixes, and the process had gone off the rails.

"Slim and fabulous, ain't she?" Lissa said, grinning in a way that *did* seem faked, if Jem was any judge. "I push out one kiddo and my belly won't flatten out no matter what I do. Purges, cleanses, those patches sold on Instagram… nothing works." Lissa patted her aforementioned gut, which would have been barely noticeable if not for her skin-tight striped leggings. "This lady goes on a retreat and comes back looking like a supermodel."

Jem thought Dahlia looked more like a celebrity fresh from rehab—the sort where they check in for the requisite "exhaustion" and come out announcing they're heroin-free. Her face was gaunt, cheekbones prominent, cheeks hollow. It made her look older, but definitely quite fashionable. The spottiness of her teen years was gone. So were her thick specs, replaced with contacts or eliminated by laser surgery. Makeup had been expertly applied; her long blonde hair fell over her shoulders in a timeless blunt cut. Smart trousers and a cashmere twin set completed the picture: from misfit waterfowl to sophisticated swan.

"Let's get you sat down and put a drink in your hand," Pauley said, needlessly ushering Jem into the one remaining chair between her and Dahlia. "In the pitcher, you'll find margaritas. If that doesn't suit your fancy, I have beer in the fridge, plus all the usual suspects—water, coffee, pop."

"A margarita would be lovely," Jem said. She could feel both Lissa and Dahlia studying her intently.

As Pauley poured the yellow mixture into a glass, Dahlia said, "I understand you discovered my mother's body."

Jem nodded. She tried to hold Dahlia's gaze, but the other woman's stare was so penetrating, so frankly assessing, that Jem found herself looking at her drink instead.

"I asked Chief Anderson what you were doing at Seascape House last night. It's not like you and Mum were ever friends." Dahlia pronounced this last word with a distinct edge that made Lissa stop fidgeting and Pauley sit up straighter. "The chief said you'd just popped over to accuse her of thieving."

Lissa sucked in her breath.

"I know this is a very emotional time—" Pauley began.

"No. You don't know," Dahlia snapped, turning her sharp, almost unblinking glare on her hostess. "You think because your old dad died a natural death and your mum's terminal now, you know exactly how I feel. Well, you have *no idea*. My mother was brutalized. She was murdered. And I don't like to think you could have done such a thing, Jem, but let's be honest. Twenty years ago, you ran away from St. Morwenna with your tail between your legs. And you blamed Mum instead of yourself, didn't you?" Dahlia pointed a finger in Jem's face, the tip of its French-manicured nail jabbing like a weapon. "The way the chief reckons it, you came back here hoping to get some of your own back. First excuse you had, you went looking for her after dark, when you knew she'd be alone. He doesn't know if you meant to kill her, or if things got out of hand, but if you have any decency at all, you'll confess!"

"Good God, Dahlia," Lissa cried. "Have you lost it? It was probably a drifter. A man, anyway. Think how much strength it would've taken to kill her with nothing but bare hands."

Dahlia rounded on her. "How did you know that? How Mum died wasn't in the papers or the TV reports."

Lissa shrank in on herself. That in-the-wars look returned, as if some part of her was forever on guard against the next punch or kick. "Newt told me. You know how he is. The boy can't keep a secret to save his life."

"I'll find out," Dahlia said. "If that brainless muppet has been telling people dirty little secrets about Mum's death, I'll have his job. And if he hasn't, and I find out you—you—" She broke off, covering her nose and mouth with both hands. Rising from her stone chair, she walked a few feet away from the table, showing them only her back.

"Dahlia," Pauley said hesitantly, taking a couple of steps toward her.

Still not turning, hands covering most of her face, Dahlia shook herself violently. It was a full-body rejection. An expression of loathing so total, Jem felt it viscerally, like a blast of heat. She didn't know if Dahlia truly believed that she, Jem, was responsible for her mother's death. Her intensity had shifted in a heartbeat, striking like a cobra at Lissa the moment the other woman referenced the lack of a murder weapon. All Jem could be sure of was Dahlia's pain, which pulsated too hot and bright to be mistaken.

"Dahlia," Pauley said again. "I want to help, but I don't know how."

Dahlia made a noise somewhere between a laugh and a sob. "I'm beyond help. So I'll go. You lot couldn't have enjoyed your little party with me here, anyhow." With that, she began striding purposely away from them, around Lyonesse's old wing, toward the gap in the crumbling hedgerow and the Byway just beyond.

CHAPTER THIRTEEN

"Dead to Me"

"Ye gods," Pauley said for the third time. They were gathered in Lyonesse House's 1970s-era kitchen, horrid to behold in shades of avocado and orange, but improved by the odor of homemade lasagna, cooling on the trivet. Pauley was slicing a loaf of crusty bread to toast in the oven.

"That was brutal," Lissa agreed. She sat at the round, Formica-topped kitchen table opposite Jem, hands trembling as if she was desperate for a cigarette, yet fighting hard against the urge. "I thought D.D. was going to lunge for you."

Jem nodded. The sunset confrontation with Dahlia had been sudden and electric, like a summer storm. Now Jem's rational mind kept blinking from READY to STAND BY. Like Pauley and Lissa, she felt capable of nothing more intellectually complicated than bursting out with "Bloody hell!" every couple of minutes. Perhaps if she did so regularly enough, she'd regain her emotional equilibrium.

"D.D.," Jem said. "I hadn't thought of 'Druggie Dahlia' in forever. How did that start?"

"Mrs. Lederer found a baggie of pot in her locker," Lissa said.

"No, that came later. It all started with truancy," Pauley corrected, reaching across the side for the butter dish. "I think we were in Year Seven, toward the end of the year. Dahlia skived out of maths with a tummy ache and hopped a ferry to Penzance. Spent the day with some older kids. Mrs. Reddy was in such a panic when Dahlia didn't come home after school, she practically mobilized MI5."

"MI6," Lissa said.

"Oh, I remember now," Jem said. "Chief Anderson brought her back in a state of—what did he call it?"

"Indisposition," Pauley said. "I reckon she was just puking-pissed, but of course the rumor went around that she'd been shooting up. Such is the island grapevine when the weather's too wet and there's nothing good on telly. Mrs. Reddy was furious. Going about threatening to sue everyone who misrepresented her child." She paused to slide the bread into the oven, then wiped her hands and withdrew the last bottle from her wine rack. "Beggars can't be choosers. Pinot Noir okay?"

Jem and Lissa nodded, though Lissa looked far more eager than Jem felt. Her half-finished margarita had gone down poorly.

Teenage Jem—pre-accident Jem—would've reacted to Dahlia's accusations with anger. It seemed that grown-up, housebroken, productive-member-of-society Jem just felt sick, and even a little frightened. Once upon a time, Mrs. Reddy had focused her gimlet eye upon Jem and cost her everything. Could she really do it again now? From inside a steel cadaver locker in Hugh Town?

"Fill me in on Dahlia," Jem said. "When I left, she was still called D.D., right?"

Pauley and Lissa exchanged glances.

"Not so much," Lissa said. "What happened with you and… the accident, I mean. It sort of blotted out the sun."

"You were 'that Jago girl,'" Pauley said, placing three wineglasses on the table. "Not the worst nickname. Kind of like *That Hamilton Woman*. Wasn't there a movie called that, about Lord Nelson's mistress?"

"Oooh, is he the one who got caught sniffing white stuff off the prostitutes?" Lissa asked, giggling.

"No, that was Lord Sewel," Jem said. "Lord Nelson was... never mind. And you're right, 'that Jago girl' is mild. This morning, I had to admit to someone that one of the reasons Chief Anderson hates me is because of 'Randy Andy.'"

She expected Lissa to giggle again, but the other woman's slender lips became a hard line. "Can you blame him? That cost him his marriage."

"Not to put too fine a point on it," Pauley said, the wine glug-glugging as she poured, "but according to his wife, it was the cheating, not the nickname."

"I heard he's retiring because he was forced out. Something about a groping?" Jem asked.

"Let he who is without sin cast the first stone," Lissa said virtuously. Her hand had gone right to the wineglass, but although she gripped its stem rather too tightly, she didn't bring it to her lips. She seemed determined to wait until someone else made the first move.

"A lovely sentiment," Pauley agreed, sitting down between Jem and Lissa. "Where'd you hear it?"

"Ha ha. Very funny. I heard it on *The Vicar of Dibley* and it wasn't a joke. Anyway," Lissa said, taking a sip of wine the moment Pauley did, "I do think if you're innocent, and I'm sure you are, you should go to Chief Anderson and start with a good, heartfelt apology," Lissa continued. "Let him know that you've learned your lesson and you're not a dangerous person. Also, that you don't mean to cause any more trouble on St. Morwenna."

Jem heard herself make a small strangled noise. Apparently, Teen Jem was still inside her somewhere, struggling to get out.

"Why should Jem get down on her knees and beg his forgiveness for stumbling across a dead body?" Pauley asked.

"He's the law. You have to respect his authority. If you don't, you can't be surprised to find yourself in a scrape."

Jem studied Lissa. Perhaps she'd stereotyped her, what with the punk hair and multiple piercings. But this toe-the-line mentality sounded like something Gran would've said. Not the girl who'd created havoc in biology class by showing off her freshly studded tongue.

"But Dahlia," she said, tasting her wine and feeling her stomach immediately revolt. Nope. It wasn't going to work for her. Not until she had eaten something substantial, at least. "Did she get married? Go off to university?"

"She got married right after leaving school," Pauley said. "No uni, but off to Hugh Town to live with her new husband. It didn't last long. I think it was the classic escape-your-family wedding that goes sour almost overnight."

"Mrs. Reddy didn't help," Lissa said. "She used to brag to me about it. How Dahlia married a dead idle lump of a man and needed saving from herself. She was convinced that no man could've possibly wanted Dahlia for herself, not in those days. Because she still had thick specs and she was still a bit chu—" She broke off.

"Chubby?" Pauley asked sweetly. "I know. God, I'm glad my mum wasn't like that with me. Poor Dahlia was never half my size, but she was always spoken to like she was a total whale. And the specs. What was she meant to do, just go without them? Walk into walls?"

"Mrs. Reddy used to brag to you?" Jem asked Lissa, wondering if she'd heard that wrong. Mrs. Reddy had always maintained a small coterie of hangers-on, people she called friends but who were really just yes-men, existing only to agree with her. None of them had been in Lissa's age bracket. Moreover, the Mrs. Reddy Jem had known would've despised Lissa for a variety of reasons: hair, piercings, unmarried with a child, to name only three.

The oven timer dinged. As Pauley popped up to take out the toasted bread, Lissa said with evident pride, "Mrs. Reddy was my

BFF around the start of the year. Can you believe it? I called her Edie. She called me 'Lissa, darling.'" She giggled, draining her wineglass. "Then the whole thing blew up. She told me off, said I was dead to her, and that was that. To be honest, when Dahlia turned up this evening, I thought she might accuse *me* of killing her mum. To get even, or something."

"But how did you end up so close, even for a day?" Jem asked.

"Computers," Lissa said. "Edie, the right old batty witch, wanted to learn how to use a computer. She didn't dare take a class and let people see how behind the times she was. She'd bought herself a laptop, a really nice MacBook Pro—spared no expense, as usual. Then she checked out a library book from, like, 1980 or something. It was all about MS-DOS and BASIC, for heaven's sake. She was trying to read that old shite in preparation for joining Facebook on her brand-new Mac."

"Food," Pauley said. "Let's head back outside."

After they were settled, Lissa tapped her empty glass. "Any more wine?" she grinned.

"Food first. You're getting a bit slurrish," Pauley told her. "And I didn't understand half of what you just said then. I'd forgotten you used to be our resident computer whiz."

Lissa made a grand gesture. "It used to be fun. Pulling out motherboards and rebuilding them. Making cool little bot programs. Now it's all gone away. Anybody, and I do mean anybody, can log on and get involved. The one thing I could ever really do, and it was almost gone before I even discovered it. Once we finally got decent Internet out here, I realized the rest of the world had moved on."

"I suppose you were still like a computer goddess to Mrs. Reddy, though," Pauley said, taking her seat. "Tuck in."

Jem tasted the lasagna. "Good lord. This is amazing. The sauce…" She looked at Pauley's beaming face, suddenly seeing not just an older version of her childhood friend, but an accomplished woman with twenty years of history Jem had missed. "When did you learn to cook like this?"

"When Dad was sick. And I perfected it when Mum was diagnosed. It's been a strange few years," Pauley said. "But you take the good parts where you find them."

The three of them were silent for a time. Jem and Pauley ate in earnest, demolishing the lasagna and hot, crusty bread. Lissa made a stab at eating her supper, but she was fidgety, like a child wanting to be excused from the table. After nibbling on a few mouthfuls, she asked Pauley, "Is there more of the Pinot?"

"That soldier is dead," Pauley said. "There's a bit more margarita in the pitcher, but I wouldn't vouch for it at this point."

Lissa made a dissatisfied noise. Then she looked at Jem. "Are you drinking yours? It looks untouched."

"I had a sip," Jem said. She pushed it over. "Help yourself. So about Mrs. Reddy… you said she was your BFF earlier this year. What happened?"

"Well." Lissa looked pleased to answer, though that might have just been her pleasure at receiving Jem's almost-untouched Pinot Noir. "Mrs. Reddy—*Edie*—knew nothing about computers. She saw me at Wired Java, fiddling with an old laptop I picked up for nothing, and struck up a conversation. First time in my life she ever spoke to me with anything like respect. Next time I was there for a coffee, she turned up too. Said she thought her MacBook Pro was broken. It wasn't, of course. She just didn't know what to do when it booted up. The part where it starts offering you languages to choose from? She thought that meant it was rubbish and she ought to take it back, that it didn't know to begin with English."

Pauley laughed. "I remember seeing you and Mrs. Reddy in Wired Java with your heads together, whispering over a keyboard. I thought perhaps she wanted you to make the Internet safe for the Isles of Scilly. That she'd heard about naughty pics on the web and thought it was the new frontier for her to police."

"Oh, that crossed her mind! The first time she used a search engine, she typed in the word 'pornography.' Then screamed like a banshee at what came up," Lissa said. "It was just the sort of graphics that go with articles. You know, like, 'Isn't Porn on the Internet Terrible' stories with a woman in lingerie as an illustration. I decided to distract her from the censorship crusade by introducing her to Facebook."

"I'll bet she loved all the drama," Jem said.

"That she did. Friending everyone she'd ever met. Then hunting down and confronting in real life anyone who didn't accept her request," Lissa said. She nibbled at a piece of bread, probably for show, but seemed only interested in the remainder of the wine. "I taught her how to make a secondary account with an alias, so she could spy on her enemies. I mean, I'm not proud of it. But she was buying me coffee and little presents. Giving me pocket money as a thank you whenever I helped with something, like setting up an email account or a pop-up blocker."

"I suppose she wanted to make sure you never told anyone she needed help," Jem said. It would've been typical of Mrs. Reddy to select someone she considered marginal, a woman of no influence or income, to help her get up to speed. That would be easier on her ego than the alternative—taking a class, doing assignments, and raising her hand in front of other people.

"Yes, she swore me to secrecy a dozen times," Lissa agreed. "It was fun being on her good side for once. Before the computer lessons, she used to treat my Kenzie a bit like she treated you, Jem. Always watching her. Rolling down on the beach in Big Orange to see what she was up to. Whenever a store window was broken or a boat went missing, she always acted as if Kenzie must be the prime suspect. All because Kenzie doesn't have a proper dad."

"So unfair. Kenzie's a good kid," Pauley murmured.

Jem wondered who Kenzie's father was, but felt there was no space to ask. She remembered that when she'd met the girl, something in her expressions, the way she held herself, had seemed familiar. At the time, she'd thought it might be a callback to memories of Lissa, but no—Lissa didn't resemble her daughter much, aside from stature and coloring. If Kenzie's looks seemed familiar, it wasn't because she resembled her mother.

"Where was I?" Lissa asked herself, giggling again. "Right. Phony accounts. I showed Edie how to spy on her enemies, but mostly she just spied on Dahlia. Every time Dahlia would meet someone new, Edie would invent a reason to say the man didn't really want Dahlia, was only after her inheritance, or whatever. All a bit cruel, if I'm being honest. Poor Dahlia would visit the islands every Sunday, saying look, Mum, I've lost half a stone. Look, Mum, I've switched to contact lenses. Didn't matter. She always went away gutted, because it was never enough.

"So anyway." Lissa sighed, as if brought down by her own narrative. "I started thinking, this Facebook thing had gone ugly. Let's switch it up. Then I introduced my dear friend Edie to a secret chat room. A hookup site called Nooners. I thought it would give her something harmless to obsess over. 'How dare these people get together for sex between half-eleven and half-one,'" she said, imitating a bitter old scold. "But you know what? She loved it."

"You are kidding me," Pauley said, wide-eyed.

"Were these local people?" Jem asked.

Lissa laughed. "It's the Internet, love. Who knows? Some of it probably was actual people getting together. The rest was performance art. I showed Mrs. Reddy my handle—Lillibet—and my pic, which was the face of a Page Three girl. I let her watch while I chatted with a couple of lads about how lonely I was since my soldier husband had been deployed. How I wanted them to come over and cheer me up. It was all a lark, done just to shock her. But she was like a gambler pulling the handle for the first time. Next week, when she met me at Wired Java—can you guess what happened?"

Jem and Pauley both shook their heads.

"She showed me a different chat room she'd found all by herself. Second Chance Love Café, it was called. She'd put her real name and photo on it, and she already had six different men chatting her up. A retired general, a businessman, an American cattle rancher, and three doctors."

"Oh, my God. How did you break it to her?" Jem asked. "That she was being catfished, or whatever they call it now?"

"Very gently." Lissa finished up her wine, looking mournfully back toward the kitchen as if Pauley's empty rack might have unexpectedly sprouted some new bottles. "That was the beginning. First crack in the wall. By the end of that week, she couldn't bear the sight of me any longer, because I refused to believe the retired general was a real person. She knew how to get along online and I was just some chick on benefits—no man, no money, living in a two-room flat, single mum. Goodbye."

Pauley made sympathetic noises, followed by the sort of reassurances friends always make—it wasn't fair, Mrs. Reddy was quite foolish, etc. Jem turned the idea of Mrs. Reddy, naïve about the Internet but supremely confident in her ability to control and dominate everything else in the known universe, over in her mind. Something nagged at her—another snippet or factoid, perhaps, floating in her subconscious toward the top of her mind. But even if she could feel it rising, it wasn't there yet.

"When did this split happen?" Jem asked.

"March. We had about three months as the best of friends. Then in March—dead to her. And now she's dead to me," Lissa said, with a laugh that sounded both inebriated and unpleasant.

CHAPTER FOURTEEN

Two Confessions

With the alcohol gone, Lissa didn't stay much longer. She offered to help Pauley wash up, but looked relieved when she was told there was no need, and mentioned a sudden concern for Kenzie.

"It's Saturday night, so lord only knows where she is. I've told her not to silence her mobile or I'll have it back, so help me," Lissa said, waving her own phone, an older model with a cracked screen. "No answer. I'd better go to the Square and see what's what. You don't mind, do you?" she asked Pauley, her voice taking on a wheedling tone.

"Not at all. Have you checked with Rhys? Maybe she's up at the lighthouse."

Lissa shook her head. "She's still banned from there. He's not cross with her. He's just—you know. And he won't say boo to me. You'd think we were complete strangers." Turning to Jem, Lissa gave her a melty look that proved the alcohol had done its work.

"It's *so* good to see you again," she cooed, throwing her arms around Jem, who stiffened reflexively. She had to tell herself to relax and at least pretend to appreciate the gesture.

"When I heard Pauley was at her mum's bedside, I stopped by the hospice ward to look in. Pauley said she was missing her meet-up with you, but she didn't dare leave. After she checked her mobile, I picked it up and…" Lissa shrugged, as if nasty anonymous text messages sometimes just happened, like shooting stars or tax audits.

Jem tried to look forgiving, but her face wouldn't soften.

"I shouldn't have done it, by the way. Spur-of-the-moment thing. *My bad,*" Lissa burst out with the depth of contrition known only to drunks. "I bought into the hype. I see now that you're a lovely person. You forgive me, don't you?"

"Sure," Jem muttered. She wanted to add, "Do you ordinarily spend a lot of time with Rhys?" but didn't, of course. Here she'd gone a few hours without thinking about him, and now he was back on her mind again, like the earworm lyrics of a catchy yet insufferable song.

"Sorry about that," Pauley said, leading Jem back into the kitchen to brew a pot of coffee. "I told her if she didn't confess about sending you the text message, I'd tell you myself. Of course, she had to get herself three sheets to the wind to do it. All keyboard courage, that one."

"Oh. So that's what she was confessing to," Jem said. It was a bit of a letdown to know it was Lissa who'd picked up Pauley's unguarded mobile and dashed off the message. In the end, she'd expected to discover it was Rhys, since he'd blurted out the question in person. Was it something he said often? Had he said it to Lissa?

"Don't judge her too harshly. Lissa can be fun when she doesn't have her head up her arse. You know how it is on St. Morwenna. You make allowances. It's not like we can just order new and better neighbors on Amazon."

Steaming coffee mugs in hand, Jem and Pauley returned to the stone table behind Lyonesse House.

"I love the night air," Pauley said. Then with a questioning note in her voice, she added, "And I'm sure you'll want to stargaze…?"

Jem didn't answer. The profound darkness had settled around Lyonesse House like a weighted blanket, surprising her with the feeling of security that came with it. She was tempted to look up at the constellations, but chose not to. That nagging sensation had returned. The puzzle pieces were rattling around the back of her mind, wanting her to pick them up and re-examine them.

"You know," Pauley said after a brief, faintly uncomfortable silence, "Mum was talking about you yesterday."

Jem stiffened. "Er… was she? I've been wondering how she was. I hope… I hope she's comfortable? That she likes her doctors?" She was babbling, trying to deflect.

"She's as comfortable as a person can be. She's accepted that it's almost time," Pauley said. "So have I. At least, I think so. Anyway, Mum told me something about that year you left. I mentioned you'd grown up to become a librarian, and you were taking over her project. She was shocked. She always thought of you as clever, but she reckoned you'd grow up to do something… I don't know. More dangerous."

Jem forced a laugh. "This assignment is the pinnacle of danger, as far as library jobs go."

"Anyway. She told me that you wrote to me from Penzance. I had no idea. She intercepted the letters and binned them. She thought after the accident, it was best that we both made different friends."

"I know," Jem said, surprised by how much the memory still hurt. "But it doesn't matter. You were fourteen. I was fourteen. It was… it was kid's stuff. Water under the bridge. Ancient history," she finished, now deflecting even less gracefully.

"Is that why you ignored my letters?" Pauley asked. "Because I said the words my parents ordered me to say?"

Jem pushed back in her chair. There was enough light for her to make out Pauley's face, gentle and sweet. In the twilight, she was the old Hollywood girl-next-door, loyal and true, just waiting for the right man to wake up and discover her. Jem's eyes stung. She blinked the tears away.

"You wrote to me?" She forced a laugh. "Kenneth must've intercepted my mail, too. I was always down in the basement, nose in a book with my headphones on. I looked at the post after he put it on the breakfast table, the day after it arrived. I never would've noticed."

"Too bad there wasn't social media then like there is now," Pauley said. "I rang your place once, but your dad answered and I hung up. And Mum changed our number to ex-directory, so I knew you couldn't call me." She sighed. "We shouldn't have left it so long. I wish I'd googled you the minute search engines became all the rage. I could've used you back in my life, pushing me along to bigger and better things. You went to university and London. You got married, didn't you? I saw it in your bio. And you're an expert in your field. I have a trust fund, a mansion I can't afford to keep up, and the only job I've ever had is caregiver to my dying parents."

"I'm divorced, if it helps," Jem said, reaching across the table to touch Pauley's hand. "I never looked you up or came back to St. Morwenna because… because I just couldn't," she admitted, throat going tight as tears threatened again. "When I saw Rhys last night, it was a gut-punch. He—"

"Rhys? You saw him? Was this before or after you discovered Mrs. Reddy's body?"

Jem realized she'd never given Pauley the complete chronological account of the previous night. When it came to an end, she added, "I have something else. A picture I took of the marks on Mrs. Reddy's torso."

Pulling up the picture on her mobile, Jem passed the iPhone over. "I just realized what they might be. Do you remember Burke and Hare?"

Pauley thought for a moment. "Grave robbers, right? Victorian resurrection men. They sold dead bodies to doctors studying anatomy. Only digging up dead bodies got to be too much work, right?"

"Right. They decided the easiest way to get fresh, healthy cadavers was to make them. The process was called burking. One partner, Hare, would find a vagrant or sailor passing through London—someone who wouldn't be missed. He'd invite the victim to a private place and get him drunk. Maybe add a sedative to the ale. Once the victim passed out, it was Burke's turn. He was big and strong. He leaned on the victim with his knee on his chest and a hand over his nose and mouth."

"Voilà. One asphyxiated cadaver in peak condition for medical students," Pauley said.

"Not decrepit, not decayed, and not bloodied or disfigured," Jem agreed. "The only marks left was from the victim's shirt buttons, which were driven into the flesh by the pressure of Burke's body weight."

"Oh, now I wish I was a librarian. You like springing these little facts on people, don't you?"

"You better believe it."

"And you think someone killed Mrs. Reddy that way? They held her down with the tape over her nose and mouth, and just kept her in place until her heart gave out?"

"I think so."

"Do you think it was a drifter? Someone looking for a bit of cash?" Pauley asked. "That's what some people were saying this morning. That if a person who didn't know her burst into Seascape House and demanded money, and she spoke to them—well, like she's spoken to all of us, every hour God sends—the intruder might've lost control and shut her up for good."

"Could be," Jem said. "I never think of the Isles of Scilly that way, but I suppose lightning could strike, even here. Still… isn't it more likely that someone she knew did it? Someone she crossed once too often?"

Pauley smiled. "I suppose. But we're all so used to kowtowing," she said with a mirthless laugh. "She's turned up on Tresco and pestered the Dorrien-Smiths. She's been all over Hugh Town, picking fights with every shop she ever set foot in. There isn't a person in the Square who doesn't freeze when they look up and see Big Orange on the move."

Jem thought about that. "You *can* see Seascape House from the Square, can't you? From just behind the Ice Cream Hut?"

"Just in front, now. Some new trees have been planted, and others cut down."

I wonder if Saoirse saw anything. She was always in and out of the hut, taking pictures, Jem thought.

"Anyway, we've all learned to live within the limits Mrs. Reddy set for us," Pauley continued. "There have been times when I've been so furious with her, I wanted to scream in her face, but I've never done it. It would be like shouting at a storm. Rain falls, wind blows, and Mrs. Reddy is a right royal pain in the arse."

Jem weighed that. It was true; even her acid-tongued gran, who never seemed afraid of much, had declined to take on Mrs. Reddy head-on. Mr. and Mrs. Gwyn had politely fled from her presence, and until the accident, Harold Tremayne, father of Rhys and Cam, had avoided her like the plague. In every scenario, Mrs. Reddy held the whip hand, and others appeased her, over and over again.

"I still feel like it might have been personal," Jem said at last. "Mostly because of the way the tape was wound around her head. There's no way that anyone, least of all Mrs. Reddy, would've stood still and let someone wrap it around her head that way. Here's what I'm imagining. An argument. A roll of duct tape, lying nearby. The killer tears off a piece and slaps it over Mrs. Reddy's mouth. Not to kill her, but to silence her. To just make the words stop. Next thing the killer knows, Mrs. Reddy is lying across the bed and the killer is on top of her…"

"On top like—sexual assault on top?"

"No. I mean, ultimately that's for the police to say, but she was still fully dressed. No, I'm imagining a completely out-of-control row where the killer is demanding to be heard. To be metaphorically on top." She winced. "Now that I listen to myself, it does sound sexual." She tried not to think about Bart the Ferryman's long arms or big, powerful paws.

"It's hard for me to think of her with a boyfriend," Pauley said. "But Lissa made it sound like Mrs. Reddy jumped head first back into the dating pool."

"The fake dating pool. One of our regulars at my old library fell for that," Jem said. "She was a lovely person, very shy of men, but always dreaming about romance. When she discovered online chat rooms, it was perfect for her. She could type things she could never say, and get back a long, flowery response."

"I wouldn't trust it."

"Nor should you. It was cut-and-paste rubbish. 'I adore you, I must marry you, our souls have already become one.' I have never seen so many misspellings, or so much bad grammar," Jem said. "Before long she had an email marriage proposal from a man she'd never met. After she showed it to me, I had to say something. That he couldn't be an English neurosurgeon working in Somalia, because no native-born Brit mangles their phrases like that."

"Bet the man's picture was either a stock photo, or a real man's profile pic clipped off the web."

Jem nodded. "I searched the contents of the email, too. Turns out it really was cut and pasted. These love scams are big business in some countries. Writing a new pitch for every punter wouldn't be efficient."

"How'd the woman take it? The debunking, I mean."

"Not well. She smiled. Thanked us for being interested. Told us politely but firmly that we were wrong. Then packed up her things and never set foot in our library again."

"Sounds like a milder version of what Lissa got from Mrs. Reddy. No one likes to be made a fool of. Or to have their gullibility revealed by someone else." Pauley sighed. "Do you think Mrs. Reddy got in over her head with an online romance? Lissa said she was using her real name and photo. Could someone have visited her at Seascape House and turned violent?"

"I don't know. I feel like there are still so many possibilities," Jem admitted. "I wish ruddy Randy Andy wasn't so hostile. Last night, I was too angry over being arrested to tell him my idea about the duct tape. In my scenario, it was just one piece, stuck over her mouth and nose in the heat of anger. After she died, the killer must have realized there'd be fingerprints—at least a partial print—on the sticky side. Perhaps that's what all the extra duct tape wrapped around her face was about. An attempt to cover it up."

"In that case, the killer could've ripped it off and taken it with them," Pauley said.

"True." Jem smiled. "I've read that most murders happen on the spur of the moment, so planning and rational thought aren't much involved. But if this was personal—well. Maybe the killer preferred to cover her face rather than uncover it. Or they just couldn't bring themselves to tear off the murder weapon and carry it away with them."

"Does it scare you? The murderer was in the house while you were on the porch, knocking," Pauley said. "If they hadn't decided to leg it, who knows what might've happened."

That prompted Jem to tell the story of the handbag snatcher, which Pauley predictably found hilarious. Laughing together under the stars, their coffees untouched and mostly forgotten, made it feel a lot like old times. Of course, the proverbial elephant in the room was still with them, staring at them unblinking from across the table. They'd need to have it out, to try and come to terms at long last. But not tonight.

"I suppose I'd better go back to *Gwin & Gweli*'s. I'm planning on putting in a real day's work tomorrow, even though it's Sunday," Jem said. "If that's all right with you, I mean."

"More than all right. But plan on a half-day. I don't want you finishing this assignment too quickly. Besides, assuming I don't get a call to rush back to Mum's bedside, I intend to spend tomorrow morning looking for *A Child's Garden of Verses*. I really believed you'd find it in Seascape House."

"Me, too. Speaking of tomorrow, I'd love to invite my friend Micki over," Jem added. "I told her so much about the library, I think she'd like to have a look. Besides, she has a flat on St. Mary's and she's Clarence Latham's cousin. So practically a neighbor, in island terms."

"A new person? Please God," Pauley said enthusiastically. The knee-jerk warmth set off a little squeeze in Jem's chest. She'd missed Pauley so much, and for so long, she was afraid of enjoying the moment too much. But apparently the schism had never been as final as she once believed. Every sailor knows the wrong sort of knot can lead to a broken line. Perhaps their friendship was more like a slipknot—unraveling with a powerful tug, but ready to be looped and pulled into a stronger hitch when needed.

"One last thing," Jem said. She sounded a bit like that American sleuth, the rumpled cop who always genially asked his most devastating questions after the culprit heaved a sigh of relief. But this "gotcha" wasn't aimed at Pauley—it was simply that buried realization, breaking the surface at last.

"Lissa said she and Mrs. Reddy had a falling out in March. Bart the Ferryman said he's been in the Isles of Scilly for about three months. He also said something about always taking Mrs. Reddy places on the boat. That she was extorting him…"

"Bart says all sort of things. He's an okay fellow, maybe. *Sometimes*," Pauley said, as if negotiating his worth downward the more she considered it.

"Well, suppose he just wanted to save face? What if he was her online boyfriend? Using her for gifts and money, the way Lissa did?" Jem asked. "What if they had a fight, and he killed her?"

Pauley gave a low whistle. "I hate to think of Bart that way. But… I suppose it's possible. And the chief has to be looking into him. He's new to the Scillies. He spent a lot of time with Mrs. Reddy, even if it was just on the boat…"

"I saw a snapshot of him next to her. Very chummy," Jem said. "I don't think it's out of the realm of possibility that they had a secret May–December fling. Have you ever seen Bart melt down? Show a propensity toward violence?"

Pauley shook her head. "Still… how men behave behind closed doors has nothing to do with the face they show to the world."

There was no need to put a bow on that particular truth. "I suppose I'd better head back to *Gwin & Gweli*. Where's my mobile?"

"Oh, I still have it." As Pauley handed it to Jem, the phone unlocked. A brush of fingertips swiped past Mrs. Reddy's red-marked torso, revealing the last image on the camera roll.

"What's that?" Pauley asked.

Jem squinted. By this time of night, she needed her readers.

"Um… Mrs. Reddy's foot, maybe? Rhys tried to stop me from taking pictures. I dropped the phone and ended up with an accidental shot."

"You're lucky the chief didn't think to confiscate your phone."

"True. Randy Andy isn't used to playing in the big leagues."

"What's that lying next to her foot? Under it, almost?" Pauley asked.

To see what she meant, Jem had to pinch and zoom the photograph. Full magnification revealed a strand of what appeared to be lavender thread.

"Is that hair?"

Pauley put her face close to the screen. "I think so. Good lord. I really think it is."

A ripple of unease went through Jem. There was no point jumping to conclusions. Without being on the scene with a qualified

SOCO to collect and verify the sample, they were simply reviewing an unofficial picture of what might be a strand of lavender hair. Still, the question burned, unasked, until Jem finally said it.

"Does anyone on St. Morwenna have hair that color? Besides Kenzie, I mean?"

"No." Pauley sucked in her breath, letting it out in a loud, nervous breath. "No, she's the only one."

"Did she have any reason to go into Seascape House?"

"I don't know. Maybe. She might have been flogging something for a school fundraiser. Mrs. Reddy might have even called her into the house to tell her off about something or other. I mean, it's just one hair in a picture," Pauley said, sounding almost angry. "It doesn't mean Kenzie killed Mrs. Reddy. It doesn't mean anything."

CHAPTER FIFTEEN

Sir Knob, Also Known as Sir Tristan

On the next morning, Sunday, Jem arose at first light. She took a quick shower, twisted her damp hair into a tight double-bun, and put on her swimsuit with the previous night's sundress layered on top of it. Instead of sandals, she chose white cotton anklets and a pair of battered, supremely comfortable plimsolls that she'd had forever. Tucking her iPhone, I.D., and a few banknotes into a lanyard pouch, she slipped it over her head and inside her dress. Then she tiptoed downstairs without switching on the lights, so as not to disturb Clarence, who was still in bed.

Friday turned out to be for meeting Micki, and getting arrested. Saturday was for catching up with Pauley. Today is just for me—a chance to get reacquainted with St. Morwenna, Jem thought.

In *Gwin & Gweli's* kitchen, she found an old Christmas biscuit box on the counter. Inside were individually wrapped muffins. Taking one, along with a bottle of water, she slipped outside, using her key to lock up behind her. Once that would've felt absurd on St. Morwenna, but not anymore. Perhaps Mrs. Reddy's killer had fled. Or perhaps they were not only on the island, but rising with the sun, just like her, in hopes of settling another score.

It was a mild morning, the sunlight watered down by mist and the sea breeze. As she walked along the Byway, Jem breathed in a salty tang, always discernible even when the summer greenery closed in from both sides. St. Morwenna had its share of imported trees: palms, elders, gray sallows, and hawthorns. They fought endlessly against the encroachment of native bracken and gorse, which worked constantly to regain their territory. It made the Byway a pleasantly shaded walk, cool as springtime in London, but with the subtropical wonder of a dazzling white sand beach at its western terminus.

I didn't have to creep out at the crack of dawn to do this, Jem thought. But she did, of course, because she wanted to reacquaint herself with the other half of St. Morwenna in peace. No Saoirse to pose mortifying questions while people she'd once attended school with looked on. No pensioners eyeballing her as she passed, possibly remembering a certain Star Fest twenty years ago, when she and Gran had realized their little community would never forgive them.

Mrs. Reddy is gone forever, Jem told herself, refusing to revisit the memory. *Pauley seems to have moved on. As for Rhys… the less we see of each other, the better.*

That little pep talk didn't do as much as she'd hoped, so Jem very deliberately focused on her surroundings. The Square and Seascape House, presumably still marked out-of-bounds with yards of crime tape, were behind her, to the northeast. Ahead were flower farms and dairy farms, which were St. Morwenna's only terrestrial industries, apart from tourism. The cows, black-and-white Shetlands, moved placidly through their pastures, looking up occasionally. They had no interest in Jem, so long as she didn't interrupt the chewing of cud.

Sounds carried easily on the sea breeze, sending the faint clang of a bell after Jem as she followed the Byway up. While the Square was at sea level, Seascape House and *Gwin & Gweli* were placed many feet higher; Hobson's Farm, which bordered the island's west coast, was placed higher still. The Byway would keep rising until it reached the island's tallest point, which was topped by Tremayne Lighthouse.

And here the Byway rounds the bend, Jem thought. *Follow it northwest past the lighthouse and down to Crescent Beach. Or step onto that cobbly footpath, pick your way through the gorse and bracken, pass through the tors, and find Sir Tristan. And below him… Snoggy Cove.*

She remembered Kenzie and her mention of Snoggy Cove. Probably it had come from Pauley, who clearly liked the girl. She'd taken Kenzie's word for it about Mrs. Reddy stealing *A Child's Garden of Verses,* when a casual observer might think Kenzie herself a more likely suspect. Pauley had also shut down the suggestion that Kenzie might have been involved in Mrs. Reddy's murder.

Well, she is *only thirteen. Just because Bart called her a wild child doesn't mean anything. Besides, they called me that, too.*

Rather than examine that similarity more closely, she walked on, refocusing on Snoggy Cove, one of the Fab Four's most precious secrets. Pauley had probably spilled the beans. But could it have been Rhys? His name had come up in conjunction with Kenzie, too. Why? What did a thirty-something bachelor—he *was* still a bachelor, wasn't he?—have to do with a headstrong teen?

Maybe St. Morwenna embraced the takes-a-village theory of child rearing, Jem thought, not believing it for a minute. While island life required cooperation and a certain amount of interdependence, there were limits to what was deemed helpful and what felt like interference.

No. If Rhys is influencing Kenzie, it's because he was specifically invited to do so, Jem thought.

She stopped. Her feet had carried her unerringly along the gorse-choked, tor-dotted ridge, right to the feet of the granite monolith called Sir Tristan.

Sir Tristan was a natural pillar of granite, approximately nine feet tall, that stood more or less upright and was capped with a protuberant head like an upside-down bucket. Or, more charitably, a knight's helm. To little girls like Jem and Pauley, who'd played near Sir Tristan every day, he was clearly a valiant cavalier bewitched into stone. To little boys like Rhys and Cam, who eventually stopped reviling girls and joined them in play, the rock formation had many other names—Sir Knob being the mildest. Jem understood their boyish tendency to perceive the world as a never-ending series of phallic symbols, but to her eyes, Sir Tristan would always be a noble knight looking out to sea.

Sir Tristan stood near the edge of a cliff that fell off steeply, about twenty feet straight down. There were no handholds or obligingly strong weeds protruding from the granite face. Not in Jem's girlhood, and not now, she saw, kneeling to have a look. About sixty feet below lay serene, picture-postcard-perfect Snoggy Cove.

It was a little oasis of white sand, seagrasses, and wildflowers. Half of it was invisible from above, thanks to the overhanging rock. Just offshore, under the blue-green water, lurked the reef that had ruptured the hull of many an unwary helmsman. Snoggy Cove was the perfect place for a tryst, if you had the skill to make landfall, which meant sailing against the currents to avoid the treacherous reef. Once on the sand, you and your *amour* could spread a blanket beneath the overhang and enjoy invisibility from above. A passerby could lie flat on the overhang and try to see them, but that was it. There was no footpath down.

Until the four of us came along, Jem thought, humming to herself as she felt around the exposed roots of a nearby elder tree.

She remembered the day Rhys had dug the cache. He'd made it so deep it took a supreme effort from him or Jem to grasp the metal lockbox inside.

The lockbox, filched from the recesses of Lyonesse House, had been Pauley's contribution. Inside was the twenty-five-foot escape ladder that Jem had nicked from an unguarded yacht.

At the time, Jem had justified the theft by telling herself that if emmets got pissed in the Duke's Head, leaving their posh watercraft moored but empty, it was only natural for a pirate to climb aboard and extract a price. She'd even patted herself on the back for declining to steal the wireless, the chilled bottles of bubbly, and the half-full box of Cuban cigars. She'd only—*only!*—stolen the rope ladder, which was red and white with fiberglass rungs and high-tensile-strength webbing.

"Think it's stout enough to bear everyone's weight?" she'd asked Cam. The word "everyone" had really meant "Pauley."

"Jemmie." Cam had examined the rope ladder with reverent hands. "This is professional grade. It must be worth a thousand pounds. It could hold three of Pauley, all at the same time. You'd best put this back where you found it."

"Can't," Jem had said, typically unrepentant. "The yacht set off Sunday morning. Ten to one they never inventoried their safety kit, or realized this was missing."

"We still need to hide it. Not at one of our homes, if we don't want to end up in trouble," Cam had insisted. "Why don't we make a cache near Sir Tristan?"

"Why?" Jem had nicked the ladder in the hopes of expediting her own escapes, when a moody Gran confined Jem to her upstairs room.

"Because if I make a few alterations, I think we can use this for something really cool."

Jem smiled at the memory. A gorse bush covered with yellow flowers had grown over some of the roots; beneath it, her fingers discovered the cache. Even so, the lockbox wasn't easy to retrieve. Only by lying flat and sticking her arm in up to the elbow was Jem able to seize it. The four-digit code came back to her instantly: 1214, for the 14th of December, Cam's birthday.

She entered the numbers. At once, the box popped open. The ladder was inside, wrapped into a tidy bundle. Rising with it, she wandered back to Sir Tristan, looking at the granite statue's sturdy base.

By removing five fiberglass slats, Cam had rigged the ladder to slip over Sir Tristan and grip the base. That left a functional ladder of about twenty-two feet: long enough to get the Fab Four down the sheer granite face onto the gentler, more climbable escarpment below. Pauley had been the least keen on trying it, until Cam had assured her that Sir Tristan weighed at least two tons. It would take something a lot heavier than one teenage girl to pull the stalwart knight from his lonely post.

I could still do it, Jem thought. The notion was indefensible, childish, and reckless. But in that particular moment, she absolutely didn't care.

"No!" cried a voice from the water below. "*No!*"

Jolted back to the present, Jem shielded her eyes and looked. Down by the reef, as if drawn by her very thoughts, a small bowrider had struck the treacherous reef. Judging by the way it listed, plumes of water whipping out behind it, the engine was wide open, but the hull was stuck.

At the helm, the skipper kept shouting, either at the water or at God, shifting from fore to aft as if on a bus instead of a boat. The bowrider groaned, its transom vibrating. The engine set up a whine.

"Hey!" Jem cried, alarmed.

The skipper was back at the helm, apparently trying to steer free of the reef. More water plumed behind the bowrider as it shuddered, prow dipping deep. A wave broke over the gunwale.

"Kill the engine!" Jem shouted.

The skipper didn't look up. She wasn't surprised. The motor's whine was probably deafening up close, and the wind was against her, throwing her words back in her face. Cupping her hands around her mouth, she tried once more.

"Oi! Kill the engine!"

The bloody fool was trying to climb onto the transom. Jem had no idea what he thought he was doing. At this rate, his vessel would soon be as seaworthy as a potted geranium, with about the same horsepower.

Shaking out the rope ladder, Jem slung its yoke over Sir Tristan. Then, not stopping to weigh the risks, or even to remind herself she wasn't fourteen anymore, Jem clambered along the rock face, down into Snoggy Cove.

CHAPTER SIXTEEN

Colossal Cockup

The rope ladder's final rung dangled just above the escarpment, which was more earth than granite rocks. As a girl, Jem had often hopped down the steep path, surefooted as a mountain goat and often barefoot, clad in nothing but a swimsuit. Today she looked where she stepped, astonished at how much steeper and more perilous the descent was than she remembered it. A careless tumble could land you on the sand with a broken arm. A headlong spill could finish you with a broken neck.

Still, her body remembered what to do, and if anything, the going was a bit easier, since time had rendered the escarpment greener and softer. Jem leapt the last three feet, hitting the powdery sand with a resounding *thump* that brutalized her knees. As a teen, she'd never given her joints a second thought. At thirty-three, she gasped at the pain and wondered why she hadn't brought along paracetamol.

"Kill that bloody engine!" she bellowed at the man, who looked like he was about to dive overboard.

Finally, his head turned. It was Hack—Mr. Hot Rod Red from her first excursion on the *Merry Maid*. Of course. Only an off-islander—a particularly cocky one—would get themselves into this kind of difficulty. No doubt he'd smiled at the powerboat and said to himself, "How different can it be from a car?"

Hack appeared to have heard only the sound of her voice, not the words. Throwing herself forward, Jem broke into a sprint on the soft sand, plimsolls be damned. It wasn't easy—she almost turned her ankle—but when she reached the wet sand, she stopped, cupped her hands over her mouth, and yelled, "Shut! Off! The engine!"

At last, he heard. Though the motor's roar stole Hack's reply, he threw his hands up in a way that communicated the situation: the helm would not respond.

Jem kicked off her shoes. Peeling off her socks and sundress, she was knee-deep in the surf when Hack inexplicably chose that moment to leap overboard.

Either the sudden shift in weight did the trick, or else the whining, straining motor finally cracked the bowrider's trapped hull. Either way, the boat shuddered off the reef and shot through the breakers, unoccupied and out of control.

"Look out!" Jem shouted uselessly as the prow bore down on Hack.

It happened too fast for her to process what she'd seen. Arms flailing, Hack disappeared in a froth of white as the boat's wake splashed over him. Had she witnessed a near miss? Or a man vs. boat collision?

The skipperless bowrider chugged toward Snoggy Cove's north-west side, where another clifftop loomed. The beach itself was tiny by anyone's standards, just a half-moon of sand hidden by granite peaks. As Jem swam toward the dissipating wake—the last place she'd seen Hack with his head above water—the boat slithered up the beach. Within mere inches of the cliff face, the tortured engine emitted one last screech, gave a mighty shudder, and died.

Jem ducked under the waves and opened her eyes. It had been ages since she'd stung her eyes with salt water, but in the heat of the moment, she didn't feel a thing. There was Hack, legs kicking weakly, failing to rise to the surface.

Operating on pure instinct, Jem swam around him, seizing him beneath the arms. He fought her a little, perhaps in a daze if the boat had struck him, or perhaps with the knee-jerk panic of a weak swimmer. Either way, Jem kicked with her long, powerful legs, easily hauling him into the shallows. There she released him, allowing him to cough up water and gasp for air as she bent over, hands gripping her thighs, and panted hard. Nothing about poring over antiquarian books prepared you for scaling down a cliff to perform a half-arsed water rescue.

"I… I… I…" The man kept trying to speak, but his lungs seemed quite cross with him. They refused to take in sufficient air to permit speech.

Jem looked him over critically. He wasn't bleeding anywhere that she could see. If the boat's prow had connected with his head, surely there would have been blood all over, as scalp wounds always bleed like the devil. His arms and legs looked okay, but he was pressing a hand to his chest.

"Did it hit you in the sternum?"

Nodding, he sucked in more air and tried once more to speak. "I suppose… jumping off the boat… wasn't ideal."

Jem giggled. The unexpected adrenaline rush had made her giddy. And the way Hack delivered his self-assessment with the classic British understatement reassured her that he wasn't mortally injured. He probably wasn't an idiot, either, even if she'd just watched him behave like one.

"Take your time getting your breath back," Jem said. "Do you want me to…" Jem started to ask, "ring someone?" and then her hands flew up, searching for the pouch on its lanyard. It wasn't around her neck.

She dashed to her heap of clothes. Fortunately, it was there, yanked off along with her sundress.

"I have my mobile," she announced, returning to his side. "Is there someone you'd like me to ring to say you've had an accident?"

"God, no," he said fervently, and managed a smile. If he hadn't been so bedraggled, he would've been just as nice-looking as he'd been on *Merry Maid,* with his flashy specs and inexplicably impractical black cowboy boots. With his dark hair slicked back, the silver was a bit more noticeable. That neatly trimmed mustache and pointed goatee gave him a rakish look. If not for his contemporary clothes and the lack of a golden earring, he could be a pirate washed up from a shipwreck.

"Come on. Up you get," Jem said, offering him a hand. "Prove to me you can walk without collapsing or I'm ringing the coastguard."

He obliged her, getting to his feet a bit unsteadily.

"You're the librarian," he said, blinking at her. "Am I hallucinating? Did a librarian just come out of the sea like Ursula Andress?"

Jem chuckled. "She had a knife in *Dr. No.* And she was wearing a bikini."

"I'm well aware of what she was wearing," Hack said, as if the detail was hugely important to his life. "I wouldn't trade her for you."

There was something in his searching gaze that made her instinctively look away. "Let's sit you down somewhere."

Keeping an arm around his waist, Jem walked Hack to a patch of seagrass. There, the flat granite slab the Fab Four had often used for picnics provided them both with a dry, raised seat. If Hack had seemed truly hurt, she would've called 999 immediately, whether he wished it or not. But she suspected he wasn't so much physically injured as shocked and furious with himself. His ego was bruised. He sat and glared at the bowrider, shaking his head and sighing.

"I'm Jem Jago, by the way," she said, when she thought he'd sulked long enough. The sunlight was brighter now, and all over St. Morwenna, people were probably starting their day.

"Jim? Like, Jim Sturgess?" he coughed. "Or Gem, like a precious stone?"

"Jem, as in Jemima. And you're Hack…?" She waited.

"That's right."

"Surname?"

"Just Hack." He pressed his hand to his sternum again, which clearly still hurt. "You can't expect me to tell you my whole name, after seeing that colossal cockup."

"Is that your boat? Or a hire?"

"Neither. Borrowed it from a mate. Soon to be an ex-mate, I reckon."

"Have you… done a lot of boating?"

Hack put his head to one side. There was a hint of the arrogance she remembered from *Merry Maid*. She suspected it would already be back in full force, if he hadn't just wrecked a vessel that didn't belong to him.

"That would be a no. This was my maiden voyage."

"Really? You set out alone… at dawn?"

"Just before first light."

"From the quay?" She jerked her head to indicate the other side of St. Morwenna.

"From Hugh Town. I watched some YouTube videos," Hack said matter-of-factly, with the blithe assurance of a future Darwin Award winner. "Read a list of do's and don'ts. Thought I was ready."

"The Isles of Scilly," Jem said slowly, as if to an infant, "constitute an archipelago."

"I know that."

"I don't think you do." Jem heard herself shifting from bemused Good Samaritan to scolding librarian, but she couldn't help herself. Pointing to the water, she said, "Out there, there's about a hundred and twenty rocks. Half of them are submerged, depending on the conditions. I suppose a novice could make it from St. Mary's to St. Morwenna if he went carefully, traveling the lanes from quay to quay. But what made you think you could circumnavigate the island?"

"It looked easy?" he offered.

"Did you have your depth finder on? Your GPS?"

"Probably. I don't know. I muted one because it kept pinging."

Jem blew out a sigh.

"I heard you calling for me to kill the engine," Hack said defensively, pressing his sternum again. "It wouldn't stop. I turned the key a dozen times. Ruddy thing went rogue. How does that even happen?"

"Probably a bad powerpack. Or a corroded wire in the helm." Jem shrugged. "Like I told you on the *Merry Maid,* I've been away a long time. Haven't really kept up with boats and seamanship."

Hack sat up straighter. He was no longer coughing, and his face was losing its strained-beet color. "Oh. Yeah. Didn't I hear… I mean, are you the one who found that murder victim? First one in the Isles of Scilly since the beginning of time?"

"Since the Fowey Pirates, anyway," Jem said. "Afraid so. Not the way I imagined my first day back."

"On the ferry, you said you were going to collect a misappropriated book," Hack said. "I don't suppose… did you go to confront the person who'd taken, or allegedly taken, the book and find her dead?"

"Yes. Lucky me." There was something about Hack's gaze that felt intrusive. Probably he just wanted to turn the tables on her, if she'd made him feel like a child with her archipelago lecture.

"Now you're looking a bit steadier, let's figure out what to do next about the boat wreck. Who loaned it to you? Someone on St. Mary's, I assume. Tourist, or local?"

"Local. He knew I was curious about boating, so last night he offered me the use of his bowrider. Mind you, we were up drinking till the small hours. He might have been a wee bit suggestible when he turned over the keys. I planned to have it back before he was up to shower and shave. Now…" He stabbed an accusing finger at the boat, as if it were to blame for everything.

"Before we ring him, let's have a closer look at the damage, shall we?" Jem asked, rising.

"I don't think so. I'd rather just, you know, start a new life here," Hack said. "I'll construct a hut from palm fronds. Send out messages in bottles. Go about in ragged trousers… which is a shame, if I'm being honest, because I'm rather fond of these trousers," he added, sadly contemplating the trousers, which were the "tactical" sort that seem to have pouches sewn on top of pouches.

"Chin up. It could've been worse. The boat could have struck your head and killed you," Jem said.

"I would've preferred it."

"Or it could've zoomed out to sea, hit another rock, and exploded."

Hack appeared to consider that scenario. "I grant you, that's marginally worse." He stood up, wincing. "All right, let's eyeball the bloody thing and see what's what."

The damage was considerable, if not downright catastrophic. The hull was dented. The motor smelled like burned rubber. The helm had no power, and that didn't bode well for the electrical system, which could usually power the running lights, even when the boat was dead in the water.

"*Unforgivable,*" Hack exploded.

"Calm down. Don't assume the worst until we get an expert opinion." Turning, Jem looked up at the granite cliffs. From where they stood, Tremayne Lighthouse wasn't visible, but she knew it was close—less than a quarter of a mile away. On the other side of the cliff was Crescent Beach, where Harold Tremayne had always kept a few no-frills runabouts on the sand to rent to the emmets. In his spare time, he'd fixed them up, tinkering with motors and patching hulls. His sons Rhys and Cam had inherited those skills, becoming dab hands at boat repair, even as kids.

From her mobile, she rang Pauley at Lyonesse House.

"Jem? Wow, it's early. Is everything okay?"

"Fine. I'm at Snoggy Cove. Down on the beach, if you can believe it. There's an, er—*tourist* here who got into difficulty with his boat. Does Rhys still do bodywork?"

CHAPTER SEVENTEEN

Lost Like Lyonesse

Pauley offered to ring Rhys, whom she said was still in self-imposed exile at the lighthouse, meaning he generally accepted no visitors and took no calls. That reminded Jem of something Lissa had said—that Kenzie probably wasn't at Tremayne Lighthouse because she was forbidden to go there.

Nonchalantly, Jem asked, "Why has Rhys shut himself off from the world?"

Pauley laughed. "He'd kill me if I told you. But you'll find out soon enough. Tell you what—don't ask him, and over lunch, I'll put you in the picture." She laughed again. "That's it. Put you in the picture."

"All right," Jem said, trying her utmost to sound as if she couldn't care less. "But he'll come, won't he? He won't leave us here? I have the ladder. The man in need isn't too banged up. I think he could climb up to Sir Tristan, but his boat's another story."

"Rhys will come," Pauley said. "You mustn't think… that is…" She tailed off.

Jem thought she knew what Pauley meant. That just because Rhys would never forgive her, that didn't mean he would take it out on a stranded emmet. It occurred to Jem that she didn't even know if Pauley had forgiven her. They'd cleared the air about *how* they'd left it, not why they'd left it.

There won't be absolution, she told herself, annoyed by the squeeze of her heart. *Stop wishing for it.*

"Understood. Thanks a million, P. See you at lunch," Jem said lightly, and disconnected. Turning, she found Hack sitting on the picnic rock again, shoulders slumped, defeated.

"Rhys will be here before too long," Jem told him, dropping onto the seagrass in an easy cross-legged position. Her swimsuit had dried, and the soft morning sun was warm on her face.

"I should call him. The boat's owner, I mean," Hack said miserably.

"Not just yet," Jem said.

He frowned at her. "I'm not meant to believe this bloke you've summoned will open his tool kit and fix it up, good as new?"

"Of course not. But he can tow it back to his place. Call his friends to scope out the motor and the electrical system. When an emmet calls those shops, they get emmet prices. You want a local to ask for estimates," Jem said. "Then Rhys will look over the hull and quote you a price to restore it cosmetically. In the end, I don't think you'll be on the hook to buy your mate a new boat, full stop. But it's still going to be bad news. If you ring him now, he'll be in a rage. If you wait until you've made a plan to get everything repaired, he's less likely to go to pieces."

Hack seemed to digest that. Then he gestured over his shoulder at the red and white emergency ladder. It hung just as she'd left it, extending down the sheer granite face and anchored by Sir Tristan. "How did you even…?"

"It's something we rigged up as kids. Well. My friend Cam rigged it up, specifically. When I hiked over here this morning, I decided to see if it was still hidden close to that big rock formation. Took it out of the cache just to… well, reminisce, I reckon. I wouldn't have actually used it if I hadn't looked down and seen you in trouble."

Hack shook his head, seemingly amazed by the audacity of it. "Here I thought you were Little Miss Safety. Nobody stepped in to tell you kids it might get you killed?"

"We were beastly," Jem said, half repentant, half proud. "Chief Anderson heard a rumor, I think, but he never caught us in the act. That reminds me. The moment I have you squared away, I need to hide that rope ladder. The chief's always loathed me. If he sees that, he'll probably invent a new reason to arrest me. Interfering with a natural monument or something."

"A new reason," Hack said. "So… he's arrested you before?"

"Last night. When I found Mrs. Reddy's body, I rang 999. Then I had a look around where she died, just a little, and he called that obstructing a police officer," Jem said. "As kids, we called him Randy Andy, because he was always sniffing after some woman who wasn't his wife. He's a creep."

"Due to be replaced soon," Hack said mildly.

"I doubt the next chief will be any better, or any smarter," Jem said. "Probably a no-hoper put out to pasture in the Scillies where he can't ruin mainland investigations. Neither of them is likely to catch Mrs. Reddy's killer unless there's an out-of-the-blue confession. Or if a concerned citizen breaks the case for them."

Like me, Jem thought, though she decided to keep that part to herself.

Hack seemed to absorb that. Then his gaze returned to the damaged bowrider, and he looked miserable all over again. Despite his natural cockiness, he was a responsible person, she decided. Risking his neck was one thing. Destroying a friend's property was quite another, and he was obviously beating himself up inside.

"I ought to thank you," she ventured suddenly.

"What?"

"It's true. When I was a girl, I loved to swim. Absolutely lived for it," Jem said. "Then for a long time, I swore I'd never go back in the water. I even thought…" She stopped.

Hack raised his eyebrows, looking genuinely intrigued.

"I thought maybe I'd forgotten how. That I'd dive in and the water wouldn't hold me up anymore. That I'd be lost… like Lyonesse."

He squinted, clearly trying to peg the reference. "That's one of the vanished kingdoms of legend, right? Arising from the memory of when the Isles of Scilly was all one landmass?"

"Right. I mean, it still is, but most of it's underwater. Like that reef," she added unnecessarily, wincing inside as he blew out another torturous sigh. "Oh, don't look like that. You're not the first person to have a bad day in a boat. My last one makes yours look like nothing."

"I don't believe you."

"It's true. So bad I've never talked about it," Jem said. "I mean, I gave a deposition or two. I answered questions. But I never sat down and talked to anyone about it intimately. You know—confessionally. My grandmother died before we got around to it. And she already knew most of the details. My dad and stepmum preferred to maintain radio silence. When I went to uni, I made it a fresh start. *Tabula rasa* as far as everything that happened in St. Morwenna. I even got married without telling my husband more than the barest details about the accident."

"You're married?"

"Divorced."

"Oh. Me, too."

Jem noticed the way his shoulders loosened at her answer, but she pretended not to. They seemed right on the cusp of flirting, which worried her. Had she ever learned how to flirt? No. Her first love, Rhys, had grown out of deep friendship. Her marriage to Dean had also sprung from friendship, with none of the feints and lunges that seemed to comprise flirtation. Then again, perhaps her tendency to think of flirtation as a knife fight explained why she'd avoided learning to do it properly.

"So," Hack said.

"So."

"There's no one here but you. And me. And that bird," Hack said, nodding toward the seagull that had just touched down, black-tipped wings still ruffled. "Usually I talk enough for two or three people. Ask my ex. But right now... I have nothing. The floor is yours."

Jem realized that she was ready. It had taken almost twenty years, but she'd arrived at last. She took a deep breath, and she told him.

CHAPTER EIGHTEEN

Confrontation on Crescent Beach

"Stargazer," Rhys whispered close to her ear.

His breath on her skin was electric. Not hot—she'd been lying on Crescent Beach too long to be warmed by mere breath. Every inch of her exposed skin was browned, even the tops of her toes. Autumn and school loomed, and yet lying on her red-striped blanket, cut-off jeans over her swimsuit and straw hat propped to cover half her face, Jem believed her perfect summer would never end.

"Jemmie." This time Rhys's lips touched her skin. The charge rippled through her, like seismic rumbles beneath the sea. Could he see it, lying beside her, the way her stomach fluttered when he got this close?

He flipped her hat aside. The breeze caught it, tumbling it along the sand to the first clump of seagrass.

"Cheek!" Jem roared, sitting up.

Rhys grinned. Such a good-looking boy might've been intimidating, if not for that big, all-in grin. Rhys's laugh was even better. When something tickled him, he screwed up his eyes, threw back his head, pressed both hands to his chest, and gave himself up to pure joy. Most of the sixteen-year-olds she knew were all about the cynical laugh, the faint half-smile, the aura of world-weariness and boredom. Maybe a bloke had to look like Rhys to laugh that way, body and soul.

"Get my hat," she demanded.

"Ask me nicely."

"Get. My. Hat." She punctuated the last word with a middle finger.

He caught her hand, kissed the offending finger, and pulled her to him. Somehow their first kiss was always a little disjointed— mouth to cheek, or lips to nose, or foreheads conking together. It was still new. Still meltingly terrifying to Jem when his tongue slid against hers, or when he pressed so, so close.

But no matter how clumsily it started, once they fell into a rhythm, every little piece of her awakened, right down to the spinning electrons. There was nowhere she wanted to be but here on Crescent Beach, knees in the cool white sand, arms around Rhys as he kissed her.

An air horn blatted, making her jump. Rhys, kissing her ever more hungrily, didn't even react. He squeezed Jem tight against him as the air horn blatted a second time.

"Are you two deaf?" Mrs. Reddy bellowed.

Jem pulled her face away. Of course, she already knew that Big Orange had rolled up on Crescent Beach. The air horn was a dead giveaway. Apparently, Mrs. Reddy had overused the golf cart's original horn until it expired prematurely. Rather than learn from this, she'd gone to the Marine and Bait Shop and purchased a considerably more intrusive replacement.

But even on its fat beach-enabled wheels, Big Orange couldn't venture into the soft sand without potentially getting stuck there. As a result, Mrs. Reddy stuck to the upper portion of the beach where there was plenty of seagrass for traction. When something displeased her she honked at the offenders. If honking didn't rectify the error to her satisfaction, she clambered down from her flaming chariot, ready to go to battle.

"Ignore her," Rhys moaned.

"She's coming over," Jem shot back. Disentangling herself, she sprang to her feet. Rhys, infuriated by the interruption, turned his back and sprinted toward the breakers.

"Where does he think he's going, Miss Jago?" Mrs. Reddy demanded.

"Swimming." Jem glared at the old woman. She was dressed, as usual, in a matching tunic and capris. Today's was a red boat neck top printed with white crabs, and white capris with a red crab appliqué sewn near each hem.

"Don't you dare be sarcastic with me."

"I wasn't. See?" Jem pointed at Rhys, now bobbing like a porpoise among the breakers. It was infuriating, considering that he'd left her behind to face the music.

"Do you think I'm someone to be trifled with, Miss Jago?"

Jem didn't answer, her mouth setting into a hard line.

"I don't know what Sue's thinking of, letting you run riot like this," Mrs. Reddy continued. "I can tell you, I won't have any sympathy for what's to come. I can see the future, when you've birthed that young man's baby and Sue's warming its bottles and putting it down for naps. She'll be Muggins and you'll be off to the mainland, looking for a good time."

Too shocked to reply, Jem gaped at the woman. "You... how can you...?"

"I know, you're all innocence. You'd rather not hear it. People never want good counsel until it's too late. When they're trying to pick up the pieces of something beyond repair." Mrs. Reddy's tone softened. "Do you think that boy cares what he puts you through? You're just a plaything to him. The handsome ones are always the worst. They only want practice."

"You don't—"

"*Practice,*" Mrs. Reddy cut across her, "with a girl who won't say no. Then they'll marry a girl who will say no. Don't believe me? Ask Sue. A pretty off-island boy got his hooks in her. Your father was born nine months later, and the pretty boy was never seen in the Isles of Scilly again."

The fury rising in Jem was unbearable. She tried to say something, but words failed her. She'd known that Gran had raised her dad alone, but they'd never discussed it. She'd assumed that meant her father was the product of a brief, unhappy marriage. Now it seemed Gran and Kenneth had been abandoned. Which quite possibly had something to do with the way Kenneth had abandoned her, while consumed with grief over the death of her mother. Why hadn't anyone told her? Why had it been left unsaid so Mrs. Reddy could drop it in her lap with such evident relish?

"It's not too late for you to change your ways," Mrs. Reddy continued, apparently mistaking Jem's shocked silence for contrition. "But what I just saw shocks the conscience. Rest assured, I'll be having a word with Harold Tremayne tomorrow. And Sue, of course. If you're wise, you'll run along home and make a clean breast of it."

Various neurons flared in Jem's brain. She always prided herself on being a clear thinker—clearer than most grown-ups, in her not-so-humble opinion—but the instant her emotions were engaged, those thought processes went haywire. She wanted to tell Mrs. Reddy that she and Rhys shared something special, something pure, that no bitter old busybody could expect to recognize. She and Rhys had grown up together. They'd gone from childhood enemies to friends to something that could only be defined by a very big word, one she'd not yet said aloud.

As for Mrs. Reddy's vulgar accusations, she didn't know what she was talking about. She and Rhys were both still virgins, for heaven's sake.

Those were the arguments Jem wanted to make. But because of the neural tangle, she opened her mouth and the following words came out:

"Why don't you ask Dahlia to make a clean breast of it? She's the one taking the pill."

Mrs. Reddy jerked as if slapped. "What?" Her small eyes hardened into gray pebbles behind her spectacles.

"Ask her."

"You lying little cow," she said, staring hard at Jem and beginning to tremble all over. When she was angry, the marionette lines that connected the corners of her mouth to the outer limits of her chin deepened, making her look like a malevolent ventriloquist's dummy.

"Dahlia showed them around the class just before term ended. They were in a pink plastic compact, arranged in a circle. Twenty-eight live pills and five—"

"Lying little *cow!*" Mrs. Reddy looked as if she might lower her head and charge Jem like a bull. "Because my girl made one mistake—"

"One?" Jem, backing away, couldn't resist hurling a final truth at the woman. "We call her D.D. Druggie Dahlia. She's a pothead. Can't you smell it on her?"

Judging by the way Mrs. Reddy paled, she *hadn't* smelled the odor of marijuana clinging to her daughter over the summer break. Jem had never realized Mrs. Reddy cherished any blind spots regarding her only daughter. Indeed, she'd always seemed like Dahlia's number one critic.

A year ago, when Dahlia had been nicked for underage drinking in Hugh Town, Mrs. Reddy had been so furious, she'd refused to collect her daughter, leaving her locked up over the weekend. And Dahlia's looks, specifically her weight and acne-ridden complexion, were issues for Mrs. Reddy, too. The wretched girl hadn't eaten an ice cream in public in four years. Not since her mum had publicly shamed her in the Square, famously declaring for all to hear, "Sweets cause spots. There's plenty on your arse. Why do you want more on your face? So no one can tell the difference?"

Mrs. Reddy was still trembling all over, her face a deep red.

Deciding she'd done enough damage, Jem turned and raced for the water. Leaping into the breakers, she swam out to the first red buoy, treading water until Rhys reached her side.

"Sorry I buggered off," Rhys said. "I saw her arms waving. What was she on about?"

"She's going to tell Gran you're using me for practice. And I'll be up the duff soon, apparently."

"Oh. Wow. She's figured us out. Me, anyway," Rhys said lightly. "Stupid old cow."

He seemed completely unconcerned. They bobbed for a while, alternately floating and treading water. Jem found herself studying Rhys. In the sea, his dark blue eyes were exactly the same color as the waves. They were framed by long, dark eyelashes—longer than hers, which didn't seem fair. No matter how crazy the world was around them, looking at Rhys always made Jem feel better.

But as far as his response to Mrs. Reddy's tirade, she wasn't entirely satisfied. What more did she want from him? She didn't know. It wasn't like she expected him to march over to Seascape House and confront the old woman. He'd have better luck slaying an actual dragon than he would getting Mrs. Reddy to back down.

"She said seeing us snogging shocked the conscience," Jem continued. "She's going to speak to Gran. To your dad, too."

Rhys groaned. "And say what? We've been playing on Crescent Beach forever. Dad knows that. He'll laugh it off."

Jem didn't answer. She stared up at the sky, watching a single gull slowly circling far above. Harold Tremayne's personality had radically changed since the death of Katie Tremayne, Rhys and Cam's mother. It was a topic no one liked to broach with his sons. While Harold had never been the friendliest of neighbors, he'd been mild and quiet. When it came to the bond between Jem, Rhys, Pauley, and Cam—the Fab Four, as some called them—Harold seemed to view it as harmless.

After Katie had been struck and killed by a speeding car while shopping on the mainland, her shell-shocked boys had relied even more on Jem and Pauley, not only for distraction and solace, but for fun. Gran thought that was only natural, and Pauley's parents felt the same. But Harold Tremayne, effectively friendless without his wife, seemed to resent the Fab Four configuration. A few weeks after Katie's funeral, he was aghast to find his sons flying a kite with Jem and Pauley, laughing as their ribbon-streaming kite wind-danced over the sea. It soon became clear that overt displays of happiness were no longer welcome in the Tremayne house, and Harold expected Rhys and Cam to be there more often. He could be overheard telling the boys, "We're a family. The three of us against the world, remember?"

When Jem and Rhys's relationship began to change—a transformation so slow and seemingly inevitable, she had no idea when they'd passed from friendship to something more—Harold Tremayne ramped up his campaign to keep Rhys and Cam at home. He'd begun assigning them new chores, keeping Cam busy with the large veg garden and Rhys tied up with boat repair and the lighthouse.

These days, Harold was making noises about reactivating the Tremayne Lighthouse. Turning it into a tourist attraction, although nominally a moneymaking venture, was really a scheme to keep Rhys at home each weekend for perpetuity. It was so unfair, it made Jem want to pterodactyl-screech. Whether he consciously knew it or not, he wanted Rhys and Cam to remain with him forever.

The silence stretched out, Jem treading water and determinedly watching the sky until Rhys admitted, "If Mrs. Reddy tells my dad she saw us kissing, I might as well warn you… it could take a while to blow over."

Jem didn't answer. The neuron signals were getting tangled again. She knew Harold was still grieving, clinging desperately to his children, and for a loyal son like Rhys, it was only natural to want to treat him with kid gloves. But as her emotions swirled, she began to feel insulted that Rhys had never told Harold they were seeing each other. Shouldn't he lay down the law? Tell Harold, "Dad, you can't keep me from Jem. We won't be parted. We're in love."

"C'mon, don't look like that," Rhys said, pulling himself along the buoy's metal rim until they were chest-to-chest, faces just inches apart. "Mrs. Reddy will say she caught us snogging. I'll say it was no big deal. That we were acting a part to egg her on. Dad will be cross for a week or two. A month at the most. Then we'll take up where we left off."

"A month?" Jem burst out. "But term's almost back in session. Every day counts."

"I'll smooth-talk him. Work harder on the boats. I do good bodywork," Rhys said. "He'll come around."

"He hates me."

"He doesn't hate you. He just… doesn't like you."

"That's the same thing and you know it," she said, genuinely hurt.

"I don't mean he dislikes you personally. More the idea of you." Rhys selected his words rapidly, like a man assembling the bridge he was walking across. "Mum was my dad's best friend. His whole world. Now he thinks because I'm sixteen, I've got one foot out the door. That before he knows it, I'll be eloping with you to Benidorm…"

"Benidorm?" she erupted. "What in the name of *God* are you on about?"

Rhys grinned. "We're a thing. You know we're a thing. I… I can't be without you," he faltered, aiming a kiss at her lips and hitting the mark for once. "Besides, maybe we're getting all spun out for no reason. You didn't say anything unforgivable to the ruddy old cow, did you?"

"Only that Dahlia's on the pill. She said she was. She showed the compact around," Jem said defensively as Rhys's eyes widened. "And that she's still smoking pot. That everyone calls her D.D."

Rhys scoffed, looking like he would've sworn, except he was too shocked to do anything but make wordless noises.

"I know. I went scorched earth. But she insulted me every way she could think of," Jem protested. "If she'd known how hopeless I am at trigonometry, I'm sure she would've said that, too. I don't care what Dahlia does, if I'm being honest. I just had to speak up for myself, and it was all I could think of."

"I get it," Rhys said, now downcast. "I do. But this might be our last day together for a while."

"No," Jem said suddenly. "We still have tonight. Let's sneak out, nick a boat, and go to Annet. We can camp under the stars."

CHAPTER NINETEEN

Convincing Cam

They almost didn't do it. Not because they couldn't get their hands on a boat, or because it was too difficult to slip away from their respective homes. Because Cam didn't want to go.

Pauley, by contrast, was mad for the idea. Jem found her in her room at Lyonesse House, listening to Motown records she'd bought at a secondhand shop and finishing a dress using her old treadle sewing machine. Nothing *prêt-à-porter*, as Pauley called it, seemed to fit her properly, so she'd learned to make her own creations.

"I can't believe you went there," Pauley said, meaning Dahlia's reputation at St. Mary's School, as she switched out bobbins, replacing blue thread with white. "Did you slip into a fugue state or something?"

"More or less."

"Should've run to the water like Rhys. Great nancy of a boyfriend you have there. But never mind," Pauley added, grinning. "Is tonight the night? I never thought of Annet as a love nest for humans. Birds, yeah. Humans—more of a stretch."

Jem scowled. What was Pauley implying? A year ago, she could barely mention kissing without giggling. Now it seemed she'd been reading too many bodice-ripping romances and V.C. Andrews potboilers.

"Oh? Did I touch a nerve?" Pauley asked, batting her eyes.

"You need to quit harping on my love life and get one of your own."

"I'll get right on that," Pauley said, working the treadle again. "Just have to lose seven stone, color my hair blonde, and move somewhere that has more than ten single blokes at any given moment."

"You're a dork," Jem told Pauley. "By the way, there's a gale warning for later. Dress accordingly."

"I'm wearing my wetsuit, however the wind blows. It's slenderizing," Pauley said. "What does later mean, exactly?"

"Twelve to twenty-four hours. If it even happens. They're wrong all the time," Jem said.

Although this would be their first out-of-bounds excursion after dark, it was hardly the first time the four of them had taken a boat to one of the little isles in the vicinity of St. Morwenna. They'd been to Mincarlo, Samson, and Illiswilgig, all on their own, for a picnic or an afternoon of running wild. Annet was a bit trickier—it was a bird sanctuary, and strictly forbidden. During the day, the coastguard and ecological types buzzed around it, reporting all trespassers. But at night, Annet would be perfect for stargazing.

As usual, Jem would be in charge of bringing blankets, the mini camp stove, the Army salvage tent and emergency flares. Pauley would be in charge of snacks and sodas, because Mr. and Mrs. Gwyn had the best-stocked larder. The brothers Tremayne would be responsible for securing a powerboat, since in addition to the ones Harold repaired, he kept three rugged old soldiers parked on Crescent Beach for the emmets to hire.

When Jem rang Rhys to say Pauley was on board, he surprised her by saying Cam wasn't coming.

"What do you mean he's not coming?"

"He's doing one of his projects. He seems to think this is a you-me thing, and he'd be odd man out. I told him Pauley was coming, but he just rolled his eyes."

"This isn't a you-me thing," Jem protested. "We'll toast marshmallows. Sing songs. *Stargaze.*"

"With you there, that last is a given, Stargazer. He said you'd quiz us on the constellations again and get mad when we couldn't remember them. I don't mind if it's just the three of us. Or just the two of us," Rhys added, lowering his voice in a way that made her shiver. "But if you want to come and argue with Cam, you're welcome to. He's in the glasshouse."

Jem had cycled across the Byway to the Tremayne compound: the big, drafty house, the sheds, the sprawling vegetable garden, the glasshouse, and—of course—the lighthouse. Emmets suffered raptures over the lighthouse, snapping pics of it daily throughout the high season, but Jem had always taken it for granted. When it came to pure romance, give her the lonely sentinel of Bishop Rock, its beacon sweeping across the terrible Western Rocks, where so many ships and sailors had met their end. Tremayne Lighthouse was short, squat, and had no interesting paint pattern. It had also been deactivated for years, although the antique Fresnel prism panels were still inside, stored in the basement. Meanwhile, the glasshouse was an unsung treasure.

Her favorite part of it was the weathervane. As Jem approached, the rising winds off the sea sent it creaking into action, its two figures circling, each on a different axis. The upper figure depicted St. George on horseback; the lower was the dragon rampant, one claw lifted and a plume of fire jutting from its mouth. Enchanted as always by the sight of them jousting, Jem halted her bike and stood, watching. As the wind gusted, either the knight or the monster seemed more favorably placed for the coup de grâce. But as they'd been fashioned never to close the distance, their dance went on, eternal.

It took a minute or so for the wind to die off. Jem studied the lowering sun critically. There were no clouds yet, but she detected a whiff of ozone in the air. Her plan was for the four of them to meet up around half-ten and be back in their respective beds by half-five. It might only just be spattering rain by then, if the weather service had muffed their prediction yet again.

She parked her bike close to a row of clay pots bearing herbs. The competing scents of rosemary, basil, and lemon balm made her wrinkle her nose. Then she peered through one of the glasshouse's transparent panels. It had been constructed in the mid-1940s, in that waste-not, want-not era of sacrifice and ingenuity. Many panes were just unmatched shards of broken windows that Harold's grandad had mortared together. It gave the building a patchwork look that Jem found so endearing.

She found Cam inside, dividing daffodil bulbs. Earlier that week, he'd started digging up undifferentiated masses, many of which were huge because they'd been neglected for decades.

"I never studied meteorology, but we're due for a gale," Cam said when Jem asked him to come. As he spoke, he immersed a mammoth rhizoid clump in the galvanized steel tub, washing away the soil as his clever fingers separated the bulbs. "Besides, I'm not into it."

She was flabbergasted. He didn't sound like he was teasing. He sounded perfectly indifferent to the whole thing.

"But this is our last chance. When Mrs. Reddy gets done telling off your dad, you and Rhys will be under house arrest until Christmas. Easter, probably."

Cam gave Jem the world-weary expression he'd been cultivating for months now. Ever since the previous autumn, when his voice dropped and he sprouted three inches, he'd adopted a pseudo-adult manner she found insufferable.

"It won't be that bad. And even if it is, we'll be in school. The weather will be turning. First thing we know, it'll be half-term and all will be right with the world."

Mild Cam turned her into Pushy Jem. "Oh, I see. You're too scared to have an adventure? You'd rather muck about with *flowers* until bedtime and clutch your teddy all night while we three have fun without you?"

"Now you're listening," Cam said, completely unprovoked. "These flowers are the ticket. Dad said if I cultivate, cut, and sell them, I can keep half the money. Besides, I'm doing another ship in the bottle," he added, gently working more bulbs free. "This one's looking good enough to sell at the next arts and crafts fair."

Under ordinary circumstances, Jem was impressed by Cam's financial instincts. There was a reason he always had pocket money while she, Pauley, and Rhys were perennially poor.

"Cam," Jem said with the phony sweetness of her pushiest persona, "you can muck about with ships in bottles anytime. Tonight's your chance to be free."

He rolled his eyes. "You and Rhys don't need me. You two can handle a vee." He meant one of the V-hull runabouts kept out for hire on the lighthouse's foreshore. "Give Pauley the torch and put her on lookout for rocks and freak waves."

"But you do the maps," Jem said. Actually, Cam did the maps poorly. But there was no need to acknowledge this truth, because she planned to handle the navigation herself. There was a relatively wide channel between St. Morwenna and Annet. With her steady hand at the rudder, their runabout would stay the course, even if Cam read the map upside down.

Finished separating the rhizoid bulbs, Cam went to the glass-house's spigot to wash his dirt-caked hands.

"So let me get this straight," he said in an amused tone that told her she was winning. "I'm telling you I'd rather stay in my nice snug room. And you're telling me I need to change my plans to suit you?"

"Yes. Think of someone else for once." Jem tried to keep a straight face, but the sheer absurdity of her own words made her giggle. "All right. I'm being selfish. But seriously, it won't be the same without you."

That did it. Over the moon, Jem biked home again, to wait impatiently until it was time to fly the coop.

As usual, slipping out after curfew was easy. Gran, a late adapter to most technology, had finally bought a secondhand VHS player. Now she was upstairs in bed watching *ER,* series three, leaving the cottage's front and back doors unguarded.

Jem had hidden the blankets, mini camp stove, Army salvage tent and emergency flares outside in the shed. Her black satchel, a small vinyl affair she'd bought at a church jumble, was perfect for covert operations. In it she packed her *Reeds Skipper's Handbook;* half a sleeve of chocolate Hobnobs; a BIC lighter; chewing gum; ChapStick; an aluminum torch with new batteries; and finally, her second-best binoculars, the pair Gran had given her on her eleventh birthday.

As confident as Jem was in her own seamanship, she didn't dare risk losing her best ones in the sea. Once, on the calmest of seas, she'd leaned carelessly over the gunwale and dropped her favorite sunglasses into the drink. The water had a way of taking what it wanted.

Because Mr. and Mrs. Gwyn went to bed by ten o'clock sharp each night, Pauley was the first out of her house. Jem found her sitting on a fallen tree on the Byway, about halfway to Tremayne Lighthouse. As planned, she wore her black wetsuit, with a polka dot dress over the top. She was eating a diet meal replacement bar, which she used not to replace meals, but as a sweet treat.

Crescent Beach was just below the lighthouse. There, the half-moon shone so brightly, there was no need for torches. Rhys and Cam awaited them near the trio of boats for hire. Rhys wore a T-shirt, swim trunks, and old leather sandals. Cam wore the same, but also his high-top trainers, which made his legs look like knobbly sticks.

"You'll sweat bullets," Jem said, eyeing his fleece jacket.

"You'll freeze your arse off," Cam retorted, eyeing her thin cotton cover-up.

The three boats were all the same basic model: aluminum runabouts with transom-mounted outboard engines, a low-profile windscreen, and a thick blue stripe painted along the hull. They were ideal for two people, and acceptable for three. A fourth person was a stretch, but the Fab Four had never let such restrictions stop them before.

"Pick your poison. They're pretty much interchangeable." Rhys indicated the boats with a shrug, like the world's worst salesman. Working on better-quality yachts and earning money for it had turned him into a boat snob.

"Each has an Achilles heel," Cam said. "This one has a dodgy engine that chokes sometimes. This one has a leak. Not much of a leak, but if we take it out, we'll be bailing water at some point. This one," he tapped the third boat, "has no running lights and the steering is sludgy, but there's no leak and the engine's practically new."

"We don't need running lights," Jem said. "You two have torches, right?"

Rhys and Cam looked at each other. It was that blank, wordless exchange of mystification that only they could do, and Jem found equally endearing and exasperating.

"I have one," Pauley said.

"So do I," Jem said. She patted the runabout's hull. "Don't listen to them, babe. You're perfect. Now. Where are the life vests?"

Another glance between the brothers. "Dad keeps them locked in the shed. They're actually valuable, you know?"

"Plus I can't be arsed," Cam said.

"Same," Rhys said.

"Most of the time they don't fit me properly," Pauley said.

Jem didn't argue. If anything, she was relieved, because life vests were a pain. They were like a Day-Glo admission that you didn't know what you were doing, and she was an expert.

"Fine. It's not like we don't know how to swim."

CHAPTER TWENTY

How It Happened

The wind picked up rapidly as they set out, clouds scudding in from the north. Jem could feel the barometric pressure dropping. On the sea, the waves were white-capped, the foam breaking into spindrift as they crashed. But the channel between St. Morwenna and Annet was clearly marked by buoys along port and starboard, and the runabout's lack of lights was no big deal. Cam stationed himself at the prow, sitting directly on it while shining his torch beam into the water.

Ordinarily, Jem disapproved of such daredevil behavior, but it did free up room inside the boat for Pauley. The last time they'd piled into a boat this small, Rhys and Cam had been noticeably smaller. Now Rhys was pushing six feet, and Cam was fast on his heels. No one said anything about it, because Pauley was clearly aware. She was tucked into her place, hugging the tent pack and mini camp stove against her, visibly trying to will herself smaller. That made Cam's willingness to sit on the prow more an act of gallantry than attention-seeking.

"Hope I don't sink us," Pauley muttered to Jem as a wave broke nearby, splashing over the gunwale.

"Don't start that rubbish. We always go out as a foursome," Jem said with knee-jerk loyalty.

"We may need to cut this short," Rhys said, watching the sky. "Might not be a lot of stargazing, even if it doesn't storm."

"It won't storm until morning," Jem said defiantly. "But if you mean we should get there faster—fine." She gunned the engine, sending the little boat streaking boldly through the white caps.

Cam whooped in delight. "Land ho!"

"I see it." She didn't, but said it anyway, because she couldn't let anyone think, even for a moment, that she wasn't in control. To her eyes, there was only the sea, and far away, the Bishop Rock Lighthouse, its beacon an intermittent second moon.

"Oh my God," Pauley squealed.

"Jem! Look!" Rhys lunged for her, rocking the little boat, and forced Jem's gaze southwest. A wave twice the size of the surrounding waves, rising against the prevailing wind, loomed over them like a black wall of water.

This isn't real, her mind screamed. *This isn't happening.*

There was no evasive maneuver, no way to escape as the rogue wave rose higher. For a dreamlike moment, they were suspended in time, screaming at the sheer power of the sea. Then the mighty wave crashed down.

Jem heard rather than felt the impact. It was a bone-deep ringing in her skull, her teeth, her ribs. Black water washed over her, like the red carpet of the Drowned Lands, welcoming her into its depths. When Jem tried to breathe, her nostrils burned and her throat seized up. She saw herself drowned: a white, bloated body on a slab, choked on seawater at the age of fourteen.

Panicked by the vision, Jem kicked her feet, instinctively making for the surface.

I'm too far down—I'm blind—I'll never make it—

She didn't break the surface. Instead, the top of her head banged against something hard, something that vibrated. It took her a few seconds' pain and terror to realize she'd struck the runabout, which was now floating upside down. She'd collided with the gunwale.

Desperate for air, Jem swam free of the capsized boat, vomiting water as her face finally met the air. For what seemed like forever she just kicked, her well-honed swimmer's instinct permitting her to tread water as she bobbed with the rolling waves, coughing and gulping air and coughing some more.

Did that really happen?

Jem's brain seemed determined to find an escape hatch, to prove she was dreaming and it was time to wake up. All her life she'd heard of freak waves—they were the stuff of legend, rarely captured on video or film, appearing and disappearing so quickly, scientists could only define them in generalities.

It capsized the runabout… knocked us into the water…

Even as the word "us" sliced through Jem's confusion, reminding her of the three lives that meant every bit as much as her own, something seized her from behind.

Jem was dragged underwater, then borne up with surprising speed. Spitting out another burning mouthful of seawater, Jem realized it was Pauley.

"Oh, God. Thank God," she whispered, clinging to the other girl, too grateful to choke out another word. All she could do was hold onto her friend, trying to think, to plan, to do anything but listen, helpless, as her heart thundered in her ears.

Rhys burst out of the water, wild-eyed. The big waves were beginning to even out, but they'd already swept Jem and Pauley several yards from the runabout.

"Where's Cam?" Rhys screamed at them.

Jem looked around desperately. All she saw was waves and a couple of dark shapes protruding from the sea. That dark shape to the east—that couldn't be Annet, could it? Had they really been swept so far?

Rhys swam for the upside-down boat. After an indeterminate time, he swam back, the strokes of his front crawl made powerful by desperation.

"I can't find him," Rhys gasped. "Help me. Help me find Cam."

CHAPTER TWENTY-ONE

The Western Rocks

The freak wave had swept them into the Western Rocks. By daylight, they could seem insignificant, just an uninteresting clump of pointy islets overshadowed by Bishop Rock. In the water, in the dark of night, they were terrifying. One of them, perhaps Gorregan, jutted out of the water, practically a mountain. Other shapes—Great Crebawetham, Little Crebawetham, the Hellweathers—lurked all around, a wolf pack surrounding its alpha. Beneath them, scattered along the floor of the sea, lay proof of their power: the remains of wooden sailing ships, scattered cargo, and seafaring men who'd gone to rest in Davy Jones' Locker.

After what felt like an eternity of searching for Cam, Jem heard Pauley calling for her. She'd swum so far, shouting Cam's name until her throat was raw, that the search almost became an out-of-body experience. She knew she was bone-cold and close to exhaustion, but these were intellectual warning bells, not visceral experiences. Even the desire to weep had been replaced with a creeping nothingness, like her internal organs had dissolved, leaving her empty inside. When Pauley called for her, Jem swam back to her mechanically, too numb even to hope that the other girl had found Cam.

"I can't… keep this up…" Pauley gasped. "I'm sorry."

"It's okay. Let's go back to the boat. If we can get it righted…"

Pauley stared at her like she'd answered in Portuguese. "Jemmie, the boat is gone. It was swept away."

Unreality washed over Jem again. Absurdly, for a moment, all she could think of was how much more Harold Tremayne would despise her, when he found out she'd lost one of his boats for hire. Then she remembered the enormity of what was truly at stake, and had to choke back a shriek.

I can't let myself do it, she thought wildly. *Once I start, I'll never stop.*

Putting an arm around Pauley, Jem swam with her to the nearest patch of shingle. If her sense of direction hadn't completely deserted her, they came ashore on Melledgan. It was a cold, treeless bit of rock and sand, but it was better than spending the rest of the night in the water without a life vest.

"You're bleeding," Pauley said. With her wide eyes and pale face, Pauley looked about eight years old. She was trembling violently. "Your leg. And your head. Did you hit your head?"

Jem touched the place Pauley indicated. It didn't hurt. Neither did her leg, although it was raw to the touch. "It doesn't matter. Cam…"

"Maybe Cam isn't in the water," Pauley said through chattering teeth. "M-m-maybe he's come ashore, like we did, and is too far away to hear us calling."

It was certainly possible. There were dozens of named and unnamed bits of land in the archipelago called the Isles of Scilly, and most of them amounted to exactly nothing. Except tonight, when one might be sheltering Cam.

Jem hugged Pauley, so grateful for that hope—the permission to hope—that tears leaked from her eyes. "Please, God, I hope so."

The gale died back, taking the clouds with it. Soon the stars came out again, and Rhys bobbed up out of the surf.

"Is he there?" he called.

"No," Jem tried to shout. Only a croak came out.

"No," Pauley cried. "Come rest!"

Finding a dry patch of seagrass, they parked themselves there as Rhys staggered ashore. The transition from sea to land made Jem feel like Old Marley's ghost—wrapped in chains and weighed down with iron blocks. She clung to Pauley, who was shivering even more violently now that she was out of the water.

Rhys fell to his knees before he reached them. In the starlight, he looked like his own ghost. His eyes were wide and staring, with dark circles underneath.

"Did you two… save… anything?" he panted.

Jem spared a thought for the camp stove, the tent, the emergency flares. It was all gone, along with Cam. The water takes what it wants.

"Nothing," Pauley whispered.

Jem tried to tell him the boat was gone, too, but started coughing the moment she tried to speak. Her chest ached, throat closing spasmodically. Rhys didn't pound her on the back. He wasn't looking at her. When she turned away from them, panting, Pauley put her arms around Rhys instead. They clung together silently. After Jem finally stopped coughing, no one said a word.

"It was a rogue wave. A freak," Jem heard herself say after what felt like forever.

Pauley and Rhys broke apart. For the first time since they'd paused the search, Rhys looked Jem in the eye. He said nothing.

"It's probably still four or five hours until first light," Jem said, struggling to keep her voice steady. As kids, she and Rhys had wrestled, chased each other, and tackled one another daily. But this was the first time she'd ever feared he might hit her.

"If we made it onto land, Cam did," she insisted, desperate to make him see. "I wish we could start a fire, but there's nothing. We'll just have to sit tight until—"

"Shut it," Rhys muttered.

"Jemmie, be quiet," Pauley said.

"It's true," Jem said, shocked that the very person who'd given her such hope would speak to her that way, as if she was ranting, or embarrassing herself. "Once the sun comes up, we'll find him. Maybe he'll find us. Maybe he stuck by the boat, did you ever think about that? Talk about a godsend. There's probably no way the four of us can get back home to our beds without coming clean, but—"

"Shut your goddamn mouth," Rhys cut across her thickly.

"Please, be quiet," Pauley pleaded. "You're not helping, Jem. This is bad."

Clambering shakily to his feet, Rhys limped a few feet away. There he stood, shoulders shaking, looking out to sea.

Jem started to follow him. Pauley caught her, not in a gentle embrace but a rough, urgent grip.

"No. Leave him be."

Rhys screamed. Not Cam's name. Not words at all. Just an agonized, full-throated, unanswerable scream.

CHAPTER TWENTY-TWO

Aftermath

Rhys fell to the shingle, curled into a ball, and cried himself out. Pauley wept a little, too, although she seemed too shocked to put much energy into it. Jem sat hugging her knees, dimly aware of her wounded leg's throb.

Rhys had shown her the truth about herself. Probably that truth—her arrogance, foolishness, failure—had been evident from the day she was born. Fate had taken her mum. As for her dad, she'd long wondered how he could've dispensed with her so cruelly. To induce her to travel sweetly and pliably from Penzance to St. Morwenna, Kenneth had told Jem that the Isles of Scilly's doctors had brought her mum back to life and that if Jem was a very good girl, and didn't cry or whine on the journey, she and Mummy would soon be reunited.

When young Jem had alighted on St. Morwenna to find not her mum waiting for her, but a stern-faced stranger, she'd burst into furious tears. Kenneth had practically sprinted back to the water taxi to escape the fallout. And so Gran had scooped up Jem, kicking and shrieking, and carried her home. It was six long weeks before Kenneth worked up the courage to phone Jem. When he did, he seemed genuinely amazed that she even remembered his lie. The interval until the next call was three months. Thereafter he rang Jem twice a year, tops.

Now I know why. He saw it. He saw what Rhys sees.

She tried to watch the stars as she awaited first light, but they held themselves apart from her, twinkling with cold disdain. The constellations were cosmic beings, uninterested in the lives and deaths playing out beneath them.

As for the sea, she suddenly understood that she'd only paid lip service to its might. In truth, Jem had believed she could prevail against natural forces. There was always a response, a correction, an escape plan. But there was no defense against a rogue wave. Except to go out in the proper-sized boat, on a course known to at least one person on land, with all aboard in life vests.

These weren't new revelations. She'd known them at age eleven. She knew them even better at fourteen. She'd simply ignored them, all the while preening and giving herself airs as the most accomplished seafarer. The price? She'd killed Cam.

Killed Cam.

Cameron Tremayne, her friend of five years, was dead. He'd been someone whose life she'd treasured and yet taken completely for granted, the way she treasured her own life yet took it for granted. He'd wanted to work on his ship in a bottle, and now he was gone, because pushy Jem wouldn't take no for an answer.

Over the course of that long night Jem regained hope, and lost it, and regained it again. But the knowledge of her own guilt came in waves, inescapable, as minute after minute after minute crawled toward the dawn.

*

Rescue came about an hour after first light, in the form of a rusty little fishing vessel with a red-faced skipper. Professional rescuers arrived soon after. Jem and Pauley were wrapped in blankets, given water to drink, and taken directly to St. Mary's Hospital. But Rhys refused to go.

He argued with the rescuers, literally begging them to let him help in the search. In the end, the coastguard radioed back to St.

Morwenna and received Harold's permission to let Rhys accompany the search team.

At St. Mary's Hospital, Gran and the Gwyns awaited Jem and Pauley. They'd staked out opposite positions at the A&E entrance, maintaining a gap of more than twenty feet. On arrival, Jem was too light-headed from shock and exposure to do more than dimly register that hostile tableau. But the image would return to her later, and often. Gran stood with her back against a low concrete wall. Her sad, resigned expression made her resemble a blindfolded prisoner awaiting the firing squad. Mrs. Gwyn looked furious. Mr. Gwyn appeared to have aged twenty years.

Jem and Pauley spent the night at St. Mary's Hospital. There was no mixing, no loading of one girl into a wheelchair to visit the other's room so they could console one another. Throughout most of the process, Jem felt like she was under arrest. That she was being given medical care only due to lofty humanitarian principles, not because she was a frightened and miserable child who deserved them. She was given IV fluids, had a penlight shone in her eyes, had her blood pressure and heart rate measured and her wounds cleaned. The young doctor in charge occasionally cracked a smile, but the nurses were grim. Chief Anderson and one of his constables looked in on her, extracted a few answers, and left, frowning all the while. Gran stayed with her overnight, and like Mr. Gwyn, seemed to have turned into an old person in the process. She looked thinner and frailer than Jem had ever seen her. And she was back on the cigarettes, too, in direct defiance of her GP's orders.

The next day, as Gran and Jem exited the hospital, Jem asked to see Pauley. Gran made a noncommittal noise. Suddenly frightened, Jem had asked, "Is Pauley okay?"

"Why wouldn't she be? She's a sturdy girl." Gran always said that about Pauley. She seemed to equate body fat with Kevlar.

"Then why can't I say goodbye?"

"Because the Gwyns don't want you there," Gran said gruffly. "They're quite convinced their perfect little princess would never have involved herself in anything so wild and irresponsible. Not unless you forced her to."

Jem, still too afraid to ask after Cam, or even Rhys, was silent all the way home. On the doorstep, she finally forced the question out.

"Gran. Did they find Cam?"

"Yes."

For one unforgivably stupid moment, Jem's heart leapt. In her hospital bed, she'd developed a storyline that felt so real, it had to be true. It simply had to be. Rhys and the coastguard must've found Cam clinging to an isle in the Western Rocks. He would've been in worse shape than them, perhaps, but he was young and strong. With top-notch medical attention, he'd soon turn the corner. Then she could visit him at St. Mary's Hospital and beg his forgiveness.

Gran sighed. She'd stared hard at Jem, unblinking, but said nothing. The truth crashed over Jem like that towering rogue wave.

*

The days that followed ground Jem down to her constituent proteins. That was a Cam catchphrase—one of his STEM catchphrases, which allowed him to liken almost anything to numbers, chemistry, or machinery. Pauley sent her a note informing her they were no longer friends. A few days later, Mr. Gwyn dropped off a package of bits and bobs Jem had left at Lyonesse House. When Gran angrily told him to expect a similar package soon, he said Jem could keep anything of Pauley's. They could afford to replace anything their daughter had lost. The point was, neither Jem nor Gran was welcome at Lyonesse House, for any reason.

Soon after, Mrs. Gwyn gave a brief interview for Channel 4 News that blamed the accident on a "juvenile delinquent." A gray-faced Harold Tremayne also appeared on the news segment, but only to say he could make no comment, as his counsel was instigating criminal proceedings.

School was forever changed. Rhys was out indefinitely, helping Harold at home. Pauley had found refuge with some C-list friends, girls she'd previously only tolerated, who were suddenly promoted to besties. Jem, who'd never been especially popular, found herself persona non grata. Even Dahlia enjoyed a rest from the "D.D." nickname as schoolyard gossip prioritized Jem.

The question of criminal proceedings was soon settled. Because Jem was fourteen, and even the oldest of the group, Rhys, was under seventeen, there was no question of serious prosecution. Harold Tremayne pressed hard for Jem to receive some kind of lingering consequences, beyond the findings of misadventure and negligence published in the Royal Navy's preliminary report. But the report had dealt only briefly with Jem—"an underage person attempting to operate a runabout in unusually dangerous conditions"—before concluding that ultimate culpability lay with the adults who'd made it possible for Jem, Pauley, Rhys, and Cam to get out that night.

To some degree, the report shifted the bullseye to Gran's back. Mrs. Reddy was particularly outraged by the Royal Navy's conclusions. Because the report was written in staid, impersonal, somewhat oblique language, it was difficult for the average person to read the details and conclude it found anything but a tragic accident. But Mrs. Reddy was no average reader.

Having parsed line after line, she went about St. Morwenna telling anyone who would listen that according to the Royal Navy, Harold Tremayne was fifty percent responsible. He'd allowed his boys off the lead and provided them, via his boats for hire, with the means to go out alone. Mr. and Mrs. Gwyn, poor things, bore another quarter of the blame, as they'd allowed Pauley to slip away. That left the true culprit, that Jago girl, and her chronically checked-out, irresponsible grandmother, with the smallest shares of blame. Imagine it: Harold Tremayne, heartbroken over the tragic death of his wife and now his son, saddled with fifty percent of the blame, while Jem and Sue Jago bore only one-eighth each!

Jem heard about all this, and cared in a remote sort of way, but only for the effect it was having on Gran. Gran had spent her entire life on St. Morwenna, and in her own slightly misanthropic way, she loved the community, and believed it loved her back. Mrs. Reddy's campaign changed all that. Now Gran was held as responsible for Cam's death as Jem herself. People discussed how she'd got into trouble, brought Kenneth up on her own, and made such a bad job of rearing him, apparently, that he'd left the islands forever. It was all grossly unfair, an opportunity for St. Morwennians to demonize one of their own, and yet they seemed to revel in it. It left Gran confined to the cottage, wandering from room to room, unsmiling. More cartons of cigarettes were smoked, and the TV stayed on all day.

As for herself, Jem slept too much, ate too little, got poor marks on her exams, and thought endlessly about Cam. She'd never hear his laugh again. Never listen to another one of his lectures about what he could do with a mere twenty thousand pounds and thirty years of compound interest. Never sit with him after maths class, marveling at how easily he tackled arcane word problems. She missed Pauley, too, but at that point she'd still believed they'd one day mend fences. As for Rhys, Jem did her best not to think of him. She knew he despised her.

Mrs. Reddy's public attack of Jem and Gran at Star Fest had been the final straw. Harold and Rhys had turned their backs. Pauley had sat with her new best friends, staring at her shoes. People who'd known Gran forever listened mutely as Mrs. Reddy once again explained her unique take on the Royal Navy's report. She also said what Harold could not—that a civil suit was forthcoming, one backed by the best solicitors she knew. If that Jago girl wasn't going to serve time or wear an ankle bracelet, the community could at least know that a heavy financial restitution would soon be paid.

Jem and Gran had fled the Square, ceding Star Fest to Mrs. Reddy and her faithful listeners. That night, Gran had gone to bed early and had never gotten up again. For a brief time, Jem had no idea where she would go or what she would do. Then Kenneth Jago and his second wife, Wendy, agreed that Jem should come live with them in Penzance. The fact that it took three phone calls from two social workers didn't trouble Jem. She'd written Kenneth off long ago. Gran's death was the eclipse that blotted out the sun. In a state of numb disbelief, Jem had packed her suitcase and prepared to leave.

The coup de grâce came as she waited at St. Morwenna's Quay, suitcase parked beside her, social worker at her side. As Jem's water taxi approached, Big Orange rolled down Quay Road, parking close to the water's edge. Mrs. Reddy had disembarked, come within a few feet of the departing boat, and bawled:

"Good riddance! Never show your face on St. Morwenna again!"

CHAPTER TWENTY-THREE

The Nauseating Sword-and-Sandals Type

Jem finished her story there, allowing Mrs. Reddy's words to hang in the air. Hack, who'd followed along silently, offering nothing but the occasional nod, didn't speak at once. When he did, his dark brown eyes were kind.

"Telling a story like that is a bit like an exorcism," he said gently. "The bad spirit is rebuked and sent away."

Jem blinked at him. She'd recited most of the story slowly and carefully, trying to be accurate, to bear witness to things she'd deliberately shut out for almost twenty years. Whatever she'd expected Hack to say, that wasn't it.

"So… who's possessed?" she asked.

"You were." He put his head to one side, gazing at her with compassion. "If that woman treated anyone else the way she treated you and your grandmother, it's no wonder she was murdered."

Jem let out a bitter laugh. Maybe Hack was right to compare how she'd told the story—relived the story—as an exorcism. Something was coming loose inside her, something big and frightening that had been denied for too long.

"Remember, I'm the one who found Mrs. Reddy's body," Jem said, voice rising in frustration. "I went to confront her about that missing book, and Chief Anderson tried to pin the *murder* on me. If someone doesn't find out who really killed her, the cloud remains over me. I'm the one she told never to come back. I did anyway—and she died that very day."

"Coincidences happen." Hack reached out as if to touch her face, then seemed to stop himself. "People may talk, but they always do, whatever happens."

Jem nodded, struggling to hold back a frightening wave of emotion. She absolutely refused to perform the whole boo-hoo/ugly-cry act in front of this man.

Her face must have gone cold, because he said, "Look. You've been more than kind to me. There's something I ought to have said before now. I—"

"Ahoy," a man bellowed from the clifftop beside Sir Tristan. Jem cringed. It was Rhys's voice. Maybe there was a way to smoothly hand off Hack and his crumpled bowrider and hurry back to *Gwin & Gweli* without seriously re-engaging with Rhys.

Hack sucked in his breath. "Is this your ex? The one whose brother died?"

"If he looks a bit like Poundland Chewbacca, yes," Jem said, still looking at the sand.

"He's coming down the ladder," Hack said, rising and offering Jem a hand up.

Clasping it, she rose, enjoying its strength and warmth. On day three, St. Morwenna had served up a pleasant surprise. He was good-looking, single, and there was something she enjoyed about him.

"Not what I'd call a Wookiee," Hack muttered.

Jem wasn't looking. The Rhys of her memory always showed off when climbing down; she'd be damned if she'd act the part of adoring audience for him now.

"More like the nauseating sword-and-sandals type."

Jem looked up at last. The sight knocked the breath out of her.

Rhys was once again barefoot, clad in a grotty T-shirt and swim trunks. There the resemblance to his previous incarnation ended. He'd shaved off the overgrown beard, revealing his chiseled jaw and high cheekbones. His hair, now cut in the classic peaked style, accentuated the symmetry between his forehead and brow. When she'd known him, he was a beautiful boy. Now he'd grown into a beautiful man. And he was all muscle. The arms of his T-shirt strained against his biceps, and when he broke into a run to close the distance, his long legs demolished it in a few easy strides.

"Hiya," Hack said in a flat voice.

"Rhys," Jem muttered. The friendliest tone she could manage was not hostile. She'd assumed he'd turn up looking like he'd just been unchained from a dungeon wall, and it would embarrass her. Instead, he looked like this—and somehow she was even more uncomfortable in his presence.

"Good morning," Rhys boomed. He seemed to be in a good mood that morning, blue eyes snapping. To Jem, he added, "I see you've been released on your own recognizance. And your first act was what? Driving this poor beggar's boat straight into the reef?"

"I'm to blame," Hack said. "She rescued me. The only good thing about this tits-up disaster has been meeting her."

Rhys raised his eyebrows. "Well. Far be it from me to accuse Jem of…" He shrugged. "Not being the best thing about a tits-up disaster." Then, in a more take charge tone he said, "Let's have a look at the damage, shall we?"

From a few paces away, sundress back on top of her swimsuit and arms crossed over her chest, Jem listened as Rhys diagnosed the bowrider's ills. The motor was unsalvageable. The electrical system would have to be evaluated in the shop. The hull needed a patch. The paint job—his department—would come last, and be the least expensive part of the repairs. Step one was to call his mate in Hugh Town, who'd collect the bowrider and tow it back to St.

Mary's. Sometime tomorrow, Hack could look over the refurbished motors available and pick the one that suited his budget.

"What d'you reckon?" Hack asked Rhys in the tone of a man asking his doctor, "How much time have I got?"

Rhys made a sound that suggested both pain and commiseration with that pain. "Don't think about it," he said, giving the other man's shoulder a brotherly pat. "My mate's the best in the Isles of Scilly. He quotes a fair price, and he'll give you islander rates on my say-so. You said you borrowed this, right? It looks a bit familiar." Rhys peered into the vessel's white vinyl interior. "Who loaned it to you?"

Hack replied, but Jem wasn't listening anymore. She wished she hadn't revealed so much to Hack. She wished she'd never gathered her courage and marched over to Seascape House after dark to confront Mrs. Reddy. She almost wished she'd turned down the job cataloguing the Gwyn family collection, allowing some other Special Collections Library to have at it instead. But that was a bridge too far.

Don't be daft, she told herself. *Today's the day. As soon as I have Hack squared away, I'm off to Lyonesse House to see Pauley. And finally get my hands on that library.*

A familiar bark from the clifftop drew Jem's gaze up to Sir Tristan. Beside the granite formation stood Buck, tail lashing.

"Buck!" Rhys erupted. He swore under his breath, then shouted, "Go home."

Buck barked again, wagging his tail even harder. He seemed to believe Rhys was praising him.

"Escapee?" Hack asked.

"I can't make him understand that he doesn't get to follow me everywhere," Rhys said. "Wretched dog's like Houdini. I lock him up, leave, and he catches up a quarter hour later. Maybe I'll build a kennel with an electrified fence."

"Hush," Jem said. To the dog, she called, "I'm coming, Buck! Pets on the way."

The path from Snoggy Cove's white sands to the seagrass and up the escarpment was steeper than she remembered, but she still made it to the sheer face and the ladder without slipping. She climbed up, ignoring Hack and Rhys's calls of alarm. It *was* a bit of a workout, and far more unnerving for a grown woman than a heedless, overconfident teen. The toughest part was vaulting onto the clifftop without anyone else to lend a hand. As kids, Rhys had always gone first, then stood by the rope ladder to help the others up.

Still, Jem made it. Gritting her teeth, she pushed off with her right foot and landed on terra firma, right at the base of Sir Tristan. He towered over her, bucket-shaped head very round against the blue sky, looking more like a giant penis than ever before. She burst out laughing. It was a good sound, only faintly bittersweet, and the emotions that had threatened to overwhelm her subsided.

Buck appeared, snuffling happily, showing the self-assurance of a puppy who expects kind treatment. She pulled his ears and he licked her hands, tail going a mile a minute.

"Jem! You gave us a bit of a scare," Hack called up, his voice amplified by the cove's granite walls.

"That was dumb," Rhys added. "Why didn't you ask me to climb up and help you?"

Jem ignored them, focusing on Buck. The little dog had intelligent black-button eyes and a soft white muzzle. A bundle of friendly energy, he soon leapt into her arms.

"Buck," Rhys shouted.

"It's all right." With the dog still in her arms, Jem turned and looked down on them. Rhys was taller and broader through the shoulders, with the sort of gladiatorial bearing that explained Hack's "sword and sandals" comment. Hack was a bit shorter and perhaps ten years older, with his own curiously authoritative bearing—a pirate in temporary exile, cut off from his ship and crew.

He's someone who gives orders more than he takes them, she decided suddenly. *That would explain why he thought he could tool around in an archipelago with no experience. And why he's planning on paying for all the repairs to make amends for his mistake. A do the crime, pay the fine type.*

Pulling a mobile from the mesh pocket on his trunks, Rhys cupped his hand over the screen to examine a message.

"All right, mate," he said, addressing Hack. "My friend Owen has been a marine mechanic for twenty years. He's on his way over from St. Mary's. After he tows your boat to his shop, he'll give you a lift wherever you need to go. We'll speak again when it's time to frost the cake. I need to collect my dimwitted little dog and fetch him back home."

"Dimwitted! Don't listen to him," Jem whispered to Buck, who seemed quite pleased to be nestled in her arms.

"I can take him back to your house," she called to Rhys, who was advancing on the cliff face. "Should I just pop him in the house through the back door?"

Rhys ignored that. Leaping for the ladder, he scaled it like the human fly, arriving at the top in half the time it had taken Jem. He looked indecently pleased by the display, as if he were his own biggest fan. At least those pectoral muscles were good for something besides stretching out his shirt.

Jem averted her eyes. If she looked at Rhys too long, her flesh responded. It was that old, inevitable attraction, difficult to fight, like a magnet yearning to press against its opposite.

"Wow. Impressive," Hack called from the beach, in a flat tone that made Jem giggle.

Handing the squirming Buck off to Rhys, she called, "I'm staying at a place called *Gwin & Gweli.* It's a B&B."

"Jem Jago at Gribble and Squilly. Got it," Hack said.

"Close enough. Worst case, call the Duke's Head Inn and ask where I am. Someone in there will know. Someone in there always knows!"

"I'll do that. Thanks, Jem. You're a lifesaver. Literally," Hack called.

Something in the way he said it made Jem believe him. A little surge of pleasure brought warmth to her cheeks. Beaming, she turned to find Rhys with his brows drawn down and his feet planted well apart.

"What, did you two fall in love in the time it took for me to get here?"

A scoff rose up in her throat. "Yeah. Wedding's Thursday next. I'm on a tight schedule. Gotta fit in another murder just before."

As she spoke, she backed away from him. Without the wild mane and beard, the man was frighteningly attractive. Infuriatingly handsome.

"Murder? Who'd you have in mind?"

"It's a surprise. Sleep with one eye open," Jem tossed over her shoulder. The other places she'd planned to visit in the early morning—Tremayne Lighthouse, the glasshouse, and Crescent Beach—would have to wait. The rest of this day would be all about Lyonesse House.

CHAPTER TWENTY-FOUR

Behind the Stuck Door

Jem was within sight of Lyonesse House when her mobile rang. Fearing it might be her boss, Mr. Atherton, eager to tell her off a day early, or perhaps Chief Anderson with a new theory of how she'd murdered Mrs. Reddy, Jem ignored it. Only when it started up again instantly did she check the screen, which read PAULEY GWYN.

"Hiya. Is your mum okay?" she asked by way of greeting.

"Fine. Thanks, love. Everything's stable on the mum front," Pauley said cheerfully. "How about that lunch we talked about?"

Jem, whose stomach had been rumbling ever since scaling the rope ladder up to Sir Tristan, said yes at once. Only after she disconnected, promising Pauley she'd be there in ten minutes, tops, did she remember the state of her bank account.

My credit card still has a bit of room…

A better person would call Pauley back, beg off, and return to *Gwin & Gweli* to see if there was another muffin left in the tin. A bad person would hop on down to Sunday brunch, pay with plastic, and adopt austerity measures at some vague future date. There was no point pretending: she was already tasting eggs Benedict.

When the Byway blazed through Mrs. Reddy's land, Jem couldn't resist having a look at the house. Apparently the forensics team had come and gone, but it was still crime-taped and guarded. A constable lounged on the porch, seemingly paralyzed with boredom until he caught sight of Jem. It was PC Newt. Even from yards away, she recognized his ears.

"Miss Jago," he called in a friendly tone, like they were old friends.

"PC Newt," she returned, pausing next to one of the six-foot-tall King Protea flowers. The towering King Protea looked a bit like an alien species from a silver age TV show, ready to swivel and shoot her with stamen darts if she got too close. "Any break in the case?"

"No," he called back. "I mean, I'm not allowed to say. But, no. Chief's not best pleased. His replacement's already measuring the drapes, is how he puts it. Not that there's drapes anywhere in the police station. We have those ugly bog-standard gray blinds. Anyway. Chief wants to extend his time until an arrest is made. Not sure the powers that be will go for it."

"What do you think of his replacement?"

PC Newt shrugged. "Haven't met him. Heard different things. He's from Exeter."

"Is he a reject?" Jem asked.

"Oh, I shouldn't think so. If he's a bit green, I'll whip him into shape," PC Newt said stoutly.

"You do that," she called. Carrying on to the Square, she followed the Byway until the asphalt became cobbles, marking the start of Quay Road. The trio of pensioners were sipping their pints outside the Duke's Head Inn again—did they ever go home?—and Jem thought she heard one mutter, "Jago girl, Jago girl," as she passed. But when she stopped and shot the old men a challenging look, their gazes were all pointed elsewhere.

Hen N' Chicks faced the Ice Cream Hut and Wired Java, the coffee shop/Internet café. It had a few bistro tables outside, one of which was occupied by Pauley. When she saw Jem, she stood up and waved her over.

Everything the two of them did—hug, shake out white linen napkins, consult the menu, thank the server for tall glasses of iced water with lemon—seemed to fascinate the passersby. Most of the islanders looked determinedly bland, as if they wanted to ascertain what Jem was up to without giving her any sign as to how they felt about her return. A few others, however, whispered behind their hands or glared at her like she ought to be behind bars, not weighing the choice of sausage vs. bacon.

"I'm sorry people are so ridiculous," Pauley said. "I chose the bistro for a bit of sun. I didn't expect us to be treated like zoo animals. Fancy changing seats?" she asked, nodding at the door leading inside Hen N' Chicks.

"Not on your life. At least Saoirse hasn't dashed out of the Ice Cream Hut to ask after my confession again, though," Jem said, sparing the ice cream novelty-plastered little building a glance. The shutters were still down, causing the occasional passerby to knock before walking away. "I'm shocked she hasn't opened by now."

"She did open up, first thing this morning," a diner at a neighboring table said. That was part of island life Jem had nearly forgotten—the willingness of others to weigh in on conversations they weren't included in, as if physical proximity granted license. No lifelong St. Morwennian had any concept of politely pretending they couldn't hear what was being said, simply because it clearly wasn't directed to them.

"Did she?" Pauley, being a lifelong islander, accepted the intrusion without the slightest indignation. "I suppose she ducked out for the loo. How long has she been away?"

"Long as we've been sitting here," the diner's brunch companion said. "I wonder if her mum asked her to dash home. Bettie's been poorly ever since she went on home oxygen."

"Bettie wouldn't call Saoirse away from the hut on a sunny June day unless she was dying," the other diner said. "She'd ring 999 before she'd be the cause of a lost summer Sunday."

"Speaking of Bettie—is that her?" Jem asked, resisting the urge to point at the ungainly figure making her way downhill from the Square's oldest terraced houses toward the Ice Cream Hut.

"Good lord, yes," Pauley said, turning in her chair for a look. "Where's her little oxygen cart? She's not meant to go about without it."

The years hadn't been kind to Bettie Quick, founder of the Ice Cream Hut and one-time friend of Sue Jago, Jem's gran. Both women had been two-and-a-half-pack-a-day chain smokers, and both had suffered for it. Gran's pain had come in the form of a massive heart attack; Bettie's had come as COPD, or lung cancer, or both, Jem supposed. With age, Bettie had both widened and shrunk, turning into a beach ball on bandy legs. The stiff breeze off the quay caught the hem of her quilted robe, making it flap. That robe, along with her plastic curlers and carpet slippers, suggested she'd exited her home in a state of agitation.

"Someone ought to go to her," one of the other bistro diners said.

"I'll do it." Pauley got up. Jem, after a moment's hesitation, went with her.

"Bettie!" Pauley hurried to the old woman's side. "What's happening?"

"Saoirse won't answer her mobile, that's what's happening," the old woman cried. "I asked Barney at the Co-op to check on her, but he said he was too busy stocking dog food. Dog food!" she spat, stopping and pressing a hand to her chest. "Lissa and Kenzie aren't home. When in the name of God are they ever not home? And bloody 999 said I was calling in a false report. So here I am."

"Fair enough. Try to calm down," Pauley began.

"Calm down?" Bettie cried, voice shredding. She would've said more, but lack of wind stole the words.

"Oi!" Jem bellowed, calling on her Londoner persona to activate the many onlookers—twenty at least—who were gawping rather than offering to help. "Can one of you run back to Mrs. Quick's and fetch her oxygen?"

A man she vaguely recognized—wasn't he Declan from St. Mary's School?—said, "I will," and set off toward the terraced homes.

"What about you?" Jem demanded, pointing at one of the bistro diners, a man who looked able-bodied. "Can you go to the front of the hut and try to pry the shutter up while we try to get in the back way? The first thing we need to find out is whether Saoirse has fallen ill in there."

"Oh, aye," the man said, rising hastily and hurrying to the Ice Cream Hut.

Bettie, who was watching Jem closely, said nothing. Perhaps she was still too short of breath to speak. She resembled her daughter slightly, in the shape of her nose and mouth, though she'd never worn Saoirse's vague expression. The prime distinction between mother and daughter was intent. Saoirse offended rafts of people without meaning to. She said or asked things that were often perceived as insulting, probably because she existed too much inside herself. It was hard for her to process the clues and nonverbal warnings on which other people relied.

The man from the bistro went to work on the hut's steel shutter, which was designed to keep out thieves and seemed unlikely to budge. As he banged on it, shouting Saoirse's name, Jem and Pauley went to work on the back door—the one papered with pictures of the various frozen novelties on offer, the one through which Saoirse had dashed out when she asked Jem if she'd killed Mrs. Reddy.

"It's not locked," Pauley said, jiggling the knob. She pushed hard, leaning against the door with her full weight. "Unless there's a deadbolt."

"No deadbolt," Bettie gasped from the green metal bench where she'd been deposited to await her portable oxygen.

"Then it's stuck," Pauley said, pushing hard again and groaning with the effort.

"It gave way just a bit," Jem said. "Let's try together."

They did. Whatever was jamming the door wasn't as firm as a heavy box or even a chair under the knob. Jem could feel it give slightly with each dual push. When the man who'd tried the shutter came around back and lent his strength, the blockage gave way enough for the door to open about a foot.

"Oh, no," Jem whispered.

Pauley, shocked, gave a little cry.

The man from the bistro swore, stumbling backward. It created a chain reaction. Suddenly the Square was full of people, all buzzing and pushing to see inside the hut. From her bench, Bettie began to wail. Even before anyone told her, she knew.

The hut's interior was so small, there wasn't much to see. There was no toilet—Saoirse had to rely on her fellow shopkeepers for lavatory privileges—and most of the room was taken up by a front-loading freezer stuffed with packaged treats.

Looking around, Jem noted a soft-serve machine, boxes of soft-serve powder mix, and a small desk shoved against one wall. On the desk was Saoirse's expensive camera and the padded zip case that presumably held its additional lenses. Next to the camera was a small photo printer and a box of pictures. Individual snapshots were scattered all over the floor. Among them, on her back, lay Saoirse Quick, her spectacles crushed and her forehead bashed in. She was dead.

CHAPTER TWENTY-FIVE

Playing the Blame Game

"Oh, God." Pauley darted away. She wasn't the only person to glimpse Saoirse's corpse and immediately run off to be sick in the nearest patch of weeds or shrubbery.

Jem felt queasy, too. And not just because of the sight alone, though it was repellant enough. Saoirse was an islander. A St. Morwennian. And if it upset Jem this much to see her this way, how much worse must everyone else feel to see her this way, to know she'd died by cold, calculated violence?

The crowd, which had swelled to include virtually everyone living in the Square or passing through it that day, was rumbling, growing angrier as their collective disbelief burned away. Jem had already found herself the object of dirty looks and suspicious gazes. Of course. She was the outsider, returned under a cloud. She'd found the first dead body, Mrs. Reddy. Now she'd been involved in finding the second dead body, Saoirse Quick. Who better for a shocked, bewildered community to blame?

She took one last look at the scene, committing it to memory as best she could, storing away the particulars for later. An empty steel bracket on the wall. Boxes of soft-serve powder mix with expiry dates standing out in black numerals. Those scattered, blood-flecked photos on the floor, not unlike the unframed pictures in Mrs. Reddy's curio cabinet. And Saoirse herself, of course, killed by a terrible blow to the head.

Turning away, she found herself face to face with Declan, once her fellow pupil at St. Mary's School. Lip curling, he stepped aside quickly, as if he couldn't bear to even look at her.

Some of St. Morwenna's older residents, one-time cronies of both Mrs. Reddy and Sue Jago, were trying to keep Bettie from seeing her daughter's body. They'd succeeded in reattaching her, via plastic tubing and nasal cannulae, to her oxygen, but she still looked dreadful. She seemed to be weeping and struggling for breath simultaneously.

Jem cast about for Pauley—her friend hadn't returned to the thick of the crowd. She was sitting on the steps of Island Gifts, which had been hastily locked up by its proprietor, who was probably somewhere in the buzzing crowd, swapping details and theories.

"You're to blame for this!" Bettie screeched, stabbing a finger at Jem.

Jem's stomach dropped. For a moment, the crowd went deadly silent. It felt like barometric pressure plummeting as black clouds gather on the horizon.

"You came back for revenge." Bettie's voice was clear, apart from the occasional gasp. "First Edith. Now my Saoirse. Just because she said to your face what no one else had the guts to say!"

"I never hurt anyone," Jem said. Chin up and voice steady, she looked from face to face. Some people glared back, frankly unconvinced. Others couldn't meet her stare.

"Jem," Pauley called from the steps of Island Gifts. "Jem, I need you!"

It was an unsubtle gambit, but it worked. The crowd parted, allowing Jem to retreat to Pauley's side. Clearly, as the mistress of Lyonesse House and the current Gwyn in residence on St. Morwenna, Pauley's loyalty to her community wasn't in doubt. She could even extend that goodwill, like a halo, around Jem—at least for a time. But the tenor of the crowd's murmurings, and some of the black looks, made Jem doubt that even Pauley could protect her for long.

"What in God's name is happening to us?" Pauley asked as Jem eased down beside her. There wasn't quite enough room on the stone step to accommodate them both, but they'd spent years leaning on each other, and being shoulder-to-shoulder still felt right.

"I don't know," Jem said. "I'm trying to pull it all together."

"Mrs. Reddy's death was awful, but it wasn't shocking," Pauley continued. "She'd hurt so many people over the years. It's not hard to think someone might hurt her back. But Saoirse—Saoirse never—"

"Not deliberately," Jem agreed.

"Maybe it is just random acts of violence," Pauley said. "Some creep who landed in the Scillies and decided to take what he wants. Preying on women when he can catch them alone."

"Maybe," Jem said. Her mind was still unpicking the images she'd observed at both crime scenes, like a cryptographer with a decoder ring. After what felt like a long time, a ripple of interest from the crowd made her look up. She elbowed Pauley, pointing toward the quay. "Here comes the police boat."

It was the same black rigid inflatable that Chief Anderson had used to transport a handcuffed Jem to the Hugh Town Police Station for processing. This time, a uniformed female officer skippered while Randy Andy sat in the aft section beside another uniformed officer. For a moment, Jem thought it was PC Newt. But no… he was probably still at Seascape House, guarding the crime scene. The policeman next to Anderson was older than PC Newt, with dark hair and a neat goatee. When he climbed the water steps, he did so carefully—not surprising, since he wore what looked like black cowboy boots.

"Oh, no," Jem whispered.

"What?" Pauley looked from the boat back to Jem. "The chief can't pretend this death is down to you. You were with me this morning. And before that, you were helping that numpty in Snoggy Cove."

"Too right." Jem watched the new officer, almost certainly the chief's replacement, walk up Quay Road, sunlight glinting off the earpieces of his spectacles. Hot-rod red.

"While I was in Snoggy Cove, waiting for Rhys, I spilled my guts with complete abandon," Jem said. "I told that bloke everything about the accident. How people despised me over Cam. How much I hated Mrs. Reddy, too. And guess what? That's him." She pointed at Hack. "That's the numpty."

*

"Ms. Jago," Chief Anderson said. He made no effort to hide his dislike.

The Square was no longer a throng of rubberneckers and time-wasters. Emmets had been driven off, shopkeepers had gone back to their work, and anyone completely uninvolved had been told to move on. Bettie Quick remained on the bench with her oxygen canister and a couple of friends. Jem, Pauley, Declan, and the man from Hen N' Chicks had been corralled for questioning. Otherwise, it was just Randy Andy and PC Mel Robbins, the officer who'd retrieved Jem's shoes just before she was taken into custody. And Hack, of course, standing at the chief's elbow as the heir apparent.

"I wish I could say I'm surprised to find you in the middle of this," Chief Anderson continued. "I understand the Ice Cream Hut opened this morning at the usual time?"

"Of course it did," Bettie said. The longer she grieved, the angrier she became. "It's June, what do you think?"

PC Robbins, who was unspooling tape to mark off the crime scene until Devon & Cornwall's forensics team arrived, said, "I have confirmation from three shopkeepers that Saoirse first opened the hut's shutters around nine o'clock."

"Nine o'clock sharp. Every day. Punctual," Bettie muttered.

"Did she take breaks on a schedule, or catch-as-can?" Hack asked. Jem, who wasn't looking at him, felt her skin prickle, as though he were looking at her.

"Lavatory breaks don't happen on a schedule." Bettie dabbed at her eyes.

"Sergeant Hackman," Chief Anderson said, in the precise tones one might say "Drop dead." "As it is your first day on the job, you might let me handle the questioning. Saoirse exited the hut from time to time, when she needed the ladies' or to have a kip. Seeing the hut with its shutters down for a little while is a routine occurrence." To PC Robbins, he asked, "Did you find a witness who can swear when the shutters came down for the last time?"

"Not yet. I thought Sergeant Hackman and I might go door to door, once the scene is handed off to Devon & Cornwall," she replied.

"I can tell you when I started ringing her," Bettie said. "Nine thirty. I wanted her to take a break and pop in the Co-op for some tea bags."

Jem tried to recall where she'd been around nine thirty. Still at Snoggy Cove?

"I rang her dozens of times. Check her mobile," Bettie went on. "Check BT. I let the phone in the hut ring and ring. The killer must've struck first thing."

"While shops were opening and people were focused on other things," Hack said, making notes on his pad. "Did your daughter have any enemies, Mrs. Quick?"

"Her." Bettie pointed at Jem.

"Now, you know that's not true," Pauley said. To Hack, she added, "Saoirse had no enemies. Only friends. Sort of... held-at-a-distance friends, if you know what I mean. She was a bit of a loner. Her best friend was her camera. I think if she was here, she wouldn't disagree."

Jem forced herself to look at Hack. She couldn't tell if he was correctly interpreting Pauley's coded language or not.

"Best friend was her camera?" Bettie cried. "Are you daft? I was her best friend! I was her whole world, and she was mine."

"We understand," Hack said gently. "I hate to intrude upon your grief, but if there's anything specific you can tell me, any bit of information that I can confirm or examine, it might help us bring your daughter's killer to justice that much faster." Glancing at the eaves of the Ice Cream Hut, he asked, "Any CCTV cameras here? Or security cameras positioned to sweep the Square?"

"Saoirse was our security camera," Bettie wailed. "The only camera in the Square was hers!"

"That's right, sir," PC Robbins told Hack. "There are no CCTV cameras on St. Morwenna."

After that final outburst, Bettie became so distraught that the IoS PD officers decided that she required emergency medical transport to St. Mary's. Otherwise, the shock of Saoirse's death might put her in the grave next. Before departing with Bettie via police boat, Chief Anderson informed Jem that she wasn't to leave St. Morwenna without telling him.

"I mean it. Not one foot off this island. Not even to Penlan across the bloody tombolo," he said. "Or I'll have you."

"Michael." Hack spoke with the quiet authority of someone used to being obeyed. "That's a touch over the top, don't you think?"

The chief gave Hack a glare that would've made a lesser man spontaneously combust. "Given the sort of morning you've had, and the fact I could bring legal proceedings against you for the ruin of my runabout, you'd best keep your opinions to yourself."

"Once again. Sorry about the boat. I've promised to get it back to tip-top shape, and I will," Hack said cheerfully. "Now, since Command has asked me to assume leadership of this investigation—and in light of your decades of experience in the Isles of

Scilly," he added, overriding the chief's objection before it began, "I'd like you to personally coordinate between IoS and Devon & Cornwall. From the station. In Hugh Town."

"Hugh Town," Chief Anderson repeated.

"If you don't mind. And since you've only a few hours left on duty… I won't hold it against you if you embark on retirement a wee bit early."

"Retirement? Two murders in these islands in three days, and you think I'll just flit off into cloud cuckoo land leaving the likes of you to mop up? I care about these people! I'll be on the job until the islands are safe again. See if I'm not."

"Suit yourself," Hack said, with a hardness in his eyes that rubbed up ominously against his light tone. "Just know you'll do it from a desk in Hugh Town. Not my desk, as it will be starting tomorrow. But *a* desk. I'm sure there's a disused closet somewhere."

"Sod off, Hackman. You won't last the year," the chief said. He put all his savagery into the declaration, but it landed with a tinkle instead of a thud. Perhaps Anderson had been the big fish in the subtropical pond for too long, and had forgotten how to terrify his fellow lawmen. Or perhaps Hack had been threatened by better—and more frightening—men.

After he and PC Robbins departed with Bettie, Hack turned to Jem and Pauley as if his dust-up with Randy Andy had been mere good-humored banter. "Let's start over. Ms. Gwyn." He shook her hand. "Ms. Jago. I'm Sergeant Hackman. Nice to see you again."

"You could've told me you were a policeman," Jem said hotly. "The moment I told you my name, you knew precisely who I was. And how the chief seems to consider me his number one suspect. But you let me pour out my heart to you, just the same."

"For the record, I tried to make a clean breast of it," Hack said. "But then your big, burly ex turned up. And did me a series of good turns, damn him," Hack added with a grin. "I was all geared up to loathe the man, and he took care of everything. All I had to provide was a credit card number."

"Is Jem really the number one suspect?" Pauley asked.

"God knows what goes on in Anderson's head," Hack said. "I can't speak to his style of policing. As far as I'm concerned, the cliché is true—I'm obliged to maintain an open mind whilst following the evidence wherever it takes me. And I'm quite happy to add, I've actually worked some murder cases. My first reaction isn't to come down like a hammer on the first person I see. Or rifle through my list of acquaintances and pick the person I like least.

"He told me that you stayed in the house after being ordered to leave," he added, turning to Jem. "The chief was well within his rights to caution you, of course. But charging you with Section 89(2) was outrageous. Please accept my apologies on behalf of the Isles of Scilly Police Department."

"All charges dropped?"

"Of course."

"Expunged?"

"Consider it done."

Jem sucked in her breath. It was hard to sustain her irritation over his failure to introduce himself when the man was so charming. He knew it, too, which somehow contributed to that charm.

"So it's Sergeant Hackman? Not Chief Hackman?" she asked.

"Just sergeant. Some people have been in the job so long, they've hung onto designations that were reconfigured a long time ago. The rank of sergeant is perfectly appropriate for command of Hugh Town Station. Besides, isn't that what you expected? Some 'no-hoper,' I believe you said? Put out to pasture in the Scillies where I can't ruin big investigations?"

"Good memory," Jem muttered. "Anyway. About Saoirse. I think the murder weapon was a fire extinguisher."

"Because…?"

"Because there's an empty bracket on the wall. The killer must've come in through the back door, pulled down the fire extinguisher, and bludgeoned her to death with it."

Hack's face assumed that uniquely copper-like blankness. Did they practice it in the mirror each night?

"I had the feeling you were trying to slip me a note about Saoirse," he said. "Speak plainly now. What was she like?"

"Unusual." Pauley smiled. "Mind you, so am I. I might be the only goth in the Isles of Scilly. I love the sun but I have to wear factor seventy sun cream. I sew all my own clothes. Unusual isn't an insult in my book. But Saoirse drew a bit of abuse. She had a way of looking at people that made them uncomfortable. A sort of vague, uncertain expression."

"Like she couldn't figure out how they'd escaped a photograph and gone 3-D," Jem said.

"Exactly. And photography was her passion," Pauley said. "When Jem and I were little, Saoirse was grown up, technically, but she never went dancing or to the cinema. All she did was take pictures. Half of them were the most boring things you've ever seen. Grass. Leaves. Gravel."

"Didn't she save all of them?" Jem asked, remembering.

"*All* of them," Pauley agreed. "Used to be, she had to save her money to buy film and have the film developed. Then digital came along, and she could store all her pictures. Then Instagram came along, and she could subject the entire world to her feed. Which never changed. We all had to follow her to make her happy."

"But she was still printing out some of them," Jem said. "She must have been sorting them with her back to the door when someone came in and… you know."

"Oh, God," Pauley whispered, as if the realization had just washed over her again. "She's gone. Really gone. We'll never see her again."

Jem put her arms around Pauley. With a gap of twenty years, she didn't mourn Saoirse's loss in the same way. But there was a great upwelling of fury at the person who'd taken her life. He or she had no right to destroy such a gentle woman, much less in such a brutal manner. It was more than wrong. It was an act of incomprehensible cruelty.

I hope Hack's up to finding the killer. And if he isn't… I am.

CHAPTER TWENTY-SIX

Burying the Hatchet

After Hack released them, going back to Hen N' Chicks for their half-eaten brunch was unthinkable. Jem and Pauley returned only to settle the bill, and then walked up to the Duke's Head Inn for the only immediate solace that came to mind—a drink.

"I hope it turns out to be a stranger," Pauley said fervently, once they'd settled into a booth with their pints of Double Drowned ale. "Some drug-crazed nutter who got stranded in the islands and is on a rampage because he's just plain evil. It has to be. It can't be someone who lives in the Isles of Scilly."

Jem didn't answer. She felt a bit like there was an abacus buried in the lower recesses of her brain, the beads clicking along on four different bars. The answer hadn't come to her yet, but she could sense the computations happening just below the level of conscious thought.

"I mean, there *are* homicidal maniacs. That's why the term exists," Pauley continued, as if trying to convince herself. "And most murders happen over money, don't they?"

"Love or money, I'm sure," Jem said. "I don't know about Mrs. Reddy, but we know robbery wasn't the motive with Saoirse."

"How do we know that?" Pauley asked, glass stopping halfway to her lips.

"Because the killer didn't take her camera. It had to be the most valuable thing she owned. A Nikon, I think, with a case full of attachment lenses."

"Huh. You're right. You never did miss much. Notice anything else in the hut?"

"Yeah. Her boxes of soft-serve mix were outdated. They looked rather beat-up, like they'd been around the world. The expiry dates said 2010."

"You mean, like… the year 2010?" Pauley asked.

Jem nodded.

"Well, that would explain why the ice cream hasn't been as good. And why Saoirse didn't have to do a price rise this spring, when every other shop keeps jacking them up just to stay in business another season." Pauley sipped her ale. "People wouldn't have been happy with her if they'd known. Someone would've reported her to the Ministry of Food, or whatever you call it. But they wouldn't have slipped into the hut and killed her over geriatric Mr. Whippys."

"I should hope not."

"I wonder where she bought the stuff. Surely it's against the law to sell foodstuffs that far beyond the pale," Pauley said.

"Think Bettie made a deal with someone?" Jem asked.

"Maybe. But since her health took a turn, she's been mostly at home. For the last couple of years, Saoirse's run the hut alone."

They lapsed into silence. The pub was occupied to the limit. Everyone was talking loudly, and mostly about the murders. Jem was uncomfortably aware of people glancing her way and nodding in her direction. Were they seriously accusing her? The islanders must think her a cool customer, a true psychopath, if she could murder Saoirse in the morning and settle down to a nice pint in the afternoon.

"It won't always be like this," Pauley said, glancing around. "When folks first heard you were coming back, they were stirred up. Not much happens on St. Morwenna that isn't peaceful, and gorgeous, and a little dull sometimes. But I think they'd have warmed up already if not for the murders. It's a lot to process. And you know they aren't going to suspect the people they see every day when they can focus on you."

Jem made a noncommittal sound. Intellectually, she understood. Emotionally, she wasn't ready to absolve her former community. Not yet.

"How's your mum?" she asked.

"The same. The charge nurse thinks it won't be long now. Then I'll be free." Pauley sighed. "At this point, I'm numb to the idea, but if losing Mum is anything like losing Dad, it'll hit me like a ton of bricks after the fact. That's how it was for Rhys, too, when Harold died."

"Harold? Jeez," Jem said. "Seems like we're a bit young to all be orphaned so soon. I assumed Harold was still living at the lighthouse."

"Orphaned? You mean your dad died, too?"

Jem bit her lip, darkly amused by her own unconscious error. "Er, actually, no, he's alive and well and doing whatever he does in Penzance. Still married to Wendy. I haven't spoken to either of them in fifteen years. But the twins still get in touch sometimes, through social media. When I went to live with them, I expected David and Victoria to treat me like a disease. But they're good kids. Or maybe anyone would seem good, next to Kenneth." She waved that aside. "What happened to Harold?"

"Died by suicide," Pauley said quietly. "He never really got over Mrs. Tremayne's death. After Cam… well, I think the lawsuit gave him something to hold onto. Which wasn't fair to you, of course. But he had Mrs. Reddy spurring him on, and pursuing it was something he could do besides sit around and think about what he'd lost."

Looking down at the tabletop, Jem traced a design on the varnished wood. After seeing Saoirse's corpse, her emotions were too close to the surface. But she wasn't going to break down in the Duke's Head Inn, surrounded by so many potentially hostile witnesses. She just wasn't.

"If I'm being honest—none of us were fair to you, Jem," Pauley said. Reaching across the table, she took Jem's hand gently in hers. "We made you the scapegoat. Me, Rhys, our parents… the whole island. I hope you'll forgive me."

Jem's eyes stung. She struggled to moderate her breathing.

"I've been working up the courage to say this," Pauley added. "I don't know how long it will take Rhys to do the same. But I know that, deep down, he feels the same way."

A surge of anger rescued Jem, sweeping away her tears.

"He accused me of killing Mrs. Reddy," she whispered fiercely. "He asked me if I ever thought of Cam. Just like Lissa. Only he never apologized."

"I know you've been through hell. But he has, too. And I don't think he's come out the other side yet," Pauley said. "I'm not making excuses for him. I'm just trying to explain."

Jem no longer wanted her beer. But even without looking, she could feel the occupants of nearby booths watching her. She forced herself to sip it, avoiding Pauley's gaze.

"Anyway. This is what I want to say," Pauley said, with a strength and determination she'd rarely shown as a girl. "About the night of the accident. Yes, it was your idea. But you didn't force me to go. I chose to, because I thought it would be fun. Same with Rhys. I know you talked Cam into it, and people made a lot of that, but Cam was his own person and he never gave way unless he wanted to. You didn't threaten him, you persuaded him. It was still his choice in the end.

"Remember when we climbed into the boat?" Pauley continued. "The moment I got in, I knew I was too large. That with three other people, it was seriously overloaded. I weighed thirteen stone, you know," she added with a smile. "But back then, I was too self-conscious and ashamed to say a word. And none of us cared that we didn't have life vests. I remember that distinctly."

In her mind, Jem heard Cam say he couldn't be arsed. Until she recounted the story to Hack, she'd completely forgotten that moment. It had been lost, along with so many other details, in the mythology of her own wickedness.

"So, yes, we shouldn't have done it," Pauley said. "But you know what else? My parents didn't check. Your gran didn't check. Harold didn't check. They all knew how we were. That we roamed all over the island and sometimes off it. Harold kept those boats unlocked on the beach, for heaven's sake. And the truth is, we would've made it just fine, and skated past the devil yet again, if not for that freak wave. The storm blew in quicker than expected, and..." She tailed off.

"We shouldn't have been out," Jem said stubbornly.

"I said that. But we were kids. Kids do stupid stuff. Jemmie," Pauley said in a commanding tone that startled Jem. "Sometimes you have to throw off the chains. No one will do it for you."

Jem met Pauley's eyes. She meant what she was saying. She wasn't smoothing things over. She was speaking the truth as she saw it.

"Mrs. Reddy loved to make trouble," Pauley went on. "Plus, she wanted to take the focus off Dahlia. And Harold was still gutted over Mrs. Tremayne's death when he lost Cam. It was too much for him. He could've blamed himself. He even could've blamed Rhys, who was sixteen. Two years older than the rest of us. But he blamed you because it was easier. Everyone blamed you because it was easier. The alternative was looking in the mirror. That, or accepting that sometimes life breaks your heart for no good reason. Now." Pauley dashed away a tear and smiled. "Do you forgive me?"

"There's nothing to forgive," Jem said. Her eyes burned, her chest ached, and she'd never felt happier in her life.

CHAPTER TWENTY-SEVEN

"Handsome Men Are the Worst"

"Tea," Clarence Latham announced, placing the pot in the middle of the kitchen table. "Micki, my love, be mother. I'll arrange the biscuits on the plate. Or would you rather have sandwiches?"

"Either," Jem said.

"It's figured into your bill, dear," Micki said. In casual clothes with her curly hair streaming around her shoulders, she looked younger and pretty, she had a glow. "Biscuits *and* sandwiches, Clar. Make it snappy."

"Eat glass and die," Clarence retorted cheerfully. A sixtyish man with dark skin and a big belly, he had close-cropped gray hair and deep crinkles around his eyes. "I can offer you roast beef. No white, but there's half a loaf of wheat. Mustard? Fair play. Roast beef on wheat with mustard coming up."

Micki poured three cups of builder's tea. Rising to bring Clarence his cup, she dumped the biscuits on a platter and brought them back to the table. They were nothing extravagant, just Vanilla Viennese, but Jem attacked them like she hadn't eaten for days.

"Clar, are you starving this woman?" Micki asked, sitting down again.

"I'm not. She's barely been in residence. Didn't even ring for breakfast this morning."

"I snagged a muffin on the way out," Jem said. "I wanted to see the island before everyone was out of bed. Just St. Morwenna—no peanut gallery. Instead, I fell down the rabbit hole of murder. Again."

After their heart-to-heart in the pub, Pauley had experienced a sudden desire to see her mum and break the news about Saoirse herself. She would've preferred Mrs. Gwyn spend her last days in peace, but island life wasn't created for keeping secrets. Someone would be sure to spill the beans, and in that case, Pauley wanted to do it. She'd offered to let Jem start work on the library alone, or even bring Micki along, but that seemed wrong-footed. Besides, Jem was strung out by her adventurous morning, the horror of discovering another dead body, and twice discussing Cam's death after twenty years of keeping those emotions buried. She'd gone back to *Gwin & Gweli,* asked Micki to pop over for tea, and told them all about her long, strange day.

"Not to make light of Saoirse's death. I've seen her from time to time, and I'm sure she was a good person," Clarence said, slicing bread with a long, serrated knife. "But I think our Jem must attract drama the way a lightning rod attracts raw energy. Not only did you discover a murder—another murder!—but you met a man. That's an accomplishment. I've rambled over the Isles of Scilly at all times, in all weather, and all I've come across are happily married blokes and spoiled birds looking for a handout."

"When the moment is right, the bloke will appear," Micki said sagely. "What about that one you mentioned before—Captain Kernow?"

"Captain Kernow. Now there's a beauty," Clarence declared, removing a jar of mustard from the fridge. "Muscle-bound. Perfectly proportioned. Who needs Captain America when we have our very own superhero on St. Morwenna? He ought to be out bringing killers to justice and whatnot."

Jem's mouth twisted. There was only one man on St. Morwenna who fit that description. "That's Rhys. The man we called to help Hack with his wrecked boat. What do you know about him?"

"Nothing deep," Clarence said, grinning, as if he very much wished otherwise. "When I was negotiating to buy this place, I saw him daily, either in the Duke's Head, or running on the beach. Soft-sand running in bare feet." Clarence made a noise of deep appreciation at the memory. "The day I moved in, I thought, let me find out where this man lives and say hello, neighbor. That's when I heard he was taking, and I quote, a sabbatical. From what, I ask. Nobody says nothing. They closed ranks because Captain Kernow is a lifelong islander, and I'm just a nosy parker from the mainland." He stared hopefully at Jem, as if she might do what the St. Morwennians would not.

"I don't know anything about his sabbatical. I've been trying to puzzle it out," Jem said. "All I really know is, he owns the lighthouse, he still does bodywork on boats, and he has a sweet little doggo named Buck. Oh, and he turned up right after I found Mrs. Reddy's body."

That detail piqued the cousins' interest, so Jem explained. So much had happened since meeting Micki on Friday night, it was hard for her to keep straight what she'd told to whom.

When she was done, Micki said, "You heard someone knock over a cabinet, went inside, and five minutes later he appeared? From the direction the killer ran? I mean, it's not impossible he killed the old woman himself, went off a little ways and doubled back."

"It hurts my heart," said Clarence, finishing up the sandwiches by cutting off their crusts, "to hear you speak ill of such a handsome man."

"Handsome men are the worst," Micki shot back.

"Yes, but I know Rhys," Jem said. "I can't imagine that he'd kill Mrs. Reddy. And think about the mechanics of it. Why do her in on Friday night, hear me coming, knock down the curio cabinet, climb out a window, then double back five minutes later? And why bring along his little dog? You don't bring a dog to a murder."

"I know people who bring their ruddy dogs everywhere," Clarence said.

That rang a bell. That morning, when Buck showed up at Snoggy Cove, hadn't Rhys called the dog an escape artist that followed him everywhere?

"If we're going to accuse attractive men who elevate the Isles of Scilly experience with their mere presence," Clarence said, bringing over the sandwiches and taking his seat, "what about this other bloke? Hack, the man who wouldn't tell you his full name until he turned up in uniform?"

Jem shrugged. "He's Randy Andy's replacement."

"In mysteries, it's the one you least suspect."

"You always suspect the police," Micki told Clarence.

"Oh. True. Then I suppose it's you, my darling."

Micki shrugged. "Maybe. So tell us about the new top cop, Jem. Is he sexy?"

Jem blushed, hesitating before answering. "Yes. But also—"

"Snoggable? In the legendary Snoggy Cove, no less?" Clarence suggested.

"Maybe," Jem said. She kept her voice neutral, but her lips curved into a smile.

The sandwiches were delicious. Jem devoured hers right down to the crumbs, then went in for some more Vanilla Viennese biscuits.

"By the way, Chief Anderson was interviewed on telly this morning, before the second victim was found," Micki said, rising to clear up. "He said his office was working closely with Devon & Cornwall. That citizens should expect an arrest soon."

Jem didn't know whether she should groan or cheer. "I hope that means they have a real lead, and not just talk. When I saw him in the Square, he seemed ready to double down on persecuting me."

"Well, I didn't know if I should tell you. But Mrs. Reddy's daughter was interviewed. Blonde. Pretty, in a brittle sort of way."

"Dahlia?" Jem questioned.

"She kept dabbing a handkerchief to her face and turning away from the camera," Micki continued, stacking crockery in the sink. "Mentioned something about a person who'd always had it in for her poor mum who recently came back to St. Morwenna. Then the chief shut down the interview and steered her away."

Jem let out her breath. "God. You know, we didn't like each other as kids. I'm sure I was a brat to her, and I probably ought to say sorry for that. But this is ridiculous."

"Just because she said it doesn't mean she seriously believed it. People grasp at straws when they're angry," Clarence said. "Everyone knows that. If I were investigating, I'd look into Kenzie and her mum."

"Really? Why?" Jem asked.

"Because Lissa had a very public falling out with Mrs. Reddy. They stood in the middle of the Square and called each other every rude name in the book," Clarence explained, smiling as if he'd enjoyed every minute of it. "It was like *The Real Housewives* of St. Morwenna. Kenzie didn't care for that, so she tried to break it up, and Mrs. Reddy told her…" He paused dramatically, like a radio presenter determined to keep his listeners on tenterhooks. "She said, and I quote, 'You're the reason your mum will never marry. Her new bloke won't take on another man's problem.'"

"Whew!" Micki sat down, appalled.

"Oh, that's vintage Edith Reddy," Jem said. "She said something like that to me once, about my grandmother. My gran raised my dad alone. But I never knew until she threw it in my face."

"Someone ought to talk to Lissa," Clarence said. "Maybe she went to Seascape House to have it out and things took a turn."

Jem sipped her tea. "Maybe. Lissa doesn't strike me as very strong, physically. Kenzie seemed stronger. Kid has a good grip. And whoever was inside the house pushed over that curio cabinet. Probably in hopes the commotion would scare me off."

"Or maybe to destroy it, for some reason?" Micki suggested.

"What would be in a curio cabinet that would have to be destroyed?" Clarence scoffed.

"I don't know. I'm not the sleuth. I'm just spitballing. What do you think, Jem?"

"I don't know. Saoirse's death makes it so much harder. Assuming it's connected to Mrs. Reddy's," she added. "I mean, there's a world where maybe Rhys snapped with Mrs. Reddy. But not with Saoirse. As for Lissa and Kenzie, I suppose I'd need to find out if there was any friction between either of them and Saoirse. Although Bettie Quick did say…" She tailed off.

"What?" Clarence and Micki asked, almost in unison.

"When she couldn't get Saoirse on the phone, she tried to find a neighbor to go check on her. She looked for Lissa and Kenzie, but they weren't home. She said something like, 'When are they ever not home?' She seemed genuinely shocked by it," Jem added thoughtfully.

"Another person I'd check into is Bart the Ferryman," Clarence said. "He's a crook wrapped in a cheat inside a criminal."

Jem and Micki dissolved into laughter. Jem said, "Now that I think of it, I saw something interesting in Mrs. Reddy's house. The whole house looked like it was in the midst of a sell-off, if I'm being honest. All the china and silver missing. Photographs pulled from their frames. One was of Bart the Ferryman and Mrs. Reddy posed together. Like they were friends. Or sweethearts."

Micki and Clarence exchanged glances. Then they both emitted a low "Oooh," like schoolchildren witnessing something naughty.

"Did you ask Bart about this yesterday?" Micki asked.

"Yeah. He said they used to despise each other, but he'd ingratiated himself with her."

"Did he seem upset by the loss?" Clarence asked.

"No. He told me when they first met, Mrs. Reddy found out he was engaged in some practice that wasn't on the up-and-up—"

"Which is every single thing he does," Micki put in.

"And so Mrs. Reddy took the opportunity to extort him. Demanded he give her free rides back and forth to Penzance. He said she would set off with a bag full of items and come back with a fatter purse."

"So there *was* a sell-off. Well, well, well," Clarence said. "Ruddy cow always treated me like I was an interloper on St. Morwenna. Like I had no right to run a B&B in her kingdom without her personal endorsement."

"Do you think she was trying to intimidate you?" Jem asked.

"What else?" Clarence laughed. "She told me she was the richest woman in St. Morwenna, with the best solicitors money could buy. That she'd sue me until I went up in a puff of smoke."

"Maybe she had fallen on hard times," Micki said. "Where'd her money come from, anyway?"

"Her late husband," Jem said. "He died thirty years ago. Long enough for her to run through it."

"Even so, I wouldn't take anything Bart says at face value without independent confirmation. He can be diverting, especially when there's a drink on the house in it for him, but he lies the way other people breathe," Micki said. "I wouldn't put it past him to romance a dotty old lady in hopes of emptying her bank account. Isn't that a crime?"

"Yes. Undue influence," Clarence said. "He's a big bloke, too. Jem, wasn't it a bare-handed job, apart from duct tape?"

Jem nodded.

"Well, it seems none of us are above suspicion, at least when it comes to Mrs. Reddy's murder," Clarence said breezily. "I clashed with her. Lissa and Kenzie despised her. You were her sworn enemy from way back," he told Jem, "and even the perfectly resplendent Captain Kernow looks a bit dodgy with regard to the old lady, if not Saoirse. Micki, did you do it?"

She shrugged. "Not as I recall."

"What about your stylish friend?" Clarence asked Jem. "The one who knows how to carry off a fit-and-flare dress?"

"Pauley?" Jem sat up straight. "Oh, no. I've known her forever. She could *never*."

"I'm sure you're right," he replied in an arch tone that conceded nothing. "But you said she was missing a book. The most valuable book in her collection. If Mrs. Reddy took it, well—you did say everyone on the island already despised her. That's two motives."

"But Pauley was at St. Mary's Hospital on Friday," Jem said. "Her mum's there, in the hospice unit. Mrs. Gwyn could go at any time."

"Might be worth mentioning Friday to a nurse or technician," Micki said. "Make sure she never ducked out for an hour or two. And don't look at me that way. Just spitballing, remember?"

"I mean, it's a long shot," Jem said. "But, yes, I suppose Pauley could've ducked out of the hospital, taken a boat back to St. Morwenna, murdered Mrs. Reddy in cold blood, and run away—not running into Rhys and Buck in the process, let's not forget—only to take a water taxi back to Hugh Town and her mum's bedside."

Clarence shrugged. Micki pushed back her chair. "Well, since we're putting off the library, I think I'll head back to Hugh Town. There's a new club that plays good music. Fancy a night of dancing, Jem?"

"I'm forbidden from leaving St. Morwenna," Jem said. "Besides, I need to ponder all this. We've run through all the obvious details, but there has to be more."

"Lucky there's a new copper on the job, since we failed to solve the case, eh?" Micki said with a smile.

"Sergeant Hackman. First name: to be determined. Condition: snoggable. If I were you, Miss Jemima Jago, I'd find an excuse to brainstorm with him. You might not bring anyone to justice, but it still might prove worthwhile," Clarence said, and winked. "Now you haven't left out any clues, have you?"

"Oh! You know what? There is one more thing." Jem pulled out her mobile. Quickly, she located the accidental snap of Mrs. Reddy's feet, pinch-zooming it so the lavender strand was easy for Micki and Clarence to see. "Of course, we don't know this was left behind by the killer, but it seems possible, don't you think?"

"So who has pale purple hair on this island?" Micki asked.

Jem sighed. "Kenzie DeYoung. I can't believe she'd be capable of something like this. I showed this picture to Pauley, and she doesn't believe it, either. But there it is. A single strand."

Clarence made a disbelieving noise. "I hate to think it could be that little girl. Just because most folks don't have the nerve to dye their hair that shade doesn't mean they're off the hook. You know who has a wig that exact color?"

"Who?" Jem and Micki asked together.

"Me. Give me two shakes." Clarence disappeared up the stairs, humming as he went, and reappeared with a lavender wig on his head. It was styled in a retro bob that curled under at chin-length.

"You look like a lavender Carol Channing," Micki said.

"Thanks, love," Clarence said, pulling off the wig and hanging it on the coat hook between his sou'wester hat and waterproof mac. "I bought it last month for a party. Half price at Island Gifts. I snagged the second-to-last. But someone else must've bought the other one. I was in there yesterday, and the sale rack was entirely wig-free."

CHAPTER TWENTY-EIGHT

On Crescent Beach

After tea, Jem went up to her room for a nap. When she woke, Saoirse's violent death seemed so impossible, she thought for a moment that she might have dreamed it. Then the full weight of the two murders struck her again. If the killings were connected, was the culprit done? Or would there be a third death soon? Perhaps of someone far closer to her than Mrs. Reddy or Saoirse Quick?

It's useless to sit around moping, Jem thought. *I need to do something. Anything.*

She decided to drop by Island Gifts and check on the lavender wig. The clerk, an off-islander who'd been hired as a fill-in while the owner was away, was no help. She admitted to selling one of the wigs to Clarence, but claimed not to recall the second buyer.

"Was it a woman?" Jem asked.

The fill-in clerk shrugged.

"I don't suppose you keep records of sales?" Jem asked, though the question sounded ridiculous the moment she uttered it. Retail shops weren't like libraries, after all. Anonymous purchasing was the norm.

The clerk looked over her glasses at Jem like an owl spying a mouse. "Beg pardon? If you're going to interrogate me, hadn't you better demonstrate the authority to do so?"

"I'm sorry," Jem backpedaled hastily, giving the clerk what she hoped was a winning smile. "I'm just eager to borrow a wig that color, and Clarence said no. So I wanted to track down the other one."

"May I suggest Internet shopping? Or a trip to Penzance?" the clerk sniffed.

"Of course, and I will. I know this probably sounds over the top, but…" Jem gestured to an old-fashioned surveillance system mounted near the ceiling. It was the bulky sort with a black-and-white screen that displayed the current occupants of the shop in real time. Above it was mounted a hand-lettered sign: SMILE, YOU'RE ON CAMERA.

"But what?" the clerk prompted.

"I don't suppose you might have footage…?"

The clerk folded her arms across her chest. "If you don't leave this minute, I'm ringing the police."

The frostiness of the woman's tone convinced Jem that the threat was genuine. After offering her most humble apology, which was neither accepted nor acknowledged, Jem exited Island Gifts into the late afternoon sun. In real life, it seemed, amateur sleuthing was more difficult than simply asking strangers to spill what they knew, or lurking around hoping to overhear something damning.

What next? Ordinarily, her go-to was reading. She had three paperbacks in her suitcase and over fifty unread e-books on her mobile app, though she would've claimed it was only ten if anyone had asked. But it was June, it would still be daylight for a couple of hours, and she was police-ordered to remain on an island with white sandy beaches and turquoise tide pools. It was time to venture out. And if people stared, or pointed, or had something to say—so be it.

With her floppy hat and dark sunglasses in place, she made her way to Crescent Beach, on the northwest side of St. Morwenna. News of the murders seemed to have depressed the usual emmet traffic, because the beach was sparsely populated. Some teenage boys ran up and down, tossing a ball and shouting at the top of their lungs. Here and there, solitary older women sat under umbrellas reading books. Beneath the short white bulk of Tremayne Lighthouse, a row of old runabouts were offered for hire. They were chained up, as they always should have been, with a nearby sign proclaiming that all boaters must wear a life jacket.

After spreading out a towel, then shedding her cover-up, hat, and sunnies, Jem walked into the surf. It felt glorious. The sun was low and the sky was already turning orange, but the sea was calm and perfect.

She told herself she only meant to wade, but before she knew it, she was front-crawling to the closest buoy, then back to the shore, then out to the buoy again. As a girl, she'd swum effortlessly, like a porpoise, or a mermaid. Now she was out of practice, slow and quick to tire, but nevertheless exhilarated. Every dip beneath the waves was a leap of faith; every breach of the surface, a rebirth. By the time the sky purpled and the first star appeared, she emerged from the sea smiling and blissfully spent.

Glancing up at the lighthouse, she spied a tall figure on the observation deck. Although Jem couldn't make out the man's face or expression, it had to be Rhys. He was simply standing there, hands on the rail, looking out to sea. Had he been watching her?

It crossed her mind to wave at him. Not to signify that his behavior at Seascape House was forgotten, or suggest a desire to mend fences. Mostly just to treat Rhys as she would've treated any acquaintance, with passing courtesy. Proof his existence wasn't significant enough for her pointedly to ignore. Or something like that. But her hand refused to rise, and as she walked toward her towel and little pile of possessions, another person joined him on the deck. It was a woman, small and delicate, dressed in a bikini.

Lissa?

Something in Jem's chest twisted. Bettie had mentioned Lissa and Kenzie not being at home that morning. In the summer, a thirteen-year-old girl might be off doing anything. But had Lissa been across the island, on an "adult sleepover?"

When she reached her towel, she risked one more quick look up. A third figure was now on the deck, the shape of her fauxhawk unmistakable. Kenzie. Did that mean it was only a visit? Friends of Rhys, taking advantage of the lighthouse's view?

They look like a family, Jem thought. The twist came again, harder.

Determinedly turning her face away, Jem settled on her towel to dry off. Before long, the twilight beach-walkers began to appear. It was a phenomenon familiar to anyone lucky enough to dwell by the sea; as the sun melted against the horizon and the winds picked up, all sorts of people came out to walk along the shore. Pensioners in clamdiggers or jeans; young families with preschoolers carrying plastic buckets and scoops; couples of all sorts; the occasional teenager walking with their eyes glued to their phone screen. There was some hardwired fascination with the sea that called to humans at twilight. Even people who didn't swim or sunbathe came to exercise, or take in some fresh air, or ramble within earshot of the crashing waves.

Jem was looking up, trying to pick out the individual points of the constellation Hercules in the night sky, when a familiar voice asked, "Think our fates are in the stars?"

It was Hack. He was still in uniform, his cowboy boots encrusted with sand.

"My mum adores astrology. Won't hear a word against it," he continued. "I told her it doesn't seem terribly scientific. But her view is, science hasn't caught up. She reckons the magnetic fields around the planets and the cosmic energy and whatnot determine our destinies. Moreover, the cosmos might deign to help us, if we get on the right wavelength," he added with a smile. "So in her view, the stars watch over us."

"Only if there are space aliens," Jem said, rising. "Astrological divination is bunk. Fun, but bunk. Before I moved to Special Collections, I worked at Kensington Central Library in London. The wait lists were always loaded with zodiac books. The silly things got nicked a lot."

"Not a romantic?" Hack probed.

"It's not that. I like romance. But the stars are indifferent. See that one?" Jem pointed at Polaris, the North Star. "It's about seven hundred light years away from Earth. So the light we perceive right now isn't in reply to anyone's actions, or telling us that tomorrow will be better. It was released around the time Richard III usurped the throne."

"Maybe it's a late telegram saying, 'Crookback. Don't usurp that throne?'" Hack suggested.

"In that case, you'll receive a dispatch with the name of Mrs. Reddy and Saoirse's murderer after you've been dead for seven centuries."

"So you theorize it's one perpetrator? Not two?"

"I want to think so." Jem's hair, although still in its bun, was dripping down the back of her neck. Picking up her towel, she shook out the sand and draped it over her shoulders. "Did you find out anything by going door to door in the Square?"

He made a dubious sound, as if signaling that she'd overstepped her bounds.

"Sorry. Since I met you as a private citizen, I keep thinking I can chat with you like one," Jem said. "Anyway, there's something you should know, if you haven't heard already. On Saturday, after Bart the Ferryman dropped me off at the quay, Saoirse came out of the Ice Cream Hut to ask me if I killed Mrs. Reddy."

He nodded. "So I heard. Why do you think she did that?"

"Because she had no filter. And because of my history with Cam. So I wonder if Saoirse didn't also ask the wrong person if they did it," Jem continued. "I mean—the correct person. And the result was a second murder to cover up the first one."

He seemed to take that in. "People described Saoirse to me the way your friend Pauley did. Bit of an odd duck. Cordial to people, especially repeat customers, but only really close to her mum. How would she know who the culprit was?"

"She might have overheard something. The Ice Cream Hut is smack in the middle of everything," Jem said.

"Sergeant!" The woman's voice was so commanding, Jem's brain first identified it as Mrs. Edith Reddy's. Shocked, she whirled to see who was approaching from Crescent Beach's south end. Naturally, it wasn't the dead woman, but another Reddy—her daughter, Dahlia.

"It's good to see you're still in uniform, Sergeant," Dahlia said. She was moving slowly, perhaps because of her smart trouser suit, which would have been appropriate in a boardroom but looked jarring on a beach. Her long blonde hair was tied with a floral scarf. As she drew close, Jem noticed she was wearing a lot of makeup. Lipstick, rouge, eyeshadow, and feathery mascaraed lashes. Even so, her cheekbones stood out starkly, as if her skull was expanding in grief.

"I assume you're out here questioning Ms. Jago. Not chatting her up?" Dahlia asked.

"Hello again, Ms. Reddy." Hack slipped into his lawman's demeanor. "I can assure you, when you see me in uniform, my only object is keeping the peace."

"Yes, well, the proof's in the pudding, isn't it? I'm sorry for what happened to Saoirse, really I am, but the woman worked with the public and served all kinds. Anyone might have jumped her. We've been telling her for years to lock that back door," Dahlia said. "My mother, on the other hand, was St. Morwenna's first citizen. Her death takes priority. The fact that no definitive arrest has been made will only embolden more off-islanders to do copycat crimes."

"A slow and methodical investigation provides the best outcome in Crown Court," Hack said.

"As for you…" Dahlia pivoted toward Jem. "Have you done a moment's work since coming back? Or is it all sun, fun, and corpses?"

"You remind me so much of your mum," Jem said in a sweet tone full of malice. "I start work on Pauley's library tomorrow. It would have been today, but Mrs. Gwyn is poorly and takes precedence."

"Ms. Jago seems like such a respectable lady, doesn't she?" Dahlia asked Hack. "A librarian, of all things. Dig into her history and you'll find stolen boats, a family that couldn't cope with her, and a young man who died long before his time. Hard to believe it. But even as a girl, she carried herself like she was too good for the rest of us. Certainly never gave me the time of day."

Jem suffered an unexpected pang of conscience. Not because she'd been a boat thief and scofflaw. She'd accepted those facets of her youthful persona. But she *had* treated young Dahlia like bad news, not simply because of her tendency to grass on her schoolmates, but because of her mother. She had a sudden vision of Dahlia in Year Seven, dressed in the requisite white blouse and blue skirt of St. Mary's School, flashing a brave little fake-it-till-you-make-it smile, only to have Jem roll her eyes and turn away.

Maybe I ought to say sorry. Not now, in front of Hack. But before I leave the island.

"Anyway." Dahlia dismissed her accusations with a wave of the hand. "Sergeant, I fear I was never provided with your full name. PC Newt gave me an information card with Chief Anderson's name struck through. Yours was scribbled below it as *I, Hackman*. Rather like I, Claudius."

Hack smiled. "PC Newt's penmanship will never win any cups. It should be I, full stop, Hackman."

"And the letter I stands for…?"

"I, Hackman. Or I full stop Hackman. Either one."

Dahlia frowned at him. "Your full name. Now."

"That's my name," he said calmly. "Now. I don't suppose you've thought of anything else that might help our inquiries? An event or personal interaction that seems newly significant in light of Mrs. Reddy's death?"

Dahlia looked pointedly from Hack to Jem.

"If you'd like to consult with Sergeant Hackman privately, I can head back to *Gwin & Gweli*," Jem said.

"No need. I imagine it's common knowledge that my relationship with my mother was often that of a barrister and a hostile witness," Dahlia said. "When I was home in Penzance, she said I was neglecting her. When I visited her at Seascape House, she said I was obstructing her daily life. Given the way she used to gallivant around the islands in the *Merry Maid*, I reckon Bart the Ferryman knows more about her final months than I do."

"Bart Bottom's name is on my list to be interviewed," Hack said. "He—"

"I'm sorry," Jem said. "Could you repeat…?"

Hack's eyes gleamed. But in a staid, professional tone he said, "Bart the Ferryman's legal name is Bartholomew Winston Bottom."

Jem bit her lip.

"While we're on the topic, Ms. Reddy, an uncomfortable but necessary question: did your mother have a romantic partner?" Hack asked. "A boyfriend, as it were?"

"Why do you ask?"

"Because we always ask, after a woman dies by violence. The world we live in, I'm afraid," Hack said.

"Sergeant Hackman, my mother was in her mid-seventies. I don't know if her GP officially diagnosed her as cognitively declining, but anyone could see it. I thought she spent time on Bart's ferry because it was cheap, and got her out of the house. If you think perhaps it was something else… Something sick and tawdry…" With a fresh flare of anger, she asked, "I presume you'll be interrogating Bettie Quick to determine whether or not Saoirse was carrying on with Bart?"

"There's no indication of a connection between Ms. Quick and Mr. Bottom."

"Yes, there is," Jem said suddenly, the words tumbling out before she knew she would speak. "Check the cargo hold of the *Merry Maid.*"

Hack and Dahlia both looked at her, eyebrows raised.

"I was down there yesterday," Jem said. "I think Mrs. Reddy was in the cabin from time to time. I saw duct tape mending the head's mirror, and a crisp packet—Oink Me Lad—identical to ones in Seascape House. I also saw white powder on the floor. At the time, I thought maybe Bart had been transporting drugs on the ferry. And maybe he has. But in the Ice Cream Hut, I noticed that Saoirse's been making soft-serve with powder that's ten years out of date. No one from the Co-op would've sold her that. But it's not hard to imagine Bart offering spoiled goods. And since times have been tough in the islands, Saoirse might have been desperate enough to agree."

Dahlia's lip twisted in a way Jem remembered. It was the look that always crossed young Dahlia's face when someone accused her of grassing—and she had.

"You knew about it, didn't you?" Jem said. "Did your mum notice, and hold that over Bart's head? Or was it you who caught on and grassed, so Mrs. Reddy could extort Bart into unlimited free passage?"

"Let's not get ahead of ourselves with accusations," Hack said. "I'll look into it tomorrow, first thing."

Dahlia's eyes narrowed. She seemed too angry to speak. But the loathing glare she turned upon Jem was more eloquent than any words.

CHAPTER TWENTY-NINE

The Library at Lyonesse

"It hasn't changed," Jem said, gazing through the iron bars at the sprawling, slate-roofed Lyonesse House.

"It has. It's falling down a little more each day," Pauley said.

"I wouldn't say no if you decided to sign over the deed," Micki said. "Besides, flaws give a place character."

The three of them had gathered after breakfast just outside the gates of the Gwyn ancestral home. Pauley and Micki had taken to one another right away, which didn't surprise Jem in the least, since they were both tip-top people and friendship was only natural. As it was Monday, Micki could only remain on St. Morwenna until mid-afternoon. Then she'd hop a water taxi back to St. Mary's, to begin her evening shift at the Kernow Arms around four p.m.

"Character, eh? I'll have to remember that one," Pauley said with a rueful laugh. "See the right-hand gate? Just there, where it's broken away from its pillar because the hedgerow has crumbled? You'll find that sort of character all over this heap."

"Hard to fix?" Jem asked.

"No idea. A mason's coming out to look at it next month. It was supposed to be last month, but I had to postpone," Pauley said. "The only working toilet we have left got clogged and, as you can imagine, the loo took precedence. Managing this house means eternally juggling three options: put it off, pay for it, or pretend it isn't happening."

Jem sighed. On second look, Lyonesse House did appear to be sinking, like the legendary lost country for which it was named. Her eyes followed the roofline from its highest point—the "new" wing, which dated from the 1970s—to its lowest point, the middle of the "old" wing, which dated from the 1840s. The library was located inside the old wing, more or less dead center.

The large wing's roof looked on the verge of falling in. As for the small wing, it was worse than she remembered. Besides the stark contrast its red bricks and ghastly artificial shingles made with the house's stately older sections, both its front-facing windows were boarded up.

"You're thinking of the first time we played in the library," Pauley told Jem, a fond note in her voice.

It was true. When they were ten years old, Jem and Pauley had crept into the out-of-bounds library while Mrs. Gwyn picked daffodils in the garden. It was stuffed with three hundred and fifty years' worth of knowledge: leather-bound classics, Gwyn family Bibles, hand-drawn maps of shipwrecks around the Western Rocks. There were Captain Mortimer Gwyn's diaries, prettily bound Victorian trilogies, post-war "pocketbooks," and chests full of Gwyn family papers. For girls who loved to read, it was Candyland.

For perhaps an hour, they'd run riot inside, delving into volumes that smelled rich and mellow, like a stretch of happy years compressed into a talisman you could hold in one hand. Most of the leather chests were locked tight, but one battered old sea chest opened for the girls, revealing crumbling yellow letters written in a strange, elongated, yearning hand. It felt like chancing upon a spell scroll.

After unrolling several antique nautical maps and accidentally creasing one, they'd decided to climb the towering ladder for a look at what was stashed on the uppermost shelves. Jem was on the top step and reaching for one of those books, loyal Pauley steadying the ladder's base, when Mrs. Gwyn came in with a bowl full of flowers and caught them in the act.

"Can you really afford to keep living here?" Jem asked.

"Savage," Micki protested with a little laugh.

"It's a question I ask myself more or less daily," Pauley said. "I used to fantasize about a rich buyer making me an offer I couldn't refuse."

Jem and Micki followed Pauley up the gravel path to the front door, ushering them into her three-hundred-and-fifty-year-old family home. As they stepped into the foyer of Sir Mortimer Gwyn's original house, Pauley produced a key and locked up behind them. She struggled to make the mechanism turn.

"First time I've locked up in—well, ever," she said with a nervous laugh. "But with two murders in less than a week, I suppose we'd all better get used to it."

The original portions of Lyonesse House had changed considerably since Jem's childhood. Gone were the 1990s-style wood paneling and electric lights. In its place, she found something very close to the original white plaster walls, decorated only with simple brass candle sconces. The 1980s-era parquet floor had been pulled up to reveal the original stone floor, rough and uneven.

"Good lord. Look at that," Micki said, going to the massive Victorian-era range, a black cast-iron affair that looked straight out of an illustrated Dickens novel. "Does it work?"

"Deactivated," Pauley said.

"But still ideal for little girls with devious minds," Jem said, smiling over it. In their imagination, the range's big iron pot had been the fearful cauldron *Pair Dadeni,* capable of restoring dead warriors to life. It had been the centerpiece of their rainy-day fantasies.

"My Aunt Brenda heard that I liked to play with it," Pauley told Jem and Micki, "and sent me a calico pinafore as a gift. I cut it up in pieces and sewed a soft toy."

"Calico!" Jem cried. She was absurdly happy to see the stuffed cat sitting on a rustic wooden stool, looking as beat-up as if it, too, hailed from centuries past.

"That poor thing looks like it went through a lot," Micki said.

"Mum and I planned to put the range in storage," Pauley said, picking up Calico and dusting between her ears. "Captain Gwyn's original hearth is bricked up behind it. Once we had things completely back to period in here, we wanted to renovate the large wing into a Victorian exhibition, since tourists always want to view Victorian rooms. Now I reckon I'll have to auction it off. Maybe just to get the boarded-up windows reglazed." She shook her head, as if the responsibility was too much to contemplate. "Ready for the main event?"

Nodding, Jem followed Pauley, with Micki bringing up the rear.

In Lyonesse House's large wing, time had stopped around 1880, apart from some clumsy electric retrofitting. The wall décor was a hodgepodge of Victoriana, the furniture draped in white dust cloths. Many of the rooms were overtly masculine, with trophy animal heads, exotic fur rugs, and a long gun hung over a mantel.

"Here we are." Pauley turned the library's crystal doorknob. "Yours at last."

In fairy tales and Gothic stories, libraries are special rooms. Intended to contain and protect knowledge, they're also meant to be beautiful. To feed the eyes and the soul with graceful lines, warm hues, and soft, inviting silence. The shelves climb the walls like ivy; the ladders roll on whisper-quiet wheels; the balustrades and railings undulate with flourishes fit for a king. In a such a library, the books themselves, the library's heart and soul, may become merely an afterthought, or a backdrop. The marble floors, the painted ceiling, and the graceful statues make such a library a destination, not a resource.

As for the Gwyn family library, it was nothing but a giant book hoard. And it was glorious.

"Okay, this is not what I was expecting," Micki said.

Jem barely heard her. She was making a beeline for the very ladder whose siren call had got her banned for life all those years ago.

The ladder faced the library's north wall, which contained the room's largest and most eclectic conglomeration of books. Over time, Jem's memory had begun to play tricks, transforming it into one made of polished oak and bolted to the shelves, like something from university. Now she beheld what it really was: a freestanding ten-foot metal A-frame, the type used by house painters. Once upon a time, someone had dragged it into the library to fetch down a book, or possibly change a light bulb—the chandelier dangled from a sixteen-foot ceiling—and left it there. It had stood on that patch of Persian rug for so long, it had worn deep gouges in the burgundy fabric.

Mounting the first step, Jem bounced to test the ladder's steadiness. It seemed fine, but the bottom of her sandal slipped. She kicked them off and started to climb.

"Are you seeing this?" Micki asked Pauley.

"I'm used to it. Hang on, Jem. Let me steady you," Pauley said, catching hold of the ladder and gripping it tight.

"Thanks, love," Jem called, and kept climbing, inspecting the north wall's floor-to-ceiling shelves as she went. Heavier items, like sets of encyclopedias and reference books, were closest to the floor. Less substantial items, like picture books and paperbacks, were stacked closer to the ceiling.

When she reached the ladder's top step, Jem turned carefully, taking in the library as a whole.

The west wall was dominated by a gargantuan mahogany desk. It was the very spot where Captain Gwyn had written coded letters pledging support for Charles II. Safe from prying eyes, he'd sat behind it in the windowless library and logged entries in his "salvage ledger," which had probably been a record of pirated goods. If only she could find proof! It was the sort of thing Cornish historians would happily chew on for decades.

At the desk, Captain Gwyn had counted out trade tokens and golden guineas, signed contracts, and drawn up maritime charts, marking the deadly rocks around Cornwall and the Scillies for future mariners.

Behind the desk was the great man's original library: eight beautifully constructed, inset shelves that even today housed many volumes once treasured by the captain, his son, and his grandsons. These, probably the oldest specimens, would have to be handled with care. Jem would don white cotton inspection gloves and be sure to pull out each book from the middle, not the top, so as to protect the fragile spines. For unexceptional works, the RIC had empowered her to rehinge loose covers with Filmoplast tape. Everything of value would be transported to the mainland and delivered safely into the hands of a professional book restorer.

Like the north wall the ladder faced, the east wall was a free-for-all, much of it Gwyn family records and ephemera. Jem found herself smiling as she took it in.

Weeks, she thought. *Weeks of work. Twilight walks on the beach. Dips in the ocean. Stargazing each night.*

Then she remembered Mrs. Reddy, Saoirse, and Chief "Randy Andy" Anderson's desire to pin their deaths on her. Her boss, Mr. Atherton, had been ice cold during their call that morning. He'd made it clear that if the police charged her again, or spoke of her in the media as a person of interest, she'd be reassigned for good.

She cast her gaze to the south wall. Though it was free of books, it was crowded with other items Jem found every bit as tantalizing. There were old file cabinets, a huge apothecary desk that appeared to be stuffed with eye of newt and toe of frog, and a battle-scarred sea chest that surely was direct from Davy Jones' locker.

"Come down from there!" Micki said sternly. "I feel as if I'm babysitting my big sister's incorrigible urchins."

As Jem climbed down at last, Pauley said, "We might as well let her wallow about. I've really only shown you a few rooms, Micki. Care to see the rest of the place, and maybe have a spot of tea, while Jem burrows into the books?"

Off they went, leaving Jem to wander about, touching and reaching to her heart's content. When she'd first entered this magical place, she was a little savage, more interested in sand and sea than anything found in a book. But as she grew older, reading had become a passion, even a saving grace. After leaving St. Morwenna and being relocated to Penzance, the Morrab Library, established in 1818, had become her touchstone. It was no exaggeration to say books had saved her. Maybe it was a clichéd old sentiment, the kind of thing you saw printed on a tasseled bookmark: *When I was lost, I found myself in books.* Yet for Jem, it was true.

She'd been a wallflower in the Regency drawing room where Elizabeth danced with Darcy—and returned, armed to the teeth, when the zombies broke in. She'd dreamed of Manderley with Daphne du Maurier's nameless heroine and glimpsed the future via Octavia Butler. She'd faced the same madwoman in the attic from opposite sides: in *Jane Eyre,* and in *Wide Sargasso Sea.* She'd fallen in love with the magician Jonathan Strange, embarked on a journey with Aziraphale and Crowley, and delved into the *Heart of Darkness.* And between these seminal moments, there were clever mysteries, time-traveling romances, thrillers, and YA books of all genres, many of which were better written and conceived than plenty of so-called adult fiction.

After the accident, Jem had lost St. Morwenna. She'd lost Cam, Gran, Pauley, and Rhys, as well as herself—the fearless, invincible girl she'd once been. But the books were always there, classic and new, during those lost years. They would be with her in this time of restoration, too.

CHAPTER THIRTY

Procreation, Moss, and Other Literary Topics

Even though they took a late lunch, it seemed to come almost instantly for Jem. Reluctantly peeling off her white gloves, putting her notes in order, and closing her laptop, she joined Pauley and Micki in the small wing's kitchen, where Pauley had dished up *bourride,* a white fish stew made with garlicky *aioli.* The moment Jem inhaled the aroma, she realized just how hungry she was.

As they ate, they chatted about Hack and his boat fiasco, which led Jem to tell Pauley and Micki about her meeting with Hack and Dahlia on Crescent Beach the previous night. After they had a laugh over Bart the Ferryman's legal name, Bartholomew Winston Bottom, Jem told them her theorized connection between Bart, the white powder she'd noticed in *Merry Maid*'s cargo hold, and Saoirse's boxes of ancient Mr. Whippy mix.

"I can't believe you held that back," Micki said.

"Not to mention the photo," Pauley said. "Bart and Mrs. Reddy. Wow. I think Dahlia was right to say her mum was losing it. I just didn't imagine her losing it quite that much."

"I'm not holding anything back from you lot on purpose," Jem said, poised to start on her second bowl of *bourride.* "Only it's been a fire hose of events. Clues. General weirdness. As Mr. Atherton was telling me off this morning, he asked if I'd had any luck tracking down the book. He meant *A Child's Garden of Verses.* For a hot second I had no idea what he was on about."

"I hope you didn't promise him anything," Pauley said. "I've gone everywhere and asked everyone. I think it's safe to say I've insulted every single St. Morwennian and half of Hugh Town." Pushing back from the table, she stretched, crossing her legs to reveal black lace-up boots that would've been appropriate on any formally attired witch. They suited her lace top and flouncy black skirt to a T.

"If the old lady nicked it, she sold it," Micki said. "You might want to give up on the bloody thing."

Pauley winced. "I was counting on auctioning it off, assuming the poem 'Isola' was really written by Wilde. Now that you've had a look around, you can see why I need the money. And I imagine giving up on the book wouldn't make Jem's higher-ups very happy."

"Nope," Jem agreed. "It would be such an awful loss. I know Hack's up to his neck with two murders, but I got the impression Randy Andy was postponing his retirement. Should you give him a ring and remind him the book may have been in Mrs. Reddy's possession when she died? The forensics team that processed Seascape House might have it under lock and key right now at the station."

"I tried. I had to leave messages because he won't take my calls," Pauley asked. "He was on telly again this morning, making big promises of an imminent break in the case. Puffed up like a basking shark." Holding her breath, she blew out her cheeks to make Jem laugh. "I know. I'll drop a word in Lissa's ear."

Jem and Micki glanced at each other. "Why Lissa?"

"Because she's been seeing Randy Andy," Pauley said. "Didn't I tell you that? Sorry, Jem. It really is a fire hose of news every day, like you said. But, yeah, Lissa and the chief have been an item since Christmas. I don't think it will go anywhere. Once a cheat, always a cheat, at least in my book. But poor Lissa seems invested."

"Huh." Micki folded her arms across her chest. "That puts her in a new light, doesn't it? If there's extracurricular activities between

Lissa and Chief Anderson, we can't expect him to pursue her if she's guilty. He'll look around for someone more convenient."

Jem turned that over in her mind. By Lissa's own admission, she'd gone from Mrs. Reddy's unlikely BFF to her sworn enemy. And in typical fashion, Mrs. Reddy had been unable to simply walk away. Instead, she'd attacked Lissa personally, in front of a large audience in the Square. She'd brought Lissa's child, Kenzie, into it, too. If Lissa *had* gone to Seascape House to get some of her own back, and had somehow ended up killing the old woman, would she have confessed to Chief Anderson? Was he, in turn, so loyal to Lissa, and so supremely corrupt in the discharge of his duty, that he would help her escape justice? Not to mention seize on Jem as the ideal scapegoat?

"My cousin Clarence thought Lissa was a bit iffy. What sort of person is she?" Micki asked Pauley. "Do you consider her a friend?"

Pauley shrugged. "I don't know. I felt drawn to her when Kenzie was born. Kenz was such a sweet little thing. Born a bit early and so vulnerable, you know? And Lissa was alone in the world and desperate for support. So I've stuck by her for Kenzie's sake, and for Rhys's."

Jem blinked at Pauley. Unbidden, she saw the silhouetted trio on the lighthouse observation deck: Rhys, Lissa, and Kenzie, looking for all the world like a family. "What's Rhys got to do with it?"

Pauley opened her deep red lips and closed them again. "Well. Only that he adores Kenzie. She used to follow him around like that little dog, Buck." Pitch rising, her words tumbled out faster. "In point of fact, I think he adopted Buck because Kenzie's become more independent. Have you met Buck? Such a spoiled little creature. Rhys is always shouting orders at him and then giving him whatever he wants," she added, forcing a chuckle. "He has only to whine and Rhys melts."

Micki was nodding along, but Jem said nothing, forcing Pauley's overbright attempt to change the subject to die in silence.

Her stomach twisted unpleasantly. But it was none of her affair. Her confusion over Rhys was nothing but a relic. A holdover response from when they were kids—the emotional equivalent of a vestigial tail.

Even in the throes of first love, they'd never crossed the line. Although their sexual awakening happened in tandem, consummation hadn't followed. No matter how much he despised her after Cam's death, some part of Rhys probably felt the same unconscious pull. It would fade, surely, as they both got on with their lives.

*

After the clearing and the washing-up, Pauley decided to ring her mum for an afternoon chat. Jem and Micki returned to the library, where the non-librarian exhibited beginner's luck by making a remarkably on-the-nose find.

"Must be kismet. Look at this."

Going to Micki's side, Jem examined the antique book. The worn leather-bound edition exuded a heady scent, as if it might be decomposing before their very eyes. On the cover in gold was etched the words *Life of Phineas Justinian Latham,* but the title page unspooled in typical eighteenth-century majesty: *Some Account of the Life of Phineas Justinian Latham, A Godly Man of Three Wives and Seventeen Children, Late of St. Ives in Cornwall, Great Britain. Also, the Letters of P.J. Latham, Addressing the Matter of Evangelism by Works; to Wit, by Means of Procreation.*

"The title's practically a book in itself." Micki laughed, delighted by her find. "No wonder there are so many Lathams in the world. Would it be okay if I sat down and had a look? It isn't terribly valuable, is it?"

"I suspect it's of value only to you," Jem said.

"See, that's funny. If I were hard up, I would've nicked it when I nicked the *Garden of Verses* thingy," Micki said. "But maybe slipping out with a truckload of books was too difficult, so Mrs. Reddy just picked the one everybody was buzzing about."

"I don't know what she thought she'd do with it," Jem said, drifting back to the shelf she'd been sorting. "Antiquarian books are presented carefully, with documentation, to a small group of collectors. A random thief can't just pop up with one, even on eBay, without people catching on."

"Ooh, eBay's a thought. I supposed you've had a peek?"

"I have an alert set on my mobile."

"Well, it sounds as if Lady Doom Buggy was too desperate for cash to put in that much effort. In which case, she might've palmed it off on some used bookseller for a fiver."

Jem groaned.

"I'm quite serious," Micki said. "If Mrs. Reddy didn't have the time or patience to auction it properly, she might've gone to a used bookshop. There isn't one in Hugh Town. Is there one on St. Morwenna?"

"I don't think so," Jem said.

"What about Tatteredly's Bookshop in Penzance?" Micki asked. "It's near the promenade. I know the lady who owns it—my ex-sister-in-law, if you want to get technical. Let me give her a ring."

*

Gina, proprietor of the used bookshop, proved unavailable, so Micki left her a detailed message. As Jem studied ecclesiastical finds, including a Gwyn family Bible that predated the *Book of Common Prayer*, Micki did her best to read her distant forebear's tome, albeit with growing frustration.

"Why do they contaminate these old books with Fs instead of Ss?" She put down the book and pinched the bridge of her nose.

"It's the medial S. Holdover from Old English."

Micki shuddered. "It's ghastly. And as far as P.J.'s theories of godliness, well…"

"Don't hold back," Jem said with a chuckle.

"Well. In my professional opinion as a barkeep and woman of the world, the man's mental status was poised between barking and doolally. He reckons he's the first person to theorize that good sex is a religious experience. So he's written all this twaddle about procreation and replacing the unbelievers with C of E children, but when you read between the lines, he's arguing for free love. If not that, for polygamy."

"You know, if you'd prefer to read that without inducing a migraine, I can get you a modernized version later," Jem said. "Everything's due to be OCR'd for online access. We'll post a facsimile, of course, but also a digital copy with Ss in their proper places."

"Maybe I'll look at it then," Micki said doubtfully. "I was really hoping to read about a secret inheritance. An X-marks-the-spot map that would lead me to a pot of gold. Or maybe a bequest for any descendant named Michaela Latham, called Micki, who tends bar and would like to move up in life."

Her mobile chimed. Jumping up, Micki stepped out of the library to take what presumably was Gina's call. She was gone for so long, Jem forgot to anticipate her return. Instead, she fell headlong into a lovely old book that had somehow been shelved with the religious writings and collected sermons of Victorian preachers: *A Synopsis of the British Mosses; Being descriptions of All the Genera and Species found in Great Britain and Ireland to the Present Date*, published by L. Reeve & Co., 1884.

Although Jem had spent her early years more or less certain the Gwyn family collection included books of magic, as a grown-up she delighted in this sort of item almost as much. As she held the little book in her hands, she tried to imagine its author, Chas P.

Hobkirk, preparing this scientific volume for the delight of readers who would never know Google or even *Encyclopedia Britannica*.

Jem thought, *We live in the age of a new library of Alexandria. Some of the ancients lived in terror of the old one. They thought it knew too much. That it might become self-aware, even. The new version might actually do that, thanks to AI. Yet it's so valuable, we've built our modern lives around it.*

"Who's the one? The one you can't do without?" Micki demanded, bursting back into the library with a whoop and a big grin on her face.

Jem, nearly bowled over, clutched her volume of British mosses and chuckled. "You, I reckon. I take it you found the book?"

"I did."

"What are you celebrating?" Pauley asked, appearing in the doorway.

"The owner of Tatteredly's used bookshop in Penzance, my ex-sis-in-law, has custody of your missing book. I got a brainwave to call her, and it paid off," Micki said proudly. "Gina bought it on Saturday morning. Said she recognized it as a first edition, and valuable. But since the woman selling it was an utter cow, she pretended it was just a facsimile. Called the poem written on the flyleaf a forgery. Gave the seller two pounds and put it under the counter."

"A woman seller," Pauley said.

"And only two pounds," Jem marveled, shaking her head. "Did your ex-in-law say what she thought of the poem?"

"Is doggerel a compliment?"

"Not exactly. Either your ex-sister-in-law is no judge of poetry," Jem said, "or she's a crack judge of it, in which case the RIC will be unhappy, because it probably isn't Oscar Wilde's." She took a deep breath. "Two ruddy pounds. Mrs. Reddy put us to all this trouble for two ruddy pounds. One last middle finger before the end."

"Oh, but you haven't heard it all," Micki said, eyes bright. "First: the woman who sold the book wasn't old. She was in her mid-thirties. Forty, tops."

"Thank God," Pauley breathed. At Jem and Micki's questioning looks, she explained. "When Jem discovered Mrs. Reddy's body, she took a picture of some marks on her torso. She accidentally took a picture of the floor at Mrs. Reddy's feet. It showed what looked like lavender-colored hair. I didn't react too well when Jem showed me. But ever since, in the back of my mind, I've been afraid Kenzie might have done something stupid."

Jem, taking that in, declined to say that the instant Micki gave the seller's age, she'd immediately pictured Lissa DeYoung as the culprit. Was she coolly examining the evidence, or jumping to conclusions because she suspected some attachment between Lissa and Rhys?

"Second," Micki said, even more triumphant. "People are in and out of the shop all day, every day. Gina generally doesn't remember names or details. But this woman wasn't a regular customer. And she was wearing a lavender wig."

*

When it was time for Micki to say goodbye, she slid her forebear's book back into the stack and said, "Monday nights at the Kernow Arms are pitiful lately. I may duck out early and come back to St. Morwenna. Clarence laughed, but I told him I'd like to stay the night at the B&B."

"Why?" Jem asked.

"Because there's been two murders and he's all alone there, apart from you," Micki said, putting her hands on her hips. "He said he can take care of himself, and he probably can, but I still worry. Lathams stick together. So if we're lucky… sleepover tonight, and a gossipy breakfast tomorrow morning."

After Micki departed, Jem continued working until well past eight o'clock, segregating the volumes that seemed most in need of swift removal from the island's hot, damp environment. At least she no longer had to worry about Mr. Atherton blaming her, however unfairly, for the loss of *A Child's Garden of Verses*. Gina at Tatteredly's took stewardship of antiquarian books seriously—she loved books enough to run a bricks-and-mortar shop in the age of e-commerce, after all—and intended to hand-deliver the book to the Courtney Library the very next day.

"I hope the poem is authentic. It'll make the auction price that much sweeter," Pauley said. Unable to reach Chief Anderson or Sergeant Hackman, she'd finally relayed the information about the woman in a lavender wig to a dispatcher at the Hugh Town Police Station. The dispatcher had promised to pass the tip up the line.

"I think they're overloaded with people calling in theories and sightings," Pauley added. "I won't go so far as to say they round-filed it, but the lady I talked to sounded about as interested as if I claimed to see the Loch Ness Monster swimming between St. Morwenna and Penlan."

"I'd be interested in that," Jem said with a smile. "I hate to admit it, but I think I'm done for the day. I can't keep my mind on the work anymore. Assuming Gina remembered correctly, the woman in the lavender wig pawned the book on Saturday morning. We've all be talking as if I interrupted the murder soon after the fact—that the killer did her in, then started ransacking, and pushed over the curio cabinet when I knocked. I think we can rule that out. Maybe the killer came to Seascape House in broad daylight, and just before I arrived that night, they returned to the scene of the crime."

"Like a mystery novel," Pauley said. "But why?"

"To look for something. Maybe to remove any traces they left at the scene, to crank down the air so time of death would be harder to pinpoint, etc.," Jem said. "But definitely to look for something."

"Does it really matter if it happened in broad daylight, or late at night?"

"Well, a morning or afternoon murder makes it impossible for me to be guilty. We know I'm not, but it would be nice to establish a timeline that shows Mrs. Reddy died while I was aboard the *Scillonian*. Or even still in Penzance. And there's one other thing."

Pauley looked at her expectantly.

"If the killer went to Seascape House in the daylight, maybe someone was walking along the Byway and saw her. If that person told Saoirse, and Saoirse let slip to the killer…"

"Then Saoirse was murdered by the same person."

"Let's go to the Duke's Head Inn for dinner," Jem said. "Lay out everything we know over a pint. I feel like I've gathered most of the pieces. I just have to assemble them into a picture."

*

It was still light in the western sky when they exited Lyonesse House, Pauley once again scrupulously locking up behind them. On Rhys's side of St. Morwenna, where Tremayne Lighthouse overlooked Crescent Beach, the sunset was painting the sea with tongues of fire. But Jem and Pauley walked east toward the Duke's Head Inn, the shadows lengthened and night was at hand. The Square looked like a ghost town. No emmets milled about, and most of the shops seemed prematurely closed. The Ice Cream Hut, usually lit by a ring of white fairy lights after sunset, sat dark and forlorn.

"I don't know what it says about us, but it'll take more than two murders to close our pub," Pauley said, opening the door for Jem to proceed her inside. "Jeez. Looks like the whole island came out for a pint this evening."

She wasn't wrong. The employees of the Co-op were there, still in their green canvas aprons. The man from Hen N' Chicks who'd helped them open the Ice Cream Hut's back door was there, eyes glued to the TV. And Dahlia Reddy was there, overdressed and sitting alone at the bar, drinking what looked like a whiskey neat.

Jem and Pauley had to wait for a table to open up. As they stood awkwardly in the pub's tiny foyer, back against a video betting machine, Jem was keenly aware of the looks thrown her way. Bettie Quick sat with several other ladies in their golden years, a cordial of crème de menthe in front of her, untouched. She was dressed in black, complete with an old black hat that looked thirty years old, and kept shifting her oxygen cannulae to dab at her eyes. Bettie didn't point at Jem, or overtly direct her supporters to accuse Jem. But mute hostility rolled off them in waves.

After Jem and Pauley were seated, their glasses of Double Drowned in front of them and their dinners ordered, Pauley said, "You know, today, at lunch, I felt like there was an elephant in the room. When we were talking about Lissa. And Kenzie. And Rhys."

Jem decided to just ask. In a soft voice, she asked, "Is Kenzie Rhys's daughter?"

"No. She's his sister."

CHAPTER THIRTY-ONE

Self-Imposed Sabbatical

"This is really Rhys's story to tell. I know that," Pauley said, keeping her words soft so the pensioners' raucous chatter obscured them for all but Jem. "But Rhys is…" She waved that away. "I'll tell it the way I think it should be told.

"I don't know why Rhys and Cam's father, Harold, was so dependent on his wife. But when Katie died, he was like a chair with one leg broken off. Some might say, so what? Three-legged stools still work, don't they? But a chair is balanced differently. After her death, Rhys and Cam weren't just Harold's sons. They were his caretakers. That last summer we were all together, in June, Harold threatened to kill himself. Did you know that?"

Jem gaped at Pauley. "June? The same month Rhys and I started going together?"

Pauley nodded.

"But he never told me. Neither of them ever let on."

"No. Harold developed a habit of putting himself out each night with a pint of whiskey. But sometimes, when he was upset to begin with, the booze turned him dark and desperate. He climbed the lighthouse one night. Not just to the observation deck… onto the roof. He told the boys he'd jump head first onto Crescent Beach, break his neck, and be done with it."

Jem struggled to take that in. Before the accident, she'd assumed that Rhys told her absolutely everything, and Cam, nearly everything. The idea that they'd endured such a secret without telling anyone astounded her. She'd spent years missing her mum and despising her dad, but she'd never kept a lid on it. Being upfront about those feelings was the only thing that made them bearable.

"What happened?"

"Rhys climbed up and talked him down. After that, he and Cam treated Harold with extra care. For a long time, they wouldn't both leave the house at once."

Jem caught her breath. "Is that why Cam didn't want to go that night? Because he didn't want Harold to be alone?"

"I don't know," Pauley said. "It was September. I think they both hoped the crisis had passed. My point is, Rhys and Cam got away that night because Harold was passed out on the settee, as usual. He didn't wake up until the coastguard rang him a dozen times. You could say his guilt was greater than your gran's, or my parents. He knew that in his house, the only parenting that had been done in ages was done by Rhys and Cam."

Their dinner, burgers with onion rings, arrived. Jem's appetite had vanished, but she forced herself to nibble an onion ring just to maintain a pretense of normality. Bettie Quick's table was still pointedly staring her way, and she didn't want to give them the satisfaction of thinking they'd put her off her food.

"So now you know a little more about why Harold pursued you the way he did," Pauley said, looking sadly at her plate as if she, too, no longer felt like tucking in. "He needed to make you the bad seed. And naturally he had Mrs. Reddy whispering in his ear."

"She never whispered," Jem said.

"No. She never did. Now about Rhys. I remember the night of the accident," Pauley said gently. "It was the longest, bleakest night of my life. I'll never forget the way Rhys screamed. Or…" She paused, her big brown eyes gentle. "Or the way he turned on you. And for a little while, I turned on you, too. I can't speak for what went through Rhys's head. He's never told me. But I was scared shitless. I thought we'd as good as murdered Cam. That I was a bad daughter and my parents would never forgive me. It was overwhelming. I couldn't shoulder my rightful share of it. So I put it on you. And I think Rhys did the same."

Jem waited for Pauley's words to sting her, but they didn't. She thought suddenly of Hack's words in the cove, likening the process of truth telling to an exorcism.

"By the time Star Fest happened, I thought it had all gone too far," Pauley continued, dabbing at the corners of her eyes and taking a sip of her neglected pint. "But then, your gran died, and you went away, and it felt like we were being punished."

"You?" Jem repeated, thinking she'd misheard.

Pauley nodded. "We'd lost the chance to make it right. Forever. That's when Rhys started to shut down. That's when he started slipping around after Harold passed out, finishing off what was left in the bottles. I'll get back to that in a moment.

"Harold rallied while he had hope that your dad would be found guilty in civil court. That he'd at least win a symbolic victory, even if he didn't actually collect any damages. When it started to go wrong, he gave up drinking only at night and started having his first one at noon," Pauley said. "He did the full mid-life crisis. That's where Lissa DeYoung comes in."

"How old was she?" Jem asked.

"Twenty-two. Legal," Pauley added, shaking her head. "But you'd never have known it. She partied all night and woke up somewhere different every morning. She and Harold got together, and it was actually good for her, in a way. Lissa was looking for a real home. She wanted to live in the lighthouse and wear a pinnie and do fry-ups over the cooker. She was thrilled to fall pregnant. But when she told him they were having a baby, he snapped."

"How'd he do it?" Jem regretted the question as soon as she asked. As much as she'd feared and resented Harold during her late teens, she wasn't sure she wanted to hear any gory details.

"Pills and booze," Pauley said. "I wish he hadn't, obviously, but I don't think it was a hard end for him. He'd been working up to it for a long time. Not since he lost Cam. Since he lost his wife. But Rhys... Rhys found him. He fell apart. Thought he'd failed to protect the last living member of his family. Except there'd soon be one last chance."

"Kenzie," Jem said. "Did people suspect Lissa was carrying Harold's baby?"

"No. Harold had become St. Morwenna's village drunk. Lissa was the wayward girl with the tongue stud. After he died, Lissa went crying to Rhys, looking for money. He asked her to marry him."

Jem blew out her breath. "Why am I not surprised?"

"He thought it was the right thing. The only thing. He could bring up his little sister, and protect her mum from the big bad world. Thank God, Lissa got cold feet," Pauley said. "She'd had a crush on Rhys forever, like most island girls. But she knew he didn't love her. She knew..." Pauley stopped. Like Jem, she fiddled with her onion rings, breaking off a bit of one and eating it slowly.

"The point is," she resumed after a moment, "Lissa was gutted over Harold. In the end, she'd loved him, not Rhys. So she said no to marrying him. But that didn't stop her from practically sucking him dry as far as help. And over the years, people just naturally assumed that Rhys was Kenzie's father. Rhys let them think so, rather than admit that Harold heard he had a child on the way and chose that moment to check out. One last act of loyalty to dear old dad."

"What about Kenzie? Doesn't she have a right to know?"

"That's between them, I reckon," Pauley said. "Anyway, since Harold died, Rhys has had three things in his life. Kenzie, painting, and booze. Kenzie can be a handful, but she's always a net positive.

His painting is positive, *if* he sticks with it. The booze—well, for a long time, it was winning."

"Rhys... paints?" Jem heard herself ask. The words ended with a childish upward lilt that made her sound like a bratty schoolgirl. True, the Rhys Jem remembered had been a doodler. Like many boys, he'd grown up copying cartoon mascots and comic book heroes, drawing them on lined notebook paper when he was meant to be taking notes. Otherwise, he'd been an entirely physical being, devoted to surfing, not sketching.

"Art therapy can have interesting results. Besides, he needed something to take the place of the water. You did, too, right? Isn't that how you ended up a librarian?"

Jem chuckled. "Of course it is."

"Well. It was about a year after Cam died, I think, that Rhys started painting seriously. He took classes. Had a tutor. And he's been selling canvases ever since," Pauley said with a note of pride. "In gift shops around Cornwall, and online. The next time we pass Island Gifts and it's open, I'll show you. Their entire back wall is devoted to his sunsets."

"Wow. All I can say is, wow."

"Mind you—he *hates* that stuff. Sunsets and lighthouses and lonely stretches of beach are how the bills get paid," Pauley went on. "Rhys's art only sells when he sticks to the formula. When he colors outside the lines, he loves the result, but no one will buy them."

"Surely it's hard to sell serious art in a tourist town," Jem said. A few hours ago, she'd been telling him to sleep with one eye open. Now she was defending his art, sight unseen. "Wouldn't he need write-ups? Some sort of patron?"

"A gallery showing at the very least," Pauley agreed. "And there just happens to be a highly reputable gallery in St. Ives. The owner says Rhys has loads of potential. But the last time they spoke, he told Rhys he expected at least ten serious pieces before he'd commit to a show. And the pieces needed to be submitted upfront. Which is fair, because did I mention…?" Pauley held up her glass and tapped it. "His work was becoming more sporadic every year."

She fell silent. Jem felt she was meant to fill the space, but before she could, the server stopped by.

"Pauley, is something wrong with the food? You two have hardly touched it."

Jem and Pauley protested that the meal was fine, which obligated them to actually taste the burgers. After they'd made a decent showing, Jem glanced around. Dahlia Reddy seemed to have left; her spot at the bar had opened up. She chanced a look at Bettie Quick's table. To her relief, she saw the old lady rise to leave, still protectively flanked by her friends. One of them paused to shoot Jem a dirty look.

Even after this is all sorted out, I could never live on St. Morwenna again, she thought. *Not if there will always be a cloud over my head.*

"So about Rhys," Jem said in a low voice. "He had a serious problem?"

"He's an alcoholic," Pauley replied. "His word, not mine. He kept saying he was going to kick it, but he drank more every year. I hoped the shot at a gallery show would motivate him to cut down, at least. But it was Kenzie who got through to him. A seven-year-old just accepts that grown-ups can be strange or self-destructive. A thirteen-year-old has *opinions.* Apparently he missed Christmas altogether last year, and she told him off for it."

Jem smiled. She knew there was something she liked about Kenzie, who was slight of stature like her mum, but full of defiance like Rhys and Cam—and like Harold, to give the man his due.

"Anyway, on the Boxing Day he rang me up and said he was off the booze. Cold turkey. Done."

"Did it work?"

"So far. He lived like a hermit all winter and most of the spring. His self-imposed sabbatical," Pauley said. "All he did was paint. Even gave up on haircuts and shaving."

"So I saw."

"Turned into a fiend for exercise, as you may have noticed. Went out soft-sand running every night in bare feet. A new compulsion to drive out the old one, that's how he put it. One night he found a puppy wandering on Porthennis Beach, desperate for scraps. An emmet must've dumped him there. Rhys took him home and named him Buck. He dotes on that animal as bad as he did on Kenzie when she was a babe in arms."

"Did the sabbatical work? As far as the serious paintings?" Jem asked. Some part of her thought she ought to pose the question with studied indifference, as if making conversation for Pauley's sake, but she didn't. There was no use trying to convince her friend—and she *was* Jem's friend—that she didn't want to know.

"I suppose we'll find out. He painted twelve canvases. Twelve serious pieces of art. I have no idea if they're any good or not, but the art gallery man will let him know. And his sobriety's worth more than an art showing, obviously," Pauley said.

"Pauley!" a voice called suddenly from the pub's foyer. "Jem!"

They looked. It was Kenzie, her fauxhawk wilted, her face frantic. She wore a rainbow jumpsuit that looked like an artifact from 1970, complete with bell-bottoms and stacked boots.

"What is it?"

"Meet me outside. It's important!"

CHAPTER THIRTY-TWO

"Just Another Day in the Ever-Unfolding Soap Opera"

"You don't have to be so dramatic, you know," Pauley told Kenzie. After settling their bill, they'd exited the Duke's Head Inn to find Kenzie sitting in the dark on the steps of Wired Java, which had closed early like every other shop. Apart from the light and noise emanating from the pub, and a few lights on boats moored within sight of shore, it was profoundly dark. None of the planets were visible above, but in the constellations, the keystone star in Hercules' belt seemed to pulse at Jem when she looked at it.

"Dramatic? *I swear to God,*" Kenzie erupted, gritting her teeth. "I am barely keeping it together here. This is wild. I don't know what to do. I don't."

Pauley sighed. "Sorry. You're amazingly calm. But does Lissa know you're running around the island after dark when there's a murderer on the loose?"

"Her?" Kenzie snorted. "She's spending the night on St. Mary's again. With her policeman boyfriend," Kenzie added in a vicious sing-song. "Old. Fat. Ugly. And everything Mum ever wanted, apparently. Besides, I'm not afraid of a murderer. I have knuckle dusters." Reaching in the front pocket of her rainbow jumpsuit, she pulled out the brass item for their inspection.

"Give me that." Pauley snatched it away. "They're illegal. Now why did you barge in the pub and drag us out here?"

Kenzie made a show of looking up and down the street. Then she led them to the municipal rubbish bin next to Wired Java, one of those heavy affairs meant to resist wind, storms, and marauding birds. Pulling off the bin's metal top, the girl reached in and pulled out three items. A red canvas tote bag. A lavender bob-style wig. And a small fire extinguisher with a dented base.

Pauley gasped. "That's mine!"

"What, this?" Kenzie made as if to lift the fire extinguisher.

"You shouldn't touch evidence," Jem told her.

"I know," the girl said scornfully.

"That's my wig," Pauley clarified. "I bought it half-price at Island Gifts. Thought it might be fun at Halloween."

"When did you notice it missing?" Jem asked.

"I didn't," Pauley admitted. "I've been so tied up with Mum, I've missed all sorts of things. I wonder if Mrs. Reddy nicked it when she took the book?"

"Probably." Jem sighed. She'd hoped to follow the wig's ownership back to the killer. But if Mrs. Reddy had taken it back to Seascape House, and the murderer had stolen it after the fact, identifying its original owner did nothing to advance the solving of the case. Except, of course, to remove Kenzie from the scene. But Jem had never seriously considered the girl a suspect, anyway.

"Forget the wig. Look at the fire extinguisher," Kenzie broke in impatiently. "Don't you see it? Take out your mobile and use the torch app. *Not* on red lens."

Jem did as she was bid. As she feared, there were dark smears on the fire extinguisher's base. Saoirse's blood, surely.

"You found this in that rubbish bin?" Pauley asked. "What were you doing digging in there?"

"And how the hell did the IoS PD miss it? They had Devon & Cornwall to help," Jem added.

Kenzie gave them the pitying stare of a thirteen-year-old who wonders how the average adult stumbles through their life each day. "I didn't find this stuff in the rubbish bin. I cached them there while I went looking for you. I went to Lyonesse. I tried your phone. I only went in the pub out of desperation, to find you gossiping with your mobiles silenced." She rolled her eyes. "I found this stuff in our bin. The one Mum and I put out on rubbish day."

"What?" Jem said.

"Your bin?" Pauley stared at Kenzie. "Like… hidden down there, under something?"

"No. Right on top. You could've seen it from space. I opened the bin to toss an empty crisp packet in and there was the fire extinguisher. The wig and tote bag were under it. I reckon I shouldn't have touched it," she admitted. "But I was so shocked, I couldn't believe what I was seeing. Someone's trying to fit me and Mum up!"

Pauley said, "Oh, come on. You really can't approach everything that happens to you like a scene from *Emmerdale*."

"She may be right," Jem said quietly. "I can't believe anyone would be cool-headed enough to pull off two murders, then leave the evidence at the top of a rubbish bin. They could've pitched it off a cliff into the sea, or crossed the tombolo to Penlan and buried it."

"Shit. I knew it. Some ruddy jerk's got it in for me," Kenzie said.

"Or they have it in for Lissa. Kenzie, are we the first people you've told?" Jem asked.

"Obviously. You used to live in London. I figured you'd know what to do with a murder weapon and whatnot."

Jem couldn't help smiling at that, although the situation was anything but funny.

"If you know Lissa is in Hugh Town with the chief, you have to ring her," Pauley said. "We need to get this evidence into the hands of the police, stat."

"I'm not ringing him," Kenzie retorted. "He hates me. Yesterday, he said I was her, reincarnated," she added, pointing at Jem, "and she isn't even dead yet. If I tell *him* I found it, he'll find a way to blame me. Put me on punishment for life somehow." Rearranging her face in what she doubtless hoped was a winning expression, she turned to Pauley and said, "Can't you tell him you found it? Here, in this bin? No one will suspect you, and that way they won't blame me or Mum, either."

"I will do no such thing. Really, Kenzie. This isn't a joke," Pauley said severely.

"I wouldn't worry about being blamed. Take it from me—being a minor in the eyes of the law is a pretty good cushion, even when you're in the wrong," Jem told the girl. "You shouldn't have moved the evidence, but you'll get off with just a sharp word. The important thing is to make sure Sergeant Hackman knows about it. The fact that someone decided to stuff the lot of it in your wheelie bin may be just as important as the evidence itself."

Pauley pulled out her mobile. "Maybe this time the IoS dispatcher will listen to me. Wait—it's ten o'clock. I wonder if that means it'll transfer to Exeter's switchboard?"

"If it does, you're in for a wait," Jem said. A flash of reflective crime tape around the Ice Cream Hut caught her eye. "Every time we pass Seascape House there's an officer there. Makes sense, given how dark the island gets at night. I wonder why they don't have someone guarding the hut."

"Not enough manpower," Kenzie replied, still in that insufferable I-can't-believe-I-have-to-say-it tone. "PC Newt always draws the short straw because he's a grade-A muppet. Or so says Mum. He paced around the Ice Cream Hut for a while. Then he went up the Byway to check on Seascape House. I was watching from up the lane. As soon as he left, I came down here with the stuff, put it out of sight, and came to the pub."

"Fine. Pauley, stick with the kid. I'll go get PC Newt."

"We should stay together," Kenzie bawled after her. "Don't you watch movies? Splitting up is dangerous."

"We'll be fine," Pauley said, putting an arm around the girl's shoulders. "Just another day in the ever-unfolding soap opera that is Mackenzie DeYoung's life."

*

It might have happened because Kenzie had been so opposed to Jem going off alone. But when she made the turn from Quay Road to the Byway's smooth ribbon of asphalt, putting the lighted windows of the Duke's Head Inn behind her, Jem thought she heard footsteps just ahead. Switching on her mobile's torch, she changed the setting from normal to red-lensed. It was important to be courteous to fellow stargazers. But no one appeared on the path as Jem traveled out of the Byway's open section and into the part shrouded by trees. She listened carefully, but there were no more footsteps, if there had ever been any. Just the occasional insect buzz or faint snap of twigs that seemed natural on a June night.

She found PC Newt behind Seascape House, pacing near the back door. Just as she was about to clear her throat—she didn't want to give the wide-eyed bunny rabbit a heart attack—he spun around, shouting, "Who goes there?"

"Good God." Jem's hands shot into the air. She half expected him to taser her, or come at her with his nightstick.

"Ms. Jago! Sorry. Thought I heard someone creeping about. I was standing very quietly, trying to draw them out. Then I did hear footsteps, quite clearly, so I was going for the element of surprise." He grinned. "Don't get to do that very often."

"It came off brilliantly," Jem assured him. "Listen. We need you down in the Square."

The grin melted away. "Not another body."

"No," she said quickly. "But maybe the means to finally catch the person who killed Saoirse. And Mrs. Reddy, too."

*

Jem and Pauley stayed with Kenzie as she repeated her story to PC Newt. Once or twice she seemed to veer into embellishment, and it was necessary to pull her back into the realm of strict, no-frills facts. PC Newt was horrified by the fire extinguisher with the dented base, which seemed to bring back the shock of Saoirse's murder all over again.

"You'll need to stick with me while I call Devon & Cornwall," he told Kenzie. "It'll be another couple of hours at least. That'll put you up well past midnight. Think you can keep awake that long, sweetheart?"

"God, yes. Obviously." Kenzie rolled her eyes at him behind his back, mouthing, "Pillock."

"You may not be tired, but I am," Jem said, stifling a yawn. "Too much excitement. I'd better be off to *Gwin & Gweli.*"

"Think again." Pauley laughed, hooking her arm through Jem's as they'd done as teenagers. "You're coming home with me. You're not leaving me alone in that big old house again. Last night was bad enough. Tonight is out of the question."

As they left Wired Java, Jem took a last look at the Ice Cream Hut, dark and forlorn in the deserted Square. Bettie was too old to man the hut even one day a week. Would she hire someone? Sell the business? Let it slip away?

As a girl, she hadn't always taken the Byway. In those days, she'd sometimes cut across country, climbing boulders and crashing her way through the brush to reach the Square in different and more interesting ways. She'd always rejoiced at her first sight of the Ice Cream Hut from above, especially if she had a few coins in her pocket. More than once she'd looked down and got a surprise—Saoirse with her camera, the long lens glinting back at her.

"Pauley," Jem said. They were already past the Duke's Head and moving toward the tree-lined Byway.

"What?"

"Remember the snapshots all over the floor of the Ice Cream Hut?"

"I should think so. Some of them were under Saoirse's body."

"Was Bettie right about Saoirse being the Square's unofficial security camera?"

"Sure. From the counter, she had a perfect view of the water, and the quay. No one could come or go in a boat without her noticing, and maybe taking a picture. And when she stepped out the back door, she could see every part of the Square. And when she looked up…" Pauley stopped.

"She could see Seascape House, couldn't she?" Jem said.

"Yeah," Pauley breathed. "That didn't seem to matter if Mrs. Reddy died at night. But if the killer came by in the daytime, and Saoirse happened to look up…"

"…and take a picture," Jem added.

"Oh." Pauley drew in her breath. "Poor Saoirse. Maybe she didn't just ask the killer if they did it. Maybe she showed them proof."

CHAPTER THIRTY-THREE

Ringing the Dinner Bell

Lyonesse House was dark and forlorn when Jem and Pauley entered, this time by the back door, which was also locked. "I'll have to learn to love futzing around with keys," Pauley said, searching in her bag. "Maybe if the Wilde poem is authentic and the book fetches a good price, I'll invest in a security system."

As she spoke, she switched on the rattan-shaded pendant light over the kitchen table. It helped, but the house still seemed dim.

There were long fluorescent bulbs installed on the ceiling above the cooker and food prep area. The switch plate had been stuck in an odd spot, just under one of the cupboards. Without even thinking about it, Jem's hand automatically snaked over the breakfast bar, found the switch and flipped it, flooding the room with garish blue-white light. She hadn't done that in almost twenty years, yet somewhere in her subconscious, the muscle memory had prompted her to perform the action she'd taken so often as young Pauley's frequent guest. Another tiny thing that made her feel home again in St. Morwenna, murders and drama be damned.

"I don't know about you, but I could use a drink. Anything, really. Would you pour us something while I visit the loo?" Pauley asked.

"Sure." Jem headed for the wine rack. "I didn't want to ask you this in front of Kenzie. But do you think Lissa could have done it? Killed Mrs. Reddy? Killed Saoirse? Then dropped the evidence in her own wheelie bin and gone on an overnight date with Randy

Andy? I know it would be crazy stupid. But after a few drinks, maybe sticking the evidence in the bin might have struck Lissa as a perfectly good way of covering her tracks."

"I hope not," Pauley said. "She's always been more self-destructive than destructive. All the bad energy is directed inward, if you know what I mean. But maybe I've fallen into the habit of giving her too much credit, for Kenzie's sake. That, or I've lived on the island so long, I think I know people better than I truly do."

Jem thought about that. Then, as she poured them each a glass of Merlot, something else occurred to her, so obvious she wondered that she hadn't thought of it before. "Pauley, where's your computer?"

*

The computer turned out to be a laptop, so Jem opened it up on the kitchen table, a glass of red wine at her hand but untouched. Pauley, meanwhile, rummaged through the kitchen cupboards.

"I ordered a nice dinner and barely ate it. Now I'm starving. Want some prawn crisps?"

"Please. Now, what was the name of that group Lissa mentioned? The hookup chat room she showed Mrs. Reddy?"

"Nooners."

"Right. And Lissa said her handle was Lillibet, right?"

"Think so."

Jem located the group easily. Nor did she have any special difficulty getting in. The only requirement was an email address and a willingness to click through an endless Terms of Service agreement—surrender privacy rights, surrender user data, surrender firstborn child, bob's your uncle, chat to your heart's delight. In no time, she'd created a "Nooners" identity with phony details and a stock photo picture with the watermark cropped out. That accomplished, she set about searching through archived threads from February and March. It didn't take long to find "Lillibet" and her grinning, chesty avatar.

"I need that drink," Pauley said, sitting down beside Jem with the crisps dumped into a crockery bowl. "So what was Lissa up to as her alter-ego?"

Jem turned the laptop so Pauley could look over a long, dispiriting column of posts by "Lillibet." Many verged on pornographic; all were poorly spelled.

"Whew." Pauley pushed the computer back toward Jem and took a swig of wine.

"I know. I'll probably need to bleach my eyes when I'm done. In the meantime, look at these posts. Lissa was unburdening herself about a certain 'old cow' who's stabbed her in the back. Read for yourself."

Pauley did, pulling faces as she skimmed the archived posts. They ran the whole gamut of Lissa and Mrs. Reddy's friendship. The early days, when Mrs. Reddy had graciously allowed herself to be schooled in computer basics, showering Lissa with small gifts in the process. Then she complained that Mrs. Reddy had jumped headlong into the world of cyber-phishing, ignoring Lissa's warnings. The online grifters liked to pose as expatriate Englishmen trapped in foreign countries, or widowed millionaires looking for a new wife, and hopeless romantics who fell in love seconds after "meeting" a woman online. Lissa was worried and more than a little hurt that Mrs. Reddy refused to accept her advice.

After that, "Lillibet's" posts turned vicious. If they couldn't be construed, strictly speaking, as promises of real-world violence, they were far too dark to be classified as humor.

"Read this one," Jem told Pauley.

"Yikes." Pauley had another swig of wine. "I guess when your group's called Nooners, there's not a lot of moderation as far as profanity and death threats go."

"Apparently not. The moderation is light to nonexistent," Jem agreed. "Maybe it's all venting and fantasy role-playing. But Lissa alternates between wishing Mrs. Reddy dead and saying she *will* die. Soon."

"Oh, dear. Give it back to me." After reading a few more of the archived posts, Pauley said, "Well, to be fair, she keeps blathering about karma and what goes around, comes around. That's classic Lissa. Whenever she's cross and helpless, she invokes karma. Maybe on Nooners she cut loose a little more, since she didn't think her real-life friends would ever see it."

Jem sighed. "You're probably right. Which means we have nothing more than we started with." She munched a prawn crisp for inspiration. "What about Saoirse? Didn't you say she had an Instagram page? Is there any chance she was uploading her digital camera roll directly to it?"

"I know she was. I don't do social media much these days, but the last time I checked, purely to make her happy, I was never so bored in my life. It was all trees and rocks and birds and—"

"And Seascape House?" Jem broke in.

"Right. Good grief. Let me check."

Jem pushed the laptop back to her, but Pauley waved it off.

"I'll use my mobile," she said, retrieving it from her bag. "Don't time me. It'll take a lot of scrolling, I promise. But if Saoirse took a picture of the killer going into Seascape House, it'll be posted there, along with six hundred other snaps of trees, rocks, and birds. If the killer didn't know Saoirse the way I do, they might not have thought to look for her on social media."

Or they might have been too frightened to think clearly. Or not terribly wise to begin with, Jem thought, envisioning Lissa on the lighthouse's observation deck next to Rhys.

I'm turning into Randy Andy, Jem thought. *Focusing on someone I don't particularly like, someone Rhys had proposed to, and trying to bend the evidence that way...*

"You know what would be really helpful? Reading what Mrs. Reddy posted online just before she died," Jem said. "Didn't Lissa mention another group? One that Mrs. Reddy discovered and joined all by herself?"

"I don't…"

"Second Chance Café," Jem said triumphantly. "Let me see if I can hunt that group down."

As Pauley worked her way laboriously through Saoirse's Instagram feed, which was purely raw photos, unaccompanied by commentary or hashtags, Jem searched for more sedate, pensioner-oriented chat groups. It soon turned up—the Second Chance Love Café.

Using her recently created fake identity, Jem joined the group. It didn't take long to find Mrs. Reddy. The old woman's last post had been only a few weeks ago, and her handle was MRSEDI-THREDDY, with a selfie of her unsmiling face and a bio that read, "Resident of Seascape House, St. Morwenna, Isles of Scilly. Widow looking for a man of mature years and independent means for matrimony. Serious inquiries only."

Jem whistled under her breath.

"What?" Pauley asked.

"Mrs. Reddy rang the dinner bell. From the day she joined, she was bombarded with men—and I use that term loosely, because who bloody knows—professing their undying love for her. Generals, retired surgeons, entrepreneurs. Most of whom seem to write their posts with an assist from Google Translate."

As Pauley returned to her scrolling, Jem speed-read the posts. Most of them were flowery and lovelorn on the part of the suitors, while fatally naïve on Mrs. Reddy's part. Was it possible that Bart the Ferryman lurked behind one of those identities with a granite-chinned avatar? How would even the slickest conman go from presenting himself as a dream husband to turning up in person as schlubby, all-too-human Bart?

What if Mrs. Reddy wasn't extorting him over the soft-serve mix? What if it was a love connection?

As Jem read on, she began to notice a pattern. Mrs. Reddy would chat with a new suitor for a while, posting several times a day. Then she would invite the general/surgeon/entrepreneur to chat with her offline by privately messaging him her email address. For anywhere from a week to a month, she disappeared from the Second Chance Love Café, then returned, her search for a mate starting anew.

The first few times this happened, Mrs. Reddy resumed posting in the forum without explanation. The third time, she seemed highly miffed, but not at the man who'd temporarily stolen her heart. This post, which was expressed in all caps like everything Mrs. Reddy wrote, was vague but intriguing:

IF ONLY I COULD LIVE MY LIFE WITHOUT INTERFERENCE. I HAVE A RIGHT TO LOVE LIKE ANYBODY ELSE. IF ANY OF YOU ARE THINKING ABOUT HAVING CHILDREN, DON'T. ALL THEY WANT IS THEIR INHERITANCE. I'M SPENDING MINE WHILE I'M STILL ALIVE.

Jem turned that sentiment over in her mind. The notion of Mrs. Reddy complaining about not being allowed to live free of interference was breathtaking. Had she ever realized the effect her meddling had on other people? Had she even once guessed what her penchant for patrolling the island had done to her neighbors?

Suddenly, an image swam up before Jem's eyes: Seascape House's kitchen in disarray, with even the cereal boxes dumped out. Hadn't she once heard about online grifters begging for cold, hard cash? Asking their lovestruck pensioners to hide the banknotes in a half-full cereal box and post them overseas?

Opening a new window, Jem googled the phrase "cash sent overseas in cereal boxes." Sure enough, it linked to a television show she'd seen; an exposé on pensioners duped into sending their money to love scammers in foreign countries.

No wonder Seascape House's rooms were stripped down and its furniture was patched with duct tape. Jem had no way of knowing how much money Mrs. Reddy had in the bank when she discovered the addictive thrill of chatting up ideal-seeming men on the Second Chance Love Café. But it probably wouldn't have taken too long for the old woman to run through a good chunk of it, if she believed the private messages she'd received and answered them by sending cash.

"Didn't someone say Dahlia lives in Penzance?" Jem asked Pauley.

"Mm-hmm," Pauley replied, still scrolling. "She started out in Hugh Town, but that was too close for comfort, I reckon. A couple of years ago, she moved to Penzance. Maybe her and her mum fell out. For a long time, we never saw her."

"Did she have a boyfriend? A new job?"

"I don't think so. Just a thirst for self-improvement, I reckon. Going off for spas and retreats. The weight loss, the hair, and so on," Pauley said, eyes still on the screen.

"What made her come back?"

"I suppose her mum needed her more, since she was getting on in years. Dahlia always looked exhausted when she passed through the quay after a visit to Seascape House."

Jem went back to reading Mrs. Reddy's sporadic posts. Unlike Lissa on Nooners, she rarely posted memes or GIFs to make a point. But one post included a JPEG depicting a support ribbon, the sort made famous by HIV awareness campaigns. It was orange.

Typical, Jem thought. *Mrs. Reddy probably assumed anyone could co-opt a ribbon for themselves. Orange was always her favorite color.*

Because the color had halted her, Jem read the word on the ribbon. Then she read what Mrs. Reddy had written to accompany it, and several pieces fell into place all at once.

"Found it!" Pauley cried.

Jem almost knocked over her untouched wineglass. "You did? Show me!"

Pauley thrust her mobile under Jem's nose.

The picture was blurry. It was past midnight. After so much effort without her specs, Jem's eyes ached. Pushing the mobile out to arm's length, she discerned the image: a zoom lens photo taken by Saoirse from behind the Ice Cream Hut. Auto-posted at 1:03 p.m. on Friday, it depicted a woman leaving Seascape House.

The woman wore blue scrubs. Her face was pale and invisible, her head covered by a lavender bob wig. In her right hand was a red canvas tote, exactly like the one found in the DeYoung's wheelie bin. It bulged with items that must have comprised everything of obvious value left in Seascape House, including Mrs. Reddy's MacBook Pro and the first edition of *A Child's Garden of Verses*.

"Is that Lissa?" Pauley asked.

"No. It's Dahlia."

"But she's so thin…"

"Leukemia will do that. I don't think she moved to Penzance for spas and weight loss. I think she moved there for medical treatment."

"But why would she kill her own mum?"

"Probably over her inheritance. Which Mrs. Reddy seems to have withdrawn in bundles of cash and shipped to God knows which country in cereal boxes. Probably while Dahlia was fighting for her life."

Wide-eyed, Pauley shook herself, as if to override paralyzing astonishment. "I'll ring 999."

"Do that." Jem stood up. "I'll dash over to Seascape House and see if PC Newt is back on guard duty. Lock the door behind me."

"Too late," said a voice from the doorway. She'd entered the small wing's kitchen from deep inside Lyonesse House, a shotgun in her hands.

CHAPTER THIRTY-FOUR

"Do You Understand?"

Dahlia looked terrible. The strain of the past three days had taken its toll. Without freshly applied makeup to cover her pallor, and wearing only a scarf instead of her expensive blonde wig, she clearly wasn't the picture of health.

"Nice job locking the kitchen door," she said, sounding coolly controlled despite the wildness in her eyes. "But I'm afraid those boards on the old wing's broken windows weren't nailed down very well."

She appeared to be dressed for travel, or perhaps dirty work: as in the picture that cost Saoirse her life, she wore light blue scrubs and trainers. Tonight, however, the scrub top's capacious front pockets bulged.

Pauley had leapt up when Dahlia spoke, spilling her wine in the process. Red liquid spread across the table, dripping slowly on the floor tiles, like a grim preview of what was to come. Hands raised and voice shaking, Pauley said, "Is that my dad's gun?"

"It is. Found it on a rack in a disused bedroom," Dahlia said. "Felt a bit like my mum, nicking it from you. I don't think the book was the only thing she lifted from here. She'd become quite the thief in her later days."

"You said she was of diminished capacity," Jem said.

"So she was. And she couldn't come to terms with having frittered away everything Dad ever earned. All she cared about was *helping* her Internet boyfriends. So she went from selling her own possessions to lifting other people's little *objets d'art* and pawning them in the junk shops around Penzance. Completely delusional," Dahlia said, with no hint of irony.

Jem's mind raced, trying to guess Dahlia's endgame. Clearly, if she just wanted Jem and Pauley dead, she would've skipped the greeting and come in shooting. Unless the shotgun was a family artifact, a deactivated piece of Gwyn history, and she was counting on them being too terrified to guess.

Pauley must've thought the same, because she said in a tremulous but defiant voice, "That gun isn't loaded."

Dahlia smiled. "What? You think I loaded up my pockets for fun?" With the shotgun still trained in Jem and Pauley's direction, Dahlia pulled a brass-tipped red cylinder from one of her bulging front pockets. Then she cracked open the shotgun's action to briefly reveal two loaded barrels.

"Shit," Pauley whispered.

Appearing to enjoy the reaction, Dahlia snapped the mechanism shut. "I used to date a man who shot clay pigeons at the Tavistock Club, you know. Don't test me unless you fancy both barrels. What happened with Mum was an accident. But after Saoirse—" Dahlia broke off, as if saying the dead woman's name was too painful to continue. "A-after that," she said, voice trembling, "it's just numbers to me."

In what she hoped was a placating tone, Jem said, "You don't have to kill anyone else. You've stopped us in time. What we learned just now—we haven't told a soul. You have time to get away. Do a runner. Escape the Scillies before the police even know it was you."

"And you'd let me do it, is that right?" Dahlia raised her sparse eyebrows. "I suppose you're feeling sympathetic, since I did what you always dreamed about."

Jem started to say that she'd never gone so far as to dream of killing Mrs. Reddy, but stopped herself. Staying alive was the point, not claiming the moral high ground.

"You said killing her was an accident. Everyone in the islands can attest to how, er, difficult your mum could be," Jem said. "It must've been a shock for you to find out what she'd been doing on the computer. If you snapped, people might not condone it, but they'd understand it."

"People? These people?" Dahlia repeated, as if Jem had said something unforgivably stupid. "When I was young and in perfect health, they treated me like a freak. My skin was too spotty. My hair was too limp. I looked like a whale in specs, remember? I don't remember who said that, only that it went round the school. Not long after that, it was 'Druggie Dahlia' on everyone's lips."

"We all got teased at school—" Pauley protested.

Dahlia lifted the shotgun and fired at the 1970s rattan pendant light hanging over the kitchen table. It exploded in an ear-splitting burst of lacquered wood, buckshot, and pulverized glass. Pauley shrieked. Jem instinctively threw herself against her friend, closing her eyes and turning her face away. Something tingled on her back, but it didn't feel as if she'd been hit. Dusted, perhaps, by hot debris.

"That's one barrel," Dahlia said from what sounded like another room. Jem's ears rang and she was shaking all over.

"Oh, God," Pauley whimpered.

Jem shushed her automatically. She'd done the same when they were kids, facing off against a bully. Perspiration had broken out across Dahlia's brow. She still sounded calm, but her eyes looked quite mad as she said, "The next person to say something stupid gets the other one."

"Dahlia, please. I know you were treated unfairly. I know I treated you unfairly, and for that, I'm truly sorry," Jem said. "Saoirse called you out, didn't she? Asked you point blank if that was you in the picture?"

Dahlia nodded, face still tight with suspicion and what seemed like rising panic. It was as if shooting the light fixture had made the possibility of shooting Jem and/or Pauley real to her, and she was wrestling with it. Working up to it.

"Saoirse wasn't taking pictures of Seascape House," Dahlia said. "She was trying for a bird. A dusky warbler, I think. Stupid bint. Rang me at home to say she'd gone through her latest crop to print the best ones and thought perhaps I was in one. Wanted to know if I'd been at Mum's on the day of the murder. Said when she showed it to Chief Anderson, he might arrest me, the way he arrested you."

Jem nodded. Dahlia's voice had broken on the word "bint," suggesting the anger contained in that insult was aimed as much at herself as at Saoirse. What must it feel like to take the life of someone so harmless? Someone who'd carved out her own little place in St. Morwenna by serving ice cream and snapping pictures.

"Did you intend to kill her when you went to the hut?"

"No," Dahlia said. "I went there to play it off, convince her to give me the photos and keep quiet about it. But I couldn't make her understand. It's hard to pull the wool over someone so literal. It made me so angry, to think I'd finally silenced Mum and got away with it, only to have her take me down. And those same damn fools who saw me post-treatment in a wig and said I looked beautiful. Who treated me like a swan only after I was half-dead from chemo!"

Jem could see the irony of it—of a woman being excoriated for her normal appearance and praised to the skies after cancer whittled her down to a painted, bewigged stick figure.

"So you pulled the fire extinguisher off the wall?"

"You know I did," Dahlia said, her voice dripping malice. "After I left the pub, I saw the little idiot Kenzie coming down the lane, carrying the things I stuffed in their bin. I didn't think they'd be in any real trouble. I just wanted to muddy the waters. The chief is useless. I'm sure his successor is, too.

"But then I looked around and saw Kenzie by Wired Java, stuffing the evidence into a different bin. I didn't have any way to stop her. I could've taken it out, but I had no plan of how to get rid of it again. Next thing I knew, she was dragging you two out of the pub and telling you all about it. That's when I realized it was over. I had to make a new plan and execute it, right away."

"It was your footsteps I heard on the Byway, wasn't it?" Jem said.

Dahlia nodded. "Coming to Lyonesse House for the gun. Took me a while to find it. Even longer to put my hands on the ammunition. Then I had to change for travel. I had the scrubs in my bag. Never travel without them, for infusion treatments and so on. People are used to seeing me dressed to the nines with long blonde hair. With the scrubs and the scarf, I'm someone else."

"You sound awfully bloody proud of yourself for a double murderer," Pauley burst out. "I know your mum could be awful, but how could you do that to Saoirse?"

"I only meant to knock her out," Dahlia said, looking stung. "To take the picture and go. But once she was down, I realized there was only one way to be safe. And that was to finish the job." As she said those last three words, a new resolve seemed to harden inside her.

"Hang on. You don't have to kill us," Jem said hastily. "You could lock us in a room. Take our mobiles and go. Get a good head start on… whatever."

"I can't chance it," Dahlia said. "This is your fault. I only broke in to take the gun. Mr. Gwyn was the only person I knew about who owned one I could handle. If you'd gone to bed or sat up watching TV, I would've left the way I came, through the window. But you had to sit there and do your Nancy Drew routine until it was too late."

Jem steeled herself. She knew what she had to do. She only hoped it would work.

"At this time of night, I suppose you'll whistle up Bart to get away. Where will you go?"

"Ireland. I've as good a chance of disappearing there as anywhere," Dahlia said. "But I figured I'd need a gun to make him do it. Now that Saoirse's dead, it doesn't matter that she was buying that expired rubbish from Bart. It was a sweet little trick, having the boat at our beck and call, but I needed new leverage."

"Pauley!" From just outside the kitchen door a man—almost certainly PC Newt—bellowed, "I heard a firearm discharge. I'm coming in!"

Dahlia whirled, pointing the shotgun at the door. This was the moment. Whirling toward the breakfast bar, Jem thrust her hand into the space, feeling for the switch.

With a snap, the kitchen's overhead fluorescents dimmed to nothing but a faint, eerie blue glow. No one could see anything. The gun went off with another thunderous *BOOM*.

Hands groping blindly, Jem tried to get hold of Pauley, intending to drag her friend out the door. But her ears ached and the acrid smell of gunpowder burned her nostrils. She couldn't see much in the near-total blackness: only the sizzling after-image of the shotgun blast. Someone was on the floor, writhing and grunting. Someone else was whimpering.

Crack. The sound of a long gun's action snapping together. Had Dahlia reloaded the gun?

"What's all this then?" a man shouted, his deep voice rolling out like a clap of thunder.

"Is someone shooting?" another voice, female, called.

"Pauley! Jemmie! What the hell's happening?" cried another man. He was out of breath, as if he'd been running. Then a volley of frenzied barking.

As a powerful flashlight cut through the gloom, Buck shot in through the kitchen door. As the light whipped here and there, Jem saw the man whose query had sounded like the voice of God. It was Clarence Latham. He was the one who'd snapped a long gun's action together. It was newer than the one Dahlia had taken, with a deadly shine to its barrel as he held it aloft, prepared to fire. The woman looking over his shoulder was Micki.

As for the man holding the powerful halogen flashlight, it was Rhys. He was heaving for breath, as if he'd sprinted across the island to get there.

Feeling behind her back for the kitchen light switch, Jem managed to flip it on with trembling fingers. The scene revealed by the garish flood of light was both less terrible than she feared and somewhat unexpected.

Dahlia was unarmed. Her stolen shotgun had skidded into the hall near PC Newt, who appeared to have fallen into the kitchen table, taking them both to the floor. On his knees, he appeared unharmed, but was in a state of distress. He must've been the person Jem had heard whimpering a few moments before. Now he was outright blubbering.

Dahlia was on her back with Pauley on top of her. To say the fight had been knocked out of her was an understatement. Pauley was sitting on Dahlia—sitting on her in the very way Dahlia must've sat astride her mother while forcing the duct tape over her mouth.

Suddenly, Jem could see the scene as clearly as if she'd been there. Dahlia going to Seascape House to confront her mum over bank withdrawals or unpaid bills. Dahlia had already known about what her mother was doing online, based on Mrs. Reddy's post about filial interference. Dahlia must've been at her wit's end, and desperate to make her mum see sense. But considering how the old woman had responded to Lissa's attempts to explain a few home truths about cyber romance, how much more abusively had she reacted toward Dahlia? To her punching bag of so many years?

Jem gave Pauley a hand up. Pauley was still wide-eyed and shaking, but with fury, not fear.

"I knew I could take her. I must have five stone on her."

Jem started to giggle. She clamped down on it, afraid that to give in would lead to complete hysteria. "You were brilliant," she managed. She turned to Clarence, Micki, and Rhys, grateful beyond words but not surprised. Only a desperate, frantic person could've shot out that pendant lamp and not realized that everyone within half a mile would hear. PC Newt had been closest, but *Gwin & Gweli* was only an acre or two past Seascape House. And islanders look after their own.

"You're okay?" Rhys asked, looking from Pauley to Jem. "Both of you?"

"Do something for him," Jem said, indicating PC Newt. It looked as if Dahlia's second shot had struck the kitchen wall, leaving only a crater in the plaster, and the young man's weeping was purely a reaction to mortal danger. Still, someone needed to check him over and be certain he was unhurt.

"I leave you two for *one minute*," Micki said, hugging first Jem, then Pauley. "Did she do it? She looks so…" Micki tailed off, staring down at Dahlia.

She lay inert on the floor, eyes half-open. The scarf was askew, and her nose was bleeding freely. Suddenly, Jem remembered how Dahlia had whirled away from her during their outdoor confrontation. She'd done the same thing on camera, while telling a TV interviewer that she suspected Jem of killing her mum. In both cases, what had looked like an attempt to tamp down her emotions had really been an effort to conceal a nosebleed. No wonder she'd left a few blood drops in Seascape House. Nosebleeds sometimes accompanied leukemia.

Jem squatted down beside her. "Was it really an accident? Your mum?"

Dahlia nodded. Her voice caught. For a second she seemed gripped by pain, tears squeezing from her eyes. "I knew she'd thrown away most of the money. When I confronted her, she... she wouldn't stop talking. I couldn't make her listen. Nothing would make her listen. So I grabbed the stupid bloody duct tape. Next thing I knew, it was over."

"You'll have a chance to tell your story," Jem said. It was an oddly flat thing to say, and certainly cold comfort, but it was all she could think of.

"No, I won't. The cancer's metastasized. I might've had six good months. Maybe a year to travel and enjoy myself on whatever legacy Mum meant for me. But there is nothing left," Dahlia said. "When I realized that, I went back to the house. Tore the place apart, looking for anything valuable. Enough to flee on. But it was all gone. She'd even torn my baby pictures out of their silver frames to sell them. I was so angry, I knocked down the curio cabinet. That's when you came in, didn't you?"

Jem nodded. Behind her, she could hear Rhys and Clarence coddling PC Newt, saying he didn't have a scratch on him and he wouldn't want the new boss to see him this way. Pauley had Buck in her arms, and Micki had her phone in hand, ringing the Hugh Town Police Station. Dahlia looked dazed, as if three days of violence, lies, and increasing madness had left her too knackered to care what happened next.

"I just wanted her to be quiet and listen," Dahlia said, suddenly fixing Jem with brimming eyes. "To be quiet. Do you understand?"

"Yes," Jem said. "I do."

CHAPTER THIRTY-FIVE

Four on the Beach

The stars were coming out. The planets, too. As usual, Venus appeared first, glowing in the west. Mars came up next, but was soon washed away in the gloaming. Lying on her back on an old woven blanket, Jem watched the cosmic players take their places, like an orchestra assembling before the show. Hack's remark about an exorcism had proved prescient. Something, some restless spark of misery and bitterness, had flown away in the long, true telling of the tale. The stars belonged to her again, as they belonged to everyone.

Pauley appeared soon after; her feet, at least, in black flip-flops adorned with little black roses. Her toenails were deep magenta, the same shade as her hair. No one had more fun expressing her personal fashion sense than Pauley Gwyn.

"Were you followed?" Jem asked as Pauley spread out her own blanket—black—and sat down on it, cross-legged.

"Ha ha. So funny," Pauley said flatly.

"He didn't send you more flowers?"

"He did. Carnations dyed purple, courtesy of a certain local dealer I'm due to have a word with. Same note. 'To the beautiful woman who saved my life. Newt McDowell.'"

"It's true," Jem said. "Gran always said you were a sturdy girl. You proved it."

Pauley made a frustrated noise. "It's weird. I wasn't even thinking of him when I rushed Dahlia. I was thinking of not dying."

"Well, here's to not dying," Micki called. She appeared over a modest dune to Jem's right, dressed in a slinky red one-piece and fluttering cover-up. What she carried—a bottle of wine and a wicker hamper, hopefully loaded with a few choice nibbles—looked promising.

Micki flopped onto Pauley's blanket, uncorking the wine while Pauley dug in the hamper. "Oh, plastic stemware. Brill."

"Technically, glassware is forbidden on all beaches," Micki said, imitating the rote recitation of a good little schoolgirl. "Or so Sergeant Hackman reminded me when I popped over to the station to congratulate him. I think he suspected I was asking around about something else."

Jem, who was enjoying the stars so much she didn't want to interrupt it just yet, even for a glass of Chardonnay, refused to take the bait.

"And I did find out," Micki added.

"Oh, look. You can just see the outline of Serpens, if you try," Jem said, doing her best to ignore her.

"What's his name?" Pauley asked.

"I didn't get it, but I did get the initial. He's always gone by nothing but his surname and first initial, as near as anyone can tell. I."

"I?" Pauley repeated. "Like I, Claudius? I, Hackman?"

"Exactly. What do you think of that, Jem?"

Jem made a noncommittal sound.

"I reckon it's something tragic. Irwin. Irving."

"Those aren't tragic." Pauley giggled. "How about Ichabod?"

"Ichabod!" Micki shrieked with laughter.

Jem was about to sit up and tell them to control themselves before they drew attention to their little stargazing soirée, but it was too late. The sound of panting and a jingling collar foretold a pending canine arrival. Rising up on her elbow, Jem squinted into the deepening dark and saw a furry, tail-wagging bullet. Then she was being licked in the face.

"Buck! Leave those cackling ladies alone," Rhys called.

"Don't be so grumpy," Pauley retorted.

"Go away," Micki said. "You're not wanted here."

Rhys smiled. "I'm just passing through. Wouldn't want to break up your hen party."

"I suppose if you want a splash of wine, we could scare up another glass," said Micki, ever the bartender. Jem, who'd told no one what Pauley had confided about Rhys's struggle with the bottle, cringed inside. But when she sat up, Rhys was shaking his head.

"Can't do it. Training. Teaching Buck to come to heel. Buck," he called.

Jem, Pauley, and Micki waited. Buck waited, too. He'd eased into a sitting position on Jem's woven blanket, and looked confused as to what Rhys was on about.

"Buck." Rhys pointed at the sand in front of him.

Buck looked back at him, blinking his shiny black eyes, and yawned.

"Right. Well. The training continues. Away from distractions," Rhys said, scooping up the little dog and tucking him under his arm. Buck let out a happy bark—this was apparently what he'd been expecting—and the two continued their trek down Crescent Beach.

"It's like they say," Micki murmured when Rhys was out of earshot. "I hate to see him leave, but I love to watch him go."

"You know," Pauley said, passing Jem her wine, "for a moment, there were four of us together on the beach again. I never thought I'd see the day."

Jem shrugged. Lots of responses occurred to her, but none seemed quite right.

"Does it have to be four? With Sergeant Hackman, there's five," Micki said.

"And with PC Newt there's six. But that's a scary thought, proving there are dangers when it comes to the indiscriminate practice of maths," Jem said. "You know what? I'd like to propose a toast." Lifting her plastic stem, she said, "To Cam Tremayne. My friend."

"To Cam," Pauley said, smiling.

"To Cam," Micki said. They tapped glasses and drank.

"You know," Pauley said. "I love having you around in the library. But the job won't last forever. After you're reassigned, if you'd like to split your time between Penzance and St. Morwenna, you could stay at Lyonesse House when you're here."

Smiling, Jem squeezed Pauley's hand. She'd been quietly hoping for an invitation like that. Not so long ago, she'd been unable to imagine herself mixing with the islanders on St. Morwenna again, unless she was getting paid to be there. The looks, the stares, the whispers of "that Jago girl"—it was all too much for her peace of mind, especially when she could go back to her little flat in Penzance. But in the past few days since Dahlia's arrest, when she picked up a pint of milk in the Co-op or browsed Rhys's sunsets on the back wall of Island Gifts, the locals, some of whom she remembered from St. Mary's School, smiled and said hello. One had struck up a conversation about e-books outside Wired Java. And in the Duke's Head Inn, Bettie Quick had insisted on buying Jem an apology pint.

"For Saoirse," she'd said. "The police will take the credit, but you're the one who brought Dahlia to justice. And don't think I'll ever forget it."

For a little while there was silence, apart from the crash of the breakers and some kids playing catch in the surf. Then Micki asked, "All right, ladies. What sort of blokes do we fancy best?"

Jem groaned. "I don't want to discuss them. Let's talk about something interesting."

Pauley and Micki swapped glances. "Like what?"

"Like books."

A LETTER FROM EMMA

Thank you so much for reading *A Death at Seascape House*. If you enjoyed it, and would like to be informed of my future releases, please sign up at the following link. I promise never to sell or reuse your email address in any way, and you can unsubscribe whenever you choose.

www.bookouture.com/emma-jameson

I chose the Isles of Scilly for my setting because it really is one of the U.K.'s best-kept secrets. It's cozy and safe yet wild in places, filled to bursting with history and interesting people. While very much a part of the modern world, in the Scillies you can feel the pull of legendary Lyonesse—that drowned land of Sir Tristan and Queen Isolde—inviting you down to the watery depths. What better place to lie on a white sand beach and contemplate a mystery?

As for my intrepid amateur sleuth, Jem Jago, I hope you enjoyed her debut. There's lots more in store for her. Not to mention her dear friends Micki and Pauley, as well as the two very different men in her life—first love Rhys and new heartthrob Hack. I do hope you'll return for future installments and discover what happens next!

One last thing. I often say the difference between a book that finds its way and a book that sinks like a stone is simple: reviews. Honest reviews are the lifeblood of books in today's competitive digital sphere. If you enjoyed *A Death at Seascape House* and would be willing to write a review, I would be eternally grateful. Thank you.

Until next time,
Emma Jameson
2021

emmajamesonbooks

@msemmajameson

emmajamesonbooks.com